Christina G. Rossetti

Time Flies

A Reading Diary   .

Christina G. Rossetti

Time Flies
A Reading Diary

ISBN/EAN: 9783337017903

Printed in Europe, USA, Canada, Australia, Japan

Cover: Foto ©Raphael Reischuk / pixelio.de

More available books at **www.hansebooks.com**

BY

CHRISTINA G. ROSSETTI,

AUTHOR OF "LETTER AND SPIRIT," ETC.

"A day's march nearer home."

JAMES MONTGOMERY.

———

PUBLISHED UNDER THE DIRECTION OF THE TRACT COMMITTEE.

———

LONDON:

SOCIETY FOR PROMOTING CHRISTIAN KNOWLEDGE,

NORTHUMBERLAND AVENUE, CHARING CROSS, W.C.

43, QUEEN VICTORIA STREET, E.C.

1895.

TIME FLIES:

A Reading Diary.

January 1.

THE FEAST OF THE CIRCUMCISION.

MOTHER Church who opens the ecclesiastical year for her children with the alarum of Advent, opens for them the civil year with a Divine example of self denial.

For whatever Christ did or suffered for us was all, first and last, the loving choice of His own free Will.

Christ met but a cold welcome into this cold world when a public inn could not take Him in; "there was no room for Him," and only a stable afforded Him shelter: thus He began His natural human life.

And He was but eight days old when He shed the first drops of His Blood: thus (in a sense) He began His spiritual life.

His natural and His spiritual life began one with privation, the other with suffering.

Let us not be too eager to lie soft and warm, or too chary of undergoing pain. Had anyone been ready to forego bed on that first Christmas Eve in favour of a poor wayfaring woman ill fitted to encounter the brunt of hardship, he also like St. Joseph would have ranked as the Lord's foster-father.

B

In these days and to the end of time the Beatitude stands open to all: "Inasmuch as ye have done it unto one of the least of these My brethren, ye have done it unto Me."

January 2.

I.

A CERTAIN masterly translator has remarked that whatever may or may not constitute a good translation, it cannot consist in turning a good poem into a bad one.

This suggestive remark opens to investigation a world-wide field. Thus, for instance, he (or she) cannot be an efficient Christian who exhibits the religion of love as unlovely.

Christians need a searching self-sifting on this point. They translate God's law into the universal tongue of all mankind: all men of all sorts can read them, and in some sort cannot but read them.

Scrupulous Christians need special self-sifting. They too often resemble translations of the letter in defiance of the spirit: their good poem has become unpoetical.

They run the risk of figuring as truthful offensively, conscientious unkindly, firm feebly, in the right ridiculously. Common sense has forsaken them: and what gift or grace can quite supply the lack of common sense?

Reverently I quote to my neighbour (and to *myself*) the grave reproof of St. James: "My brethren, these things ought not so to be."

Stars, like Christians, utter their silent voice to all lands and their speechless words to the ends of the world. Christians are called to be like stars, luminous, steadfast, majestic, attractive.

January 3.

2.

SCRUPULOUS persons,—a much tried and much trying sort of people, looked up to and looked down upon by their fellows.

Sometimes paralysed and sometimes fidgeted by conscientiousness. they are often in the way yet often not at hand.

The main pity is that they do not amend themselves. Next to this, it is a pity when they gratuitously attempt what under the circumstances they cannot perform.

Listen to an anecdote or even to a reminiscence from their lips, and you are liable to hear an exercise on possible contingencies: a witticism hangs fire, a heroic example is dwarfed by modifying suggestions. Eloquence stammers in their mouth, the thread even of logic is snapped.

Their aim is to be accurate; a worthy aim: but do they achieve accuracy? Such handling as blunts the pointed and flattens the lofty cannot boast of accuracy.

These remarks have, I avow, a direct bearing on my own case. I am desirous to quote here or there an illustrative story or a personal reminiscence: am I competent so to do? I may have misunderstood, I may never have understood, I may have forgotten, in some instances I cannot recall every detail.

Yet my story would point and clench my little essay.

So here once for all I beg my readers to accept such illustrations as no more than I give them for; true or false, accurate or inaccurate, as the case may

B 2

be.   One perhaps embellished if I have the wit to
embellish it, another marred by my clumsiness.

All alike written down in the humble wish to help
others by such means as I myself have found helpful.

January 4.

A HEAVY heart, if ever heart was heavy,
   I offer Thee this heavy heart of me.
Are such as this the hearts Thou art fain to levy
   To do and dare for Thee, to bleed for Thee?—
   Ah, blessed heaviness, if such they be!

Time was I bloomed with blossom and stood leafy
   How long before the fruit, if fruit there be:
Lord, if by bearing fruit my heart grows heavy,
   Leafless and bloomless yet accept of me
   The stript fruit-bearing heart I offer Thee.

Lifted to Thee my heart weighs not so heavy,
   It leaps and lightens lifted up to Thee;
It sings, it hopes to sing amid the bevy
   Of thousand thousand choirs that sing, and see
   Thy Face, me loving for Thou lovest me.

January 5.

CAN anything be sadder than work left unfinished?
Yes: work never begun.

"Well begun is half done," says our English proverb.

Whilst the Italians say: "Il più duro passo è quello
della soglia" (The hardest step is at the threshold):
and again, "Cosa fatta capo ha" (That which is *done*
has a beginning).

True, the final verdict depends on the ending : but

neither good nor bad ending can ensue except from some manner of beginning.

I have heard tell of a painter who sought far and wide for an atmosphere wherein to paint. At last he found an available atmosphere in Italy : and returning thither he worked ? . . . not so : he died.

A bad beginning may be retrieved and a good ending achieved. No beginning, no ending.

It is bad to work loiteringly : it may be worse to loiter instead of beginning to work at all.

January 6.

FEAST OF THE EPIPHANY.

"LORD Babe, if Thou art He
We sought for patiently,
Where is Thy court?
Hither may prophecy and star resort ;
Men heed not their report."—
  "Bow down and worship, righteous man :
  This Infant of a span
  Is He man sought for since the world began."—
"Then, Lord, accept my gold, too base a thing
For Thee, of all kings King."

'Lord Babe, despite Thy youth
I hold Thee of a truth
Both Good and Great :
But wherefore dost Thou keep so mean a state,
Low lying .desolate ?"—
  "Bow down and worship, righteous seer :
  The Lord our God is here
  Approachable, Who bids us all draw near."—
"Wherefore to Thee I offer frankincense,
Thou Sole Omnipotence."

"But I have only brought
Myrrh; no wise afterthought
Instructed me
To gather pearls or gems, or choice to see
Coral or ivory."—
　　"Not least thine offering proves thee wise:
　　　For myrrh means sacrifice,
　　　And He that lives, this same is He that dies."—
"Then here is myrrh: alas! yea, woe is me
That myrrh befitteth Thee."

Myrrh, frankincense and gold:
And lo! from wintry fold
Good will doth bring
A Lamb, the innocent likeness of this King
Whom stars and seraphs sing:
　　And lo! the bird of love, a Dove
　　Flutters and cooes above:
　　And Dove and Lamb and Babe agree in love:—
Come, all mankind, come, all creation, hither,
Come, worship Christ together.

January 7.

"Now when Jesus was born in Bethlehem of Judæa in the days of Herod the king, behold, there came wise men from the east to Jerusalem, saying, Where is He that is born King of the Jews? for we have seen His star in the east, and are come to worship Him."

Popular tradition fixes the number of the Magi or Wise Men at three. Be their number what it may, we cannot doubt that set against the total number of their countrymen it was very small.

Let us then call them three. Out of a whole

nation dwelling under one and the same sky, three individuals beheld a star, and in consequence of that sight started on a journey.

Did those three alone see the star? Presumably not. Did others seeing arise? We read of none such.

Faith and good will made all the difference between seer and seer.

As then, so now.

The starry heavens are so far like their (and our) Maker, that they answer and instruct each man according to his honest intention, his tolerated stumbling-block, his bosom-idol, as the case may be.

To some they say nothing.

Some they address through the intellect exclusively.

While to Magi (that is, to Wise Men) they declare the Glory of God, and show His handiwork.

January 8.

FEAST OF ST. LUCIAN, PRIEST: BY TRADITION, A BISHOP.

A DEGREE of obscurity invests this Saint, by some deemed a disciple of St. Peter, by others an emissary sent by St. Clement (Pope) into Gaul. Be his date what it may (3rd century?), it seems certain both that he carried the Gospel into Gaul, and that at Beauvais, of which place he has been styled the Apostle, he won the martyr's crown.

Even his identity, however, has been so far questioned that conjecturally he has been viewed as an independent saint indeed, yet, as regards the Anglican Calendar, merely as a mistake for a more noted St. Lucian, celebrated elsewhere in Christendom one day earlier.

Supposing these two holy Lucians to be cognisant of all this confusion, with what peace and pleasure must they abide within the Knowledge and Love of God, and therefore in loving unity with each other! To be done justice to on earth, is nothing now to them: is it in truth anything even now to us?

To be misunderstood by men cannot withdraw anyone from the Divine Protection or from the Communion of Saints. What can it effect: anything, or nothing?

January 9.

"Lo, the star, which they saw in the east, went before them. . . . When they saw the star, they rejoiced with exceeding great joy."

One beginning was not enough. Those Magi from afar had not only to start but to overcome subsequent doubt and discouragement; to commence, persevere, recommence.

"Who is among you that feareth the Lord, that obeyeth the voice of His servant, that walketh in darkness, and hath no light? let him trust in the Name of the Lord, and stay upon his God."

They endured as seeing Him Who is invisible. The trial of their faith worked patience, and patience experience. and experience hope. [Would their experience have worked hope in ordinary persons? in us? in me?]

The star had vanished: so, at least, we infer. For the sublime and beautiful teaching of a star they had to substitute and accept man's word. And not even a good man's or a wise man's word, but Herod's first and last, he acting towards them as mouthpiece of the Jewish priesthood. Truly might they have affirmed: "I have more understanding than my teachers." Nevertheless it behoved them to crave and follow the guidance of men who yet stood in sorer need of their guidance.

For the faithful wise may lack knowledge for a while: but alas! for the unwise learned who lack faith permanently.

"Before honour is humility." God Who was pleased first to instruct their ignorance by ordinary means, afterwards relit for them the preternatural illumination of a star.

January 10.

VIEWED in one light Epiphany seems well-nigh the most joyous of Christian Feasts: in the sense, that is, of its having no gloomy side.

For before this Festival our dearest Saviour has already made that incalculable descent which His Incarnation involved.

He has been overlooked by the first instalment of His own who received Him not: witness, His birth in a stable.

He has deigned to shed the first drops of His pure Blood, thereby "fulfilling all righteousness" in the rite of Circumcision.

All those humiliations are over.

Even Herod and his troubled Jerusalem have been weighed, found wanting, and for the moment left behind.

And now the Wise Men arrive with gifts, worship, love; their gifts sanctified by worship, their worship vivified by love.

Their love more precious than gold, more acceptable than frankincense, more needful than myrrh.

For that incorruptible Body needed not myrrh for Its preservation even in the dust of death. Whereas the loving Lord deigns to need their love,—and ours.

Theirs, to have Him in everlasting remembrance.

Ours, to celebrate His memory and show forth His Death until His coming again.

January 11.

EXAMPLE kindles enthusiasm, enthusiasm aspires to emulate.

But unfortunately pseudo-aspiration often selects points impossible to be emulated, and overlooks at least some one point within the boundary of possible imitation.

How great a dignity, how great a happiness, to have been one of the Magi!

This, however, we cannot be. Our Saviour no longer dwells in a small humble house; ready to be worshipped with men's hands as though He needed anything. Neither does any star traverse heaven as our guide. Neither does any dream enable us to mock the counsels of a king.

Nevertheless as those Wise Men offered their treasures to the Visible Presence, so can we offer ours to the Invisible.

Not frankincense or myrrh, necessarily: nay, nor gold either, necessarily. Yet such as they are, our treasures.

And though not to Christ Whom mortal eyes can look upon, yet as truly to Christ unseen in His Temple or veiled in His poor.

If not gold, then silver; if not silver, then copper.

Yet if our hearts were set on reproducing the Magi in some one particular, I suppose many of us could find gold (though it were only the *least* gold coin) for our Epiphany offering.

Perhaps many have tried to do so and have succeeded.

Perhaps not one has tried to do so and has failed.

January 12.

WHO cares for earthly bread though white?
 Nay, heavenly sheaf of harvest corn!
Who cares for earthly crown to-night?
 Nay, heavenly crown to-morrow morn!
I will not wander left or right,
 The straightest road is shortest too;
 And since we hold all hope in view
And triumph where is no more pain,
 To-night I bid good night to you
And bid you meet me there again.

January 13.

FEAST OF ST. HILARY. Chosen Bishop of Poictiers about the year
 353. Died (according to the majority of historians) 368.

THE great work of St. Hilary's public life was to
uphold Catholic truth against the Arian heresy.

The great sacrifice of his private life may have been
that severing of the marriage tie which ensued on his
becoming a bishop. To which dignity he was elevated
straight perhaps from the laity.

Before his consecration his wife had borne him a
daughter, Apra by name. Who later on being
asked in marriage, followed her father's counsel and
devoted herself rather to the exclusive love of Christ;
ceasing to live, when God pleased, without pain or
apparent disease.

Now of St. Hilary's wife I read nothing further,
beyond such a hint of her career as is involved in that

of her husband. Wherefore of her I am free to think as of one "unknown and yet well known:" on earth of less dignified name than her husband and daughter, in Paradise it may well be of equal account.

For many are they of whom the world is both "not worthy" and ignorant.

Moreover it is written: "Many that are first shall be last; and the last shall be first."

January 14.

WHERE love is, there comes sorrow
To-day or else to-morrow:
Endure the mood,
Love only means our good.

Where love is, there comes pleasure
With or withouten measure
Early or late
Cheering the sorriest state.

Where love is, all perfection
Is stored for heart's delection;
For where love is
Dwells every sort of bliss.

Who would not choose a sorrow
Love's self will cheer to-morrow?
One day of sorrow,
Then such a long to-morrow!

January 15.

"IN the beginning God created the heaven and the earth."

Both perfect, and no mention of hell.

No hell needed, while heaven and earth abode as God made them.

Hell is not a primary necessity, but a contingent necessity.

"Lo, this only have I found, that God hath made man upright; but they have sought out many inventions."

Satan's initial work is not on record for us.

Adam's initial work of production (so far as we are told) was sin, death, hell, for himself and his posterity.

Not that he made them in their first beginning: but he, as it were, re-made them for his own behoof. Never had the flame kindled upon him or the smell of fire passed upon him, but for his own free will, choice, and deed.

January 16.

LOVE understands the mystery, whereof
  We can but spell a surface history:
Love knows, remembers: let us trust in Love:
  Love understands the mystery.

Love weighs the event, the long pre-history,
Measures the depth beneath, the height above,
  The mystery, with the ante-mystery.

To love and to be grieved befits a dove
  Silently telling her bead-history:
Trust all to Love, be patient and approve:
  Love understands the mystery.

January 17.

EPIPHANYTIDE at the shortest amounts to twelve days and terminates on January the 17th.

Even when it consists of twelve only, it yet invites

us day by day to meditate upon twelve Manifestations of Christ.

His Names and Titles manifest Him as our All in all.

Emmanuel, God with us. "Abide with us."—"Lo, I am with you alway, even unto the end of the world. Amen."

Jesus, Saviour. "The Father sent the Son to be the Saviour of the world."—"Christ Jesus came into the world to save sinners."—"My soul doth magnify the Lord, and my spirit hath rejoiced in God my Saviour."

The Word. "In the beginning was the Word, and the Word was with God, and the Word was God."—"And He was clothed with a vesture dipped in blood: and His Name is called The Word of God."—"Lord, to whom shall we go? Thou hast the words of eternal life. And we believe and are sure that Thou art that Christ, the Son of the Living God."

The Way. "Jesus saith, . . . I am the Way, the Truth, and the Life; no man cometh unto the Father, but by Me."—"A new and living way, which He hath consecrated for us, through the veil, that is to say, His Flesh."

The Truth. "The Word was made flesh, and dwelt among us, . . . full of grace and truth . . . Grace and truth came by Jesus Christ."—"Every one that is of the truth heareth My voice."

The Life. "As the Father hath Life in Himself; so hath He given to the Son to have Life in Himself." —"I am the Resurrection, and the Life."—"The Life was manifested, and we have seen It."—"When Christ, Who is our life, shall appear, then shall ye also appear with Him in glory."

The Master. "One is your Master, even Christ."— "It is enough for the disciple that he be as his Master." —"Jesus, Master, have mercy on us."

The Lord. "Ye call Me Master and Lord: and .ye say well; for so I am. If I then, your Lord and Master, have washed your feet; ye also ought to wash one another's feet ... Verily, verily, I say unto you, The servant is not greater than his Lord."

The Intercessor. "He is able also to save them to the uttermost that come unto God by Him, seeing He ever liveth to make intercession for them."

The Light of the World. "God is Light."—"I am the Light of the world: he that followeth Me shall not walk in darkness, but shall have the light of life."—"In Thy light shall we see light."—"That great city, the holy Jerusalem ... The Glory of God did lighten it, and the Lamb is the Light thereof."

The Good Shepherd. "I am the Good Shepherd: the Good Shepherd giveth His life for the sheep."—"We are the people of His pasture, and the sheep of His hand."—"The Lord is my Shepherd: therefore can I lack nothing."

The Rock of Ages (Is. xxvi. 4, *margin*). "He is the Rock ... a God of Truth, and without iniquity.... The Rock of his salvation."—"Thou shalt smite the rock, and there shall come water out of it, that the people may drink."—"They drank of that spiritual Rock that followed them : and that Rock was Christ."—"Blessed be my Rock ; and let the God of my salvation be exalted."

"Yea, He is altogether lovely."

January 18.

Feast of St. Prisca, Virgin Martyr.

About the year 50, in the reign of the First Emperor Claudius, St. Prisca, then aged thirteen, refusing to sacrifice to idols, by steps of ignominy and torture went up to her glorious death by decapitation.

Two prodigies are narrated as connected with her martyrdom : a lion to which she was exposed crouched harmless at her feet; an eagle protected her corpse from dogs until her fellow Christians gave it burial.

Likewise two alleged errors beset her identity: one confounds her with the admirable Priscilla, or Prisca, of St. Paul's circle; a second modernizes her date by more than two centuries.

Perhaps we feel a momentary disappointment on finding that this St. Prisca is not the beloved friend of St. Paul. Yet what follows? For one saint we were aware of, behold, we become aware of two!

Whereat, if we share the spirit of St. John the Divine, we shall rejoice. For he wrote: "I have no greater joy than to hear that my children walk in truth," speaking of all those good Christians without a shadow of favoritism.

Favoritism is quite possible, but is highly objectionable in our love of saints. "Enviest thou for my sake?" said Moses.

January 19.

JOY is but sorrow,
　While we know
It ends to-morrow :—
　Even so!
Joy with lifted veil
Shows a face as pale
As the fair changing moon so fair and frail.

Pain is but pleasure,
　If we know
It heaps up treasure :—
　Even so!
Turn, transfigured Pain,
Sweetheart, turn again,
For fair art thou as moon-rise after rain.

It is related that St. Fabian was elevated to the See of Rome under direct Divine sanction : the electing brethren, by individual mental impression. fixing upon him exclusively, despite other eligible and eminent persons there present ; and a Dove alighting upon his head, and resting there.

For sixteen years he " fed the flock of God," until in the persecution under Decius he sealed his faith with his blood.

Holy and blessed is the marvel of election to dignity by help of a visible Dove. More holy, more blessed is the mystery of each ordinary baptized Christian's election to salvation by operation of the Invisible Divine Dove. Even as Christ Himself assures us : " Blessed are they that have not seen, and yet have believed."

In accordance with which Divine standard St. Paul declares : " We look not at the things which are seen, but at the things which are not seen : for the things which are seen are temporal ; but the things which are not seen are eternal."

January 21.

By name " chaste " (Greek), and " a lamb " (Latin), this loveliest girl of thirteen, noble and wealthy, was sought in marriage by a youth of distinguished birth. But she, for spouse, would have none save the Lamb of God : Who keeping her pure alike in body and in soul, accepted her as His whole burnt offering. Nevertheless the lighted pyre on which she prayed died out of itself : and unscathed by that death, and unshackled by man, she won her victory by submitting to the sword in the persecution under Diocletian.

Her lover, at first of base mind, became afterwards ashamed: "There is a shame which is glory and grace." Wherefore since he remained accessible to shame, we may deem hopefully of him as accessible no less to honour.

And we may rejoice with St. Agnes, who along with the greater, may also these fifteen hundred years have inherited the lesser love " in spirit and in truth," in that land where " they neither marry nor are given in marriage." Even as Solomon, who discreetly choosing "a wise and an understanding heart," received with it the " riches and honour" which he asked not.

January 22.

FEAST OF ST. VINCENT, DEACON AND MARTYR.

ON this day, in the year 304, St. Vincent of Saragossa died a most true martyr, and yet not directly under any one instrument of martyrdom.

For Dacian, Governor of Spain, had done his worst by torture, by persuasion, by renewed and augmented torture, to shake the saint's constancy: he had done his worst, and that worst had failed. Then—please God, it was for pity's sake!—he changed his policy, and commanded a cessation of torment. Whereupon kind Christian persons gathered around the exhausted indomitable champion, cared for him tenderly, and provided a soft bed, whereon being laid he at once expired.

St. Vincent feared not them who could kill the body, and after that had no more that they could do. He feared (and let us fear) Him only Who is able to destroy both soul and body in hell.

"Fear God, and give glory to Him."

"JESUS ... found in the Temple those that sold oxen and sheep and doves, and the changers of money sitting: and when He had made a scourge of small cords, He drove them all out of the Temple, and the sheep, and the oxen ; and poured out the changers' money, and overthrew the tables ; and said unto them that sold doves, Take these things hence ; make not My Father's House an house of merchandise." (St. John ii. 13–16.)

In conversation lately, a friend set this passage in a light altogether new to me.

We behold the Temple cleared summarily of sheep and oxen, of their owners, and of the money-changers. These were all driven forth together when Christ "made a way to His indignation," were driven forth without one recorded word bestowed upon them, and without appeal.

Not so, as regards "them that sold doves." Them only the Lord rebuked and exhorted, giving them time to remove their live-stock.

Now it seems probable that the former classes of offenders were comparatively rich, the latter poor. To trade in beasts or in specie implies substance : to bring a few doves to market lies within the power of a mere peasant.

Wherefore my friend inferred that the rich were those more severely dealt with, because they had no stress of poverty to plead. While the poor folk, having want as a temptation, and evil example as a standard, were more tenderly dealt with by that gracious Master, Who came to preach the Gospel to the poor.

Finally, it was pointed out to me that at His second

cleansing of the Temple our Lord drew no distinction between the rich and poor traders : both classes had been chastised, both had returned to their sin, both at last had to be alike expelled :—

" Jesus went into the Temple of God, and cast out all them that sold and bought in the Temple, and overthrew the tables of the moneychangers, and the seats of them that sold doves, and said unto them, It is written, My House shall be called the house of prayer ; but ye have made it a den of thieves." (St. Matt. xxi. 12, 13.)

January 24.

MANY years ago a friend wrote and gave me a Sonnet, which now, as best I may, I reproduce from memory. I think it devotional ; perhaps others may think it so too :—

" ' Give Me thy heart.'   I said : Can I not make
    Abundant sacrifice to Him Who gave
    Life, health, possessions, friends, of all I have,
All but my heart once given ?   Lord, do not take
It from its happy home or it will break.
    ' Give Me thy broken heart.'   Can love enslave ?
    Must it be forced to look beyond the grave
For its fruition ?   Lord, for Thy Love's sake
Let this thing be : as two streams journeying on
    Melt into one and widen to the sea,
So let two souls love-burdened make but one,
    And one full heart rest all its love on Thee.
    ' Alas, frail man, for thine infirmity !
Thy God is Love.'—Then, Lord, Thy Will be done."

January 25.

Such Festivals as commemorate Divine Mysteries always excepted, the Gentile Church may surely keep this Feast of the Apostle of the Gentiles with pre-eminent exultation.

Because we are Gentiles, still more because we are Christians, let us thank God and take courage, and " run all."

O blessed Paul elect to grace,
   Arise and wash away thy sin,
Anoint thy head and wash thy face,
   Thy gracious course begin.

To start thee on thy outrunning race
Christ shows the splendour of His Face:
What shall that Face of splendour be
When at the goal He welcomes thee?

January 26.

O Christ our All in each, our All in all!
   Others have this or that, a love, a friend,
   A trusted teacher, a long-worked-for end:
But what to me were Peter or were Paul
   Without Thee? fame or friend if such might be?
   Thee wholly will I love, Thee wholly seek,
Follow Thy foot-track, hearken for Thy call.
   O Christ mine All in all, my flesh is weak,
   A trembling fawning tyrant unto me:
   Turn, look upon me, let me hear Thee speak:
Tho' bitter billows of Thine utmost sea
Swathe me, and darkness build around its wall,
Yet will I rise, Thou lifting when I fall,
   And if Thou hold me fast, yet cleave to Thee.

January 27.

I.

"NEMICO del bene è il meglio" (Better is foe to well).

Much good work has been hindered by such an anxiety to do better as deters one from promptly doing one's best.

Acquiescence in remediable shortcoming degrades : resignation to unavoidable shortcoming ennobles.

When we so set our hearts on doing well that practically we do nothing, we are paralysed not by humility but by pride. If in such a temper we succeeded in making our light to shine, it would shine not in glorification of our Heavenly Father but of ourselves.

Suppose our duty of the moment is to write : why do we not write ?—Because we cannot summon up anything original, or striking, or picturesque, or eloquent, or brilliant.

But is a subject set before us ?—It is.

Is it true ?—It is.

Do we understand it ?—Up to a certain point we do.

Is it worthy of meditation ?—Yes, and prayerfully.

Is it worthy of exposition ?—Yes, indeed.

Why then not begin ?—

"From pride and vain glory, Good Lord, deliver us."

January 28.

2.

PATIENCE! At any rate let us enquire what we propose to do instead of grappling with that distasteful duty.

Are we inclined to pray?—No, for that would end in our having to set about the evaded task.

Or to praise and give thanks?—No, for we have not put on our armour, much less are we taking it off.

Or to meditate?—No, for meditation would harp on the silenced string.

What then?—It is vain saying "what" in particular. Centuries ago an inspired Apostle summed up all alternatives for duty in a brief quotation: "Let us eat and drink, for to-morrow we die."

"From sudden death, Good Lord, deliver us."

January 29.

A LIFE of hope deferred too often is
A life of wasted opportunities;
A life of perished hope too often is
A life of all-lost opportunities:
Yet hope is but the flower and not the root,
And hope is still the flower and not the fruit;—
Arise and sow and weed: a day shall come
When also thou shalt keep thy harvest home.

January 30.

"I AM Alpha and Omega, the Beginning and the Ending, saith the Lord, which is, and which was, and which is to come, the Almighty." (Rev. i. 8.)

This is the Beginning of all beginnings, this the Origin not of species only but of genera.

The Beginning without beginning, the Beginning that endeth not.

"Before the mountains were brought forth, or ever

Thou hadst formed the earth and the world, even from everlasting to everlasting, Thou art God."

The aftercourse may perplex and trouble us : but whoso reverts and has recourse to this Beginning and takes refuge therein, and in this all-pervading Presence abides, has peace though the world be in an uproar and has stability though the world quake.

For what is it perplexes and troubles us? an intellectual obscurity. And what is it we know not? somewhat which we need not know.

January 31.

A FRIEND once put it to me that the choice of each man's free will must be unknown beforehand even to God Omniscient Himself. To foreknow would involve to preordain, and that which is ordained is not free :— so, I suppose, my friend might have gone on to argue, handling a mystery far beyond my comprehension.

Yet one thing I seem to comprehend clearly. Either we must accept God's Omniscience as compatible with man's freedom of choice, or else we in truth set human free will as a limit of Divine Omniscience.

Limited Omniscience is a contradiction in terms.

A being any one of whose attributes is limited, cannot be our Infinite Lord God.

February 1.

VIGIL OF THE PURIFICATION.

"OUR Lady of February" is one name for a snow-drop, called also "Purification Flower." The modest snowdrop hangs its head without anything to blush for : how should it blush, with green veins?

February is one of the snowy months, moreover a month of lambs: snow symbolizes purity, a lamb innocence.

This Vigil of the Purification, being the first vigil since Christmas turned all to joy, bids us watch and keep guard: for purity is soon sullied and is not easily restored.

"Blessed are the pure in heart: for they shall see God."

February 2.

FEAST OF THE PRESENTATION OF CHRIST IN THE TEMPLE, COM-
MONLY CALLED, THE PURIFICATION OF ST. MARY THE VIRGIN.

PURITY born of a Maid,—
Was such a Virgin defiled?
Nay, by no shade of a shade.—
She offered her gift of pure love,
A dove with a fair fellow dove.
She offered her Innocent Child,
The Essence and Author of Love;
The Lamb that (conceived by The Dove)
Was spotless, and holy, and mild;
More pure than all other,
More pure than His Mother,
Her God and Redeemer and Child.

February 3.

FEAST OF ST. BLASIUS OR BLAISE, BISHOP AND MARTYR.

THIS Saint was Bishop of Sebaste, a city of Cappa-
docia, and whilst fulfilling his episcopal duties found leisure for much devout retirement. Under Diocletian, his eminent position, Christian work and contempla-
tive piety naturally led him up to the glory of martyrdom, which glory he attained at an uncertain date early in the 4th century.

Now it was a hill to which St. Blaise was used to resort for holy privacy: and we may contemplate him as "set on a hill" for our edification. Or again, if we view him as an elevated candle showing light to all the household, this figure falls in with the fact that tapers and bonfires belonged of yore to the observance of his festival.

This connexion of fire with St. Blaise is not, it seems, accounted for: the fact however remains certain. A pun on his name of "Blaise" has been suggested as the connecting link, but only to be branded as "absurd" by at least one author of repute. Yet let us hope that this particular pun if baseless is also blameless.

Can a pun profit? Seldom, I fear. Puns and such like are a frivolous crew likely to misbehave unless kept within strict bounds. "Foolish talking" and "jesting," writes St. Paul, "are not convenient." Can the majority of puns be classed as *wise* talking?

February 4.

Up, my drowsing eyes!
　Up, my sinking heart!
Up to Jesus Christ! arise
　Claim your part
In all raptures of the skies.

Yet a little while,
　Yet a little way,
Saints shall reap and rest and smile
　All the day :—
Up! let's trudge another mile.

I.

FEAST OF ST. AGATHA, VIRGIN MARTYR. SUFFERED DEATH
ABOUT THE YEAR 251.

SICILY lays undoubted claim to this heroine of
piety, Catania and Palermo meanwhile disputing for
the honour of her birthplace: evidence turns the scale
perhaps in favour of Catania.

Quintianus, Consular of Sicily under Decius, loved
St. Agatha after his own fashion. When he found
her an invincible Christian, " espoused . . . as a chaste
virgin to Christ," his base love turned to hatred, and
he exhausted cruelty and torture on her person while
she set her face as a flint to endure unto the end.
The great fight of her afflictions accomplished, she
was returned to prison; and there, " more than
conqueror " through Him Who loved her, fell asleep
in the same Jesus.

The love of Christ, like a touchstone, has tested
much human affection, and over and over again has
proved it dross. Yet now and then two who have
differed—and two who differ cannot both hold the
entire truth—have loved on faithfully, believing and
hoping the best of each other, one (perhaps each)
praying for the other, both alike exercising themselves
to have always a conscience void of offence. In such
a case, where both have loved the Truth and have
accounted it "great . . . and mighty above all things,"
there surely remains a strong consolation of hope to
flee unto. For can an utter alien from God love
Truth and make sacrifices for Truth's sake ?

" I found an altar with this inscription, To the
Unknown God."

February 6.

2.

THE Triangle is a received emblem of the Most Holy Trinity in Unity.

Christians have been accused of loving and worshipping Christ to the practical superseding of the love and worship of God the Father.

If any of us have fallen into so grave an error, we do not, so far, deserve to be called Christians; "...every tongue should confess that Jesus Christ is Lord, to the glory of God the Father."

Now the Island of Sicily is in outline triangular. Let St. Agatha who, while dwelling in her three-sided native land, clave to Christ with a love strong as death, be our pattern of the true Christian adoring the All Holy Undivided Trinity.

"O Holy, Blessed, and Glorious Trinity, Three Persons and One God : have mercy upon us miserable sinners."

"The Grace of our Lord Jesus Christ, and the Love of God, and the Fellowship of the Holy Ghost, be with us all evermore.   Amen."

February 7.

WHO scatters tares shall reap no wheat
But go hungry while others eat.

Who sows the wind shall not reap grain,
The sown wind whirleth back again.

What God opens must open be
Tho' man pile the sand of the sea.

What God shuts is opened no more
Tho' man weary himself to find the door.

February 8.

1.

A HEAVEN of ceaseless music,—a monotonous heaven, a heaven of ceaseless endless weariness, say some.

Yet surely this heaven of music (if for argument's sake we may so define the Christian heaven of the Beatific Vision) is obviously and characteristically otherwise.

For is music monotonous? On the contrary, a monotone is not music.

No single note, however ravishing, amounts to music: musical it may be, but not music.

How is it to become an element of music? By forming part of a sequence. Change, succession, are of the essence of music.

Therefore, when our Christian heaven is by condescension to man's limited conceptions represented as a heaven of music, that very figure stamps it as a heaven, not of monotony, but of variety.

For in music one sound leads unavoidably to a different sound, one harmony paves the way to a diverse harmony.

A heaven of music seems rather a heaven of endless progression, of inexhaustible variety, than a heaven of monotony.

February 9.

2.

IF music, because opposed to monotony, typifies celestial ever fresh delight; vocal music, as the highest form of so high an art, exhibits special appositeness in illustration of heaven.

For the voice is inseparable from the person to whom it belongs. The voice which charms one generation is inaccessible to the next. Words cannot describe it, notes cannot register it; it remains as a tradition, it lingers only as a regret: or, if by marvellous modern appliances stored up and re-uttered, we listen not to any imitative sound, but to a reproduction of the original voice.

In St. John's vision we read of "the harps of God": but the human voices worthy of such accompanying instruments are the actual voices of the redeemed who sing the new song.

The song indeed is new: but those singing voices are the selfsame which spake and sang on earth, the same which age enfeebled and death silenced.

"And I look for the Resurrection of the Dead."

February 10.

PERHAPS one reason why music is made so prominent among the revelations vouchsafed us of heaven, is because it imperatively requires living agency for its production.

For I think that from this connection music produced by mere clockwork is fairly excluded: ingenious it may be, but inferior it cannot but be.

Music, then, demands the living voice for its utterance, or, at the least, the living breath or the living finger to awaken a lifeless instrument.

Written notes are not music until they find a voice.

Written words are words even while unuttered, for they convey through the eye an intellectual meaning. But musical notes express sound, and nought beside sound.

A silent note, then, is a silent sound : and what can a silent sound be?

The music of heaven, to become music, must have trumpeters and harpers as well as harps and trumpets, must have singers as well as songs.

" Glorious things are spoken of thee, O city of God. . . . As well the singers as the players on instruments shall be there."

February 11.

I.

"I see that all things come to an end."

No more! while sun and planets fly
    And wind and storm and seasons four,
And while we live and while we die,—
    No more.

    Nevertheless old ocean's roar
And wide earth's multitudinous cry
    And echo's pent reverberant store

Shall hush to silence bye and bye :—
    Ah, rosy world gone cold and hoar!
Man opes no more a mortal eye,
    No more.

February 12.

2.

" But Thy commandment is exceeding broad."

Once again to wake, nor wish to sleep;
    Once again to feel, nor feel a pain!—
Rouse thy soul to watch and pray and weep
    Once again.

Hope afresh, for hope shall not be vain:
Start afresh along the exceeding steep
   Road to glory, long and rough and plain.

Sow and reap: for while these moments creep,
   Time and earth and life are on the wane.
Now, in tears; to-morrow, laugh and reap
   Once again.

February 13.

TACT is a gift: it is likewise a grace. As a gift it
may or may not have fallen to our share : as a grace
we are bound either to possess or to acquire it.

Tact has, as all human good things have, a weak
side open to temptation. Its love of conciliation and
abhorrence of jars too readily incline it to overstep
the boundary of truth, or at the least to curve that
straight line of limitation.

Yet we can scarcely overstate the daily practical
value of tact, if only kept pure from insincerity. Take
a story in illustration :—

A certain man on being challenged to fight a duel
became, of course, entitled to choose his weapon.
" Javelins," said he. " But whoever heard of such a
weapon?"—"Well, that is mine." And the duel
never came off.

February 14.

FEAST OF ST. VALENTINE.

VARIOUS saints of this name are commemorated
to-day. One, a priest, was put to death for the faith
under the second Emperor Claudius about the year
270.

With St. Valentine's Day stands popularly associated the interchange of "Valentines": this custom

having its origin, we are informed, in a pagan cere-
mony wisely exchanged for a Christian observance.

And thus our social habit, even if degenerate, assumes a certain dignity : we connect it not merely
with mirth and love, but with sanctity and suffering.
The love exhibits a double aspect and accords, or
should accord, with heaven as well as with earth.

Never is interchange of affection more appropriate
than on a holy day : only let the sentiment be serious,
modest, honourable, ready for self-sacrifice. " Fair
maid of February " is a name for the snowdrop, and
seems to wed love to innocence. Valentines as pure
as snowdrops will not disgrace the Day even of a
martyr who has washed his " robes, and made them
white in the Blood of the Lamb."

February 15.

"Doeth well, . . . doeth better."—(1 COR. vii. 38.)

My love whose heart is tender said to me,
  " A moon lacks light except her sun befriend her.
Let us keep tryst in heaven, dear Friend," said she,
  My love whose heart is tender.

From such a loftiness no words could bend her;
Yet still she spoke of "us." and spoke as " we,"
  Her hope substantial while my hope grew slender.

Now keeps she tryst beyond earth's utmost sea,
  Wholly at rest tho' storms should toss and rend her;
And still she keeps my heart and keeps its key,
  My love whose heart is tender.

February 16.

Man, endowed with free will, rebels against God
and defies Him. "Who is Lord over us?" saith he.
  God, Author and Giver of free will, Whose gifts are

D

without repentance, overrides not by His own Will
that of His creature but defers to man's freedom of
choice. "Return unto Me, and I will return unto
you," He saith, and awaiteth the issue.

So also our Divine Redeemer Himself speaketh,
saying : "Abide in Me, and I in you :" thus leaving
as dependent upon man the sacred mutual indwelling.

Human free will is a profound mystery, so also is
Divine predestination. The twain being revealed co-
exist, whether or not mortal faculties avail to reconcile
them. But surely if our own conscience attests either
and not both, that one is free will rather than predestination.

We all talk of the sun rising and the sun setting :
yet in neither case is any motion of the sun really in
question, but only a revolution of the earth.

February 17.

ONE whom I knew intimately and whose memory
I revere once in my hearing remarked that unless we
love people we cannot understand them. This was
a new light to me.

Another time, after she had taken a decisive step in
religion, a friend appealed to her not to be alienated
from her regard : and she answered that goodness
wheresoever found she thought she loved more than ever.

Thus in her lips was the law of kindness. Wisdom
rooted in love instructed her how to give a right
answer.

Love is all happiness, love is all beauty,
    Love is the crown of flaxen heads and hoary,
Love is the only everlasting duty,
    And love is chronicled in endless story
    And kindles endless glory.

February 18.

"WHAT a good thing my feet are large, for so anyone can wear my boots:" such a remark I once heard made by one of the kindest-hearted of my friends.

A quaint remark and humorous, as she uttered it. I do not think she entertained an idea that she was propounding any high or deep or spiritually helpful truth.

Yet such surely we may find it to be : a key at least in part to the why and the wherefore of some irremediable blemishes, a comfort under the depression of lifelong inferiority.

For oftentimes our disadvantage promotes the welfare of others, or our weak-point nerves them to endure their own.

If really and truly we loved our neighbour as ourself, such aspects of our sorry plight would brighten its gloom and blunt its sting.

If only we could and would estimate every blameless blemish in ourselves, not as a personal hardship, but as a helpful possibility ; as, so to say, large feet in doubly available boots !

February 19.

HOME by different ways. Yet all
    Homeward bound thro' prayer and praise,
Young with old and great with small
    Home by different ways.

    Many nights and many days
Wind must blow and rain must fall,
    Quake the quicksand, shift the haze.

Life hath called and death will call
  Saints who praying kneel at gaze,
Ford the flood or leap the wall
  Home by different ways.

February 20.

A GREAT many years ago, I do not recall how many, I visited a large waxwork exhibition brilliant with costumes, complexions, and historical effigies.

And entering that gorgeous assembly I literally felt shy!

The real people present did not abash me: it was the distinguished waxen crowd which put me out of countenance.

Now looking back I laugh at my own absurdity. Why then recount it? Because it seems to furnish a parable of many passages in many lives.

Things seen are as that waxwork, things unseen as those real people. Yet over and over again we are influenced and constrained by the hollow momentary world we behold in presence, while utterly obtuse as regards the substantial eternal world no less present around us though disregarded.

Will we not rise above an awe of waxwork?

February 21.

I.

"A SQUARE man in a round hole,"—we behold him incompatible, irreconcileable, a standing incongruity.

This world is full of square men in round holes; of persons unsuited to their post, calling, circumstances.

What is our square man to do? Clearly one of two

things: he must either get out of his round hole, or else he must stay in it.

If he can get out by any lawful exit, let him up and begone, and betake himself to a square habitat.

But for one cubic man who can shift quarters, there may be a million who cannot. And this notwithstanding that many such ought never to have stepped into a circular hole at all: once in, therein they must abide.

Our permanent square tenant, then: what shall he do to mitigate the misfit which cannot be rectified?

He can turn that very misfit to account by sitting loose among his surroundings. If it brings home to him daily that "this is not our rest" it will be blessed to him. If so uneasy a present "city" moves him to seek "one to come" blessed will be his lot.

In one sense we are all alike square people in round holes, inasmuch as we are made less for our actual environment of earth and time than for heaven and eternity. Thus it appears that the main change must, after all, be wrought not in our surroundings but in ourselves: for the circle symbolizes eternity; and to fit into any round, any square must sacrifice its angles.

February 22.

2.

OR to reverse the figure. Let our man be round and let him occupy a square hole.

Let man thus appear to us as in truth he is, primarily tenant not to a finite "square" but to an infinite "circle."

He feels ill at ease in his square: or thus, at least, he ought to feel.

He abides cramped, dwarfed; he cannot expand

evenly and harmoniously in all directions with perfect balance of parts. Wherever he expands he is liable to graze and get jammed against prison confines.

Ought he to feel habitually comfortable? He ought to be incessantly thankful, contented, joyful, hopeful: scarcely, perhaps, prevalently comfortable.

We do not expect a caged eagle to look comfortable. We rather expect him to exhibit noble indignant aspiration and the perpetual protest of baulked latent power.

February 23.

VIGIL OF ST. MATTHIAS.

IT is impossible for us to disentangle the memory of St. Matthias from the memory of Judas Iscariot: impossible, at least in this life.

As impossible as for the tide not to stand connected in thought with the ebb, or light with darkness.

So, too, hope and fear tremble responsively.

To be remembered somehow, anyhow, by the righteous, seems perhaps less terrible than to be clean forgotten and out of mind.

If there is a text more dreadful than "He shall be tormented with fire and brimstone in the presence of the holy angels, and in the presence of the Lamb," is it not that which saith "DEPART from Me, ye cursed, into everlasting fire"?

February 24.

FEAST OF ST. MATTHIAS, APOSTLE.

ST. MATTHIAS is conjectured to have been at first one of our Lord's Seventy Disciples. The fall of Judas Iscariot made room for him among the Twelve Apostles. According to tradition the scene of his evangelistic labours after the apostolic dispersion from Jerusalem may have been Cappadocia, and the date of his death by martyrdom among the fierce Cappadocians about the year 64.

But for the apostacy of Judas St. Matthias must perforce apparently have occupied a less exalted station: there, doubtless, he would thankfully have remained, rather than make his stepping-stone of such a ruin; for he cannot but have been one who, at least in will, loved his neighbour as himself. A heavenly temper of primary importance, but by flesh and blood not lightly attainable.

Thus even Jonah, inspired Prophet as he was, seems to have grudged Nineveh its uncovenanted overflow of mercy: presumably on patriotic grounds, yet none the less with a resentment far removed from the Divine good pleasure.

Whenever our own personal gain depends on a neighbour's loss, do we, at least in will, steadily and practically love him as ourself?

If not, how shall we face him, though not to-day or to-morrow, yet assuredly at the last great Day of Judgment? when all things covered shall be revealed, or hidden shall be made known.

February 25.

"ONE sorrow more? I thought the tale complete."—
 He bore amiss who grudges what he bore:
Stretch out thy hands and urge thy feet to meet
 One sorrow more.

Yea, make thy count for two or three or four:
 The kind Physician will not slack to treat
His patient while there's rankling in the sore.

Bear up in anguish, ease will yet be sweet;
  Bear up all day, for night has rest in store:
Christ bears thy burden with thee, rise and greet
  One sorrow more.

February 26.

SLOTH does not at a first glance seem the deadliest
of the seven deadly sins, yet under one aspect it can
fairly be reckoned such. The others may consist with
energy, and energy may always be turned to good
account.

Sloth precludes energy.

Sloth may accompany a great many amiable tempers and skin-deep charms : but sloth runs no race.

And a race is the one thing set before us. We are
not summoned to pose picturesquely in *tableaux
vivants*, or die away gracefully like dissolving views.

We are called to run a race, and woe is us if we run
it not lawfully, and with patience and with pressing
toward the mark.

Sloth tends to paralyse the will. Blessed are those
merciful who labour to help the self-helpless slothful,
and betimes to arouse him.

It is never too early to fight against sloth in one
committed to my charge,—or in myself. It is never
too early, but ere long it may be too late.

February 27.

A HANDY Mole who plied no shovel
To excavate his vaulted hovel,
While hard at work met in mid-furrow
An Earthworm boring out his burrow.
Our Mole had dined and must grow thinner
Before he gulped a second dinner, ·

And on no other terms cared he
To meet a worm of low degree.
The Mole turned on his blindest eye
Passing that base mechanic by;
The Worm entrenched in actual blindness
Ignored or kindness or unkindness;
Each wrought his own exclusive tunnel
To reach his own exclusive funnel.

A plough its flawless track pursuing
Involved them in one common ruin.
Where now the mine and countermine,
The dined-on and the one to dine?
The impartial ploughshare of extinction
Annulled them all without distinction.

February 28.

THE difference between heaven and human attempts at describing heaven may, I think, be illustrated by the difference between pure colour and pigments or dyes.

Such colour as is cast by a prism is absolutely pure, intangible, incapable (it would appear) of analysis. It is not so much as a film: it is, so to say, a mode, a condition.

Far otherwise is it with dyes and pigments. These exhibit colour, while their substance is by no means colour, but is merely that field upon which light renders visible one or other of its component tints. Animal, vegetable, or mineral, the substance may be; oily, gummy, watery, simple, compound; however dense or however translucent, equally an appreciable body.

Now just as prismatic hues take no hold of aught on which they fall, but like the pure light which is

their parent are shifting, evanescent, intangible ; while
dyes seize on what they come in contact with and
affect it permanently : so any literal revelation of
heaven would appear to be over spiritual for us ; we
need something grosser, something more familiar and
more within the range of our experience.

The heavenly symbol attracts : what will be the
heavenly reality?

It was blessed to know Christ on earth : what will
it be to know Him not as mortal eye hath seen, or
mortal ear heard, or mortal heart conceived?

February 29.

"SEEING is believing." This proverb conveys sometimes a truth, sometimes an untruth : for less depends
on the "seeing" than on the seer.

"I have heard of Thee by the hearing of the ear :
but now mine eye seeth Thee," said pious Job ; and
forthwith abhorred his errors, repenting in dust and
ashes. His was the genuine seeing eye, for his was
the honest godly heart.

On the other hand, of the multitude who gazed on
Christ crucified, how many discerned Him? Their
chief priests and scribes said in mockery: "Let Christ
the king of Israel descend now from the cross, that
we may see and believe." Yet would He not descend
thence: even because to be that very King of Israel at
whom they cavilled, it behoved Christ to suffer those
things and by that road to enter into His glory.

"And this is the condemnation, that light is come
into the world, and men loved darkness rather than
light, because their deeds were evil."

"From all blindness of heart, Good Lord, deliver
us."

March 1.

FEAST OF ST. DAVID, Archbishop of the Welsh Church, and accounted Patron Saint of Wales. Died presumably in the year 544; at which period, according to different dates proposed for his birth, he was aged either eighty-two or ninety-eight.

To him the honour appertains of having convened in the year 529 a Synod whereby the Pelagian heresy was overthrown: which Synod was thence styled the Synod of Victory.

Glorious and happy are those champions who purge the Church from error: this is the privilege of a few, among whom St. David ranks. Meanwhile all Christians, the lofty and the lowly alike, are called to walk in daily holiness: and to such no less St. David sets a pattern. Study his portrait as handed down to us by Giraldus Cambrensis (I quote at second hand):—

"He was a doctrine to his hearers, a guide to the religious, a light to the poor, a support to the orphans, a protection to widows, a father to the fatherless, a rule to monks, and a path to seculars, being made all things to all men that he might bring all to God."

₊ My "black letter Feasts" have been studied mainly from "The Lives of the Saints," by the Rev. S. Baring-Gould; from which interesting work most of my quotations, whether at first hand or at second hand, are taken. Recording these facts, I record no less my permanent obligation to the Author.

March 2.

FEAST OF ST. CHAD, Bishop of Lichfield: born in the year 620 (?), died about 672.

HOLY in retirement and holy in public life this saint preferred lowliness to pomp, and in his first Bishoprick performed pastoral journeys not on horseback but on foot.   Some irregularity may have attended his elevation to the episcopacy : if so, this was afterwards rectified by Archbishop Theodore of Canterbury.

Bishop Chad sets us an example of godly fear :— " If it happened that there blew a strong gust of wind, when he was reading or doing anything else, he at once called upon God for mercy, and begged it might be extended to all mankind.   If it blew stronger, he, prostrating himself, prayed more earnestly.   But if it proved a violent storm of wind or rain, or of thunder and lightning, he would pray and repeat Psalms in the church till the weather became calm.   Being asked by his followers why he did so, he answered, ' Have ye not read,—The Lord also thundered in the heavens, and the Highest gave forth His voice ; yea, He sent out His arrows and scattered them, and He shot out lightnings and discomfited them ?   For the Lord moves the air, raises the winds, darts lightning, and thunders from heaven to excite the inhabitants of the earth to fear Him ; to put them in mind of the future judgment ; to dispel their pride and vanquish their boldness, by bringing into their thoughts that dreadful time when, the heavens and the earth being in a flame, He will come in the clouds with great power and majesty, to judge the quick and the dead.   Wherefore it behoves us to answer His heavenly admonition with due fear and love.' "

March 3.

LAUGHING Life cries at the feast,—
    Craving Death cries at the door,—
" Fish, or fowl, or fatted beast ?"—
    "Come with me, thy feast is o'er."—

"Wreathe the violets."—"Watch them fade."—
"I am sunlight."—"I am shade:
   I am the sun-burying west."—
"I am pleasure."—"I am rest:
   Come with me, for I am best."

March 4.

My first vivid experience of death (if so I may term it) occurred in early childhood in the grounds of a cottage.

This little cottage was my familiar haunt: its grounds were my inexhaustible delight. They then seemed to me spacious, though now I know them to have been narrow and commonplace.

So in these grounds, perhaps in the orchard, I lighted upon a dead mouse. The dead mouse moved my sympathy: I took him up, buried him comfortably in a mossy bed, and bore the spot in mind.

It may have been a day or two afterwards that I returned, removed the moss coverlet, and looked . . . a black insect emerged. I fled in horror, and for long years ensuing I never mentioned this ghastly adventure to anyone.

Now looking back at the incident I see that neither impulse was unreasonable, although the sympathy and the horror were alike childish.

Only now contemplating death from a wider and wiser view-point, I would fain reverse the order of those feelings: dwelling less and less on the mere physical disgust, while more and more on the rest and safety; on the perfect peace of death, please God.

March 5.

WHERE shall I find a white rose blowing?—
    Out in the garden where all sweets be.—
But out in my garden the snow was snowing
    And never a white rose opened for me.
Nought but snow and a wind were blowing
And snowing.

Where shall I find a blush rose blushing?—
    On the garden wall or the garden bed.—
But out in my garden the rain was rushing
    And never a blush rose raised its head.
Nothing glowing, flushing or blushing;
Rain rushing.

Where shall I find a red rose budding?—
    Out in the garden where all things grow.—
But out in my garden a flood was flooding
    And never a red rose began to blow.
Out in a flooding what should be budding?
All flooding!

Now is winter and now is sorrow,
    No roses but only thorns to-day:
Thorns will put on roses to-morrow,
    Winter and sorrow scudding away.
No more winter and no more sorrow
To-morrow.

March 6.

IN a certain little nest, built almost if not quite upon the grassy ground, having a sheltering bush behind it, and not far in front a railing, I one day saw three naked young birds consisting mainly of three gaping beaks.

Neither father nor mother in sight, there sat the three wide open birds and beaks handy and prompt in case anything edible should drop in.

There seemed a thousand chances that these particular nestlings should never attain to feathers and years of discretion; for like their own beaks their nest spread wide open, and any passing cat might in a moment "finish the birds with the bones and the beaks." Occasional cats were known to haunt those grounds.

Yet feather by feather the three became fledged; until deserting their nest they fluttered, perched, made merry, among the world-wide family of birds.

Part of all this I saw, part was told me. I had felt in doubt about the three and their prospects : but as it turned out I had better have learnt a lesson they were teaching me open-beaked.

With well-placed blind confidence they sat ready and adapted to be fed. No visible agency did *I* discern at the moment, yet *they* gaped on unabashed and unwearied. They settled themselves and persevered in the attitude of recipients, and they lacked nothing.

I might well have recalled (though I did not) that familiar verse of the Psalm : "Open thy mouth wide, and I shall fill it."

"Ask now ... the fowls of the air, and they shall tell thee."

March 7.

FEAST OF ST. PERPETUA, Carthaginian Martyr under the Emperor Severus in the year 203.

VIVIA PERPETUA of gentle birth and married as befitted her birth, favourite child of her father, and mother of a sucking baby, at the age of twenty-two was cast into prison for the faith; happy in this, that

an elect company went with her to bonds and to death.
Hard usage she sustained unflinchingly. Keener
still, she withstood her loving father's anger, his en-
treaties at her feet, his pleading her infant's helpless-
ness, his incurring a blow for her sake. She who
could triumph thus far was well able to triumph in the
arena over the wild cow which tossed but failed to
kill her, and afterwards over the unskilful gladiator
whose clumsiness prolonged her death pangs.

Noble she in every way: yet not more intrinsically
noble than the woman slave Felicitas, who enduring
with her to the end, with her likewise won a crown
"where there is neither . . . bond nor free: but Christ
is all, and in all."

March 8.

AFTER midnight, in the dark
    The clock strikes one,—
    New day has begun.
Look up and hark!
With singing heart forestall the carolling lark.

After midday, in the light
    The clock strikes one,—
    Day fall has begun.
Cast up, set right
The day's account against the on-coming night.

After noon and night, one day
    For ever one
    Ends not, once begun.
Whither away,
O brothers and O sisters? Pause and pray.

March 9.

DIRT has been hopefully defined as "something out of place."

This admirable definition applies no less encouragingly to some faults. Where actually placed, they are faults: placed elsewhere they might develop into virtues.

Let obstinacy cleave to the right side, avarice hoard in heaven, covetousness hanker after "the best gifts," rashness launch out into ventures of faith, timidity fear not them that can "kill the body, but Him Who can destroy both soul and body in hell,"—and then obstinacy, avarice, covetousness, rashness, timidity, may look up and lift up their heads for their redemption draweth nigh.

March 10.

THE Table of days upon which Easter can possibly fall, shows that there are twelve days which must in all years alike be included among the forty-six weekdays and Sundays of Lent.

Of these the 10th of March is the first, the 21st the last.

At this point a grand idea suggests itself: that for nearly nineteen centuries these twelve solemn days, like twelve Sybils arrayed in mourning robes, have year by year sounded an alarm throughout the Church's holy mountain; calling on the faithful to bewail the past, amend the present, face the future.

A grand idea if only it were a sound one! But varieties in the mode of computing Easter (not to mention any other difficulty) forbid it. So all that I can do with my "grand idea," is to set it aside: sound must give way to sense, fancy to fact.

E

For pious frauds are pinchbeck : pious honesty and accuracy are gold.

March the 10th will do us great good, if it conduces to our becoming accurate. Many other achievements may look more impressive at first sight : but let us wait and see ; for time will show, or if not time eternity. Sooner or later we are likely to find accuracy itself a solemn thing : most formidable when infringed. yet sometimes when adhered to only less formidable than when violated : a solemn duty, a solemn discipline.

March 11.

EARTH has clear call of daily bells,
   A rapture where the anthems are,
   A chancel-vault of gloom and star,
A thunder when the organ swells :
Alas, man's daily life—what else?—
Is out of tune with daily bells.

While Paradise accords the chimes
   Of Earth and Heaven : its patient pause
   Is rest fulfilling music's laws.
Saints sit and gaze, where oftentimes
Precursive flush of morning climbs
And air vibrates with coming chimes.

March 12.

FEAST OF ST. GREGORY THE GREAT, Monk and Pope. Born of an illustrious Roman family, about the middle of the sixth century, died 604.

THIS great Pope stands out among his fellow-men by the lustre of his many gifts and graces. Noble birth and wealth rendered accessible to him the high places of this world, and he became Praetor of Rome.

Nor (according to some accounts) was it without a conflict that the Grace of God weaned him from luxury and splendour, nevertheless that sufficing Grace won the victory : and after the year 574 the superb Praetor had vanished, to reappear as the self-impoverished Benedictine, the endower of monasteries, and benefactor of the poor.

As a monk he outran the austerities of his brethren and undermined his health, devoting himself to mental pursuits and to prayer.

Called in 577 to be a Cardinal Deacon, he was afterwards sent on an embassy to Constantinople, where he resided six years. Thence he returned to his monastery, and by election of his brethren he became their abbot.

In the year 590, on the death of Pope Pelagius II, the unanimous voice of Rome called him to ascend the pontifical throne. Vainly he appealed to the Emperor Maurice, vainly he fled : the voice of the nation, in this instance we may well believe the Voice of God, spake, and it had to be done.

Thus the devout monk filled the papal chair, an eminence demanding along with the spiritual graces of a saint, the dominant gifts of a statesman : nor did he fail under either aspect. He withstood and abased theological error ; he carried further the liturgical work of his predecessors by giving to public devotion its actual form of words ; he added to words the elevated musical tones which bear his name ; he influenced for good both France and Spain. Yet are we of England bound beyond others to revere his memory, for at his word St. Augustine came over and helped our heathen forefathers to turn from darkness to light.

One stain is alleged as marring the glory of St.

Gregory,—an unworthy complacency to the murder-
ous usurping Emperor Phocas. Nevertheless to ourselves he is truly a Father in God, to be venerated even
as our own Venerable Bede teaches us : " If Gregory be
not to others an apostle, he is one to us, for the seal
of his apostleship are we in the Lord."

March 13.

I.

CAN false etymology ever be of use ? I think in
one instance it has been of use to me.

"Lent."   Good as it is to understand one's own
language, I feel neither incited nor helped to observe
Lent by being referred to a German root.

But when once (however erroneously) I connect the
word with "a loan " : that which is lent, that which
being lent, not bestowed, will some day be with-
drawn : then it sounds an alarm in my ears.

Forty chances to be used or abused.

Forty appeals to be responded to or resisted.

Forty battles to be lost or won.

Forty days to be utilized or wasted.

And then the account to be closed, and the result
registered.

March 14.

2.

OR again, and yet more solemnly.

Lent : a loan of forty days : but such a loan as is
terminable at the pleasure of the Lender.

Lent : a loan of unguaranteed duration : the beginning, by God's mercy, ours ; the end not assured
to us.

Lent : a period set us wherein specially to prepare

for eternity: forty days long at the longest: can forty days be accounted long when eternity is at stake?

"In the Day of Judgment, Good Lord, deliver us."

March 15.

THY lilies drink the dew,
Thy lambs the rill, and I will drink them too;
    For those in purity
And innocence are types, dear Lord, of Thee.
    The fragrant lily flower
Bows and fulfils Thy Will its lifelong hour;
    The lamb at rest and play
Fulfils Thy Will in gladness all the day;
    They leave to-morrow's cares
Until the morrow, what it brings it bears.
    And I, Lord, would be such;
Not high, or great, or anxious overmuch,
    But pure and temperate,
Earnest to do Thy Will betimes and late,
    Fragrant with love and praise
And innocence through all my appointed days;
    Thy lily I would be
Spotless and sweet, Thy lamb to follow Thee.

March 16.

THE Impious Cudweed,—how can any weed have earned so grim a title?

In a very simple manner.

This cudweed puts forth a blossom which in its turn puts forth around itself other blossoms.

The first-formed blossom stands like a father encircled by his children, their stock and source.

But the blossoms of the second generation lengthen

their necks, and hold their heads high : they overtop
their parent : in a figure, they look down upon him.

For which loftiness our wise forefathers stigmatised
this plant as the Impious Cudweed.

March 17.

WHAT is it Jesus saith unto the soul?—
" Take up the Cross, and come and follow Me."
One word He saith to all men : none may be
Without a Cross yet hope to touch the goal.
Then heave it bravely up, and brace thy whole
    Body to bear ; it will not weigh on thee
    Past strength ; or if it crush thee to thy knee
Take heart of grace, for grace shall be thy dole.
Give thanks to-day, and let to-morrow take
Heed to itself ; to-day imports thee more,
    To-morrow may not dawn like yesterday :
    Until that unknown morrow, go thy way,
Suffer, and work, and strive for Jesus' sake :—
Who tells thee what to-morrow keeps in store?

March 18.

FEAST OF ST. EDWARD, King of the West Saxons. Born about
the year 962 ; murdered, 978 or 979.

WE are happy in that the Anglican Calendar does
not appear to define this good young monarch as a
martyr, though elsewhere he has been styled such.
By a popular account he fell a victim to the jealousy
of his stepmother Elfrida, who, wishing her own son
to mount the throne, opened a way by causing Edward the elder half-brother to be stabbed.

Great is our privilege as members of the English
Church, in that we are not commanded, or invited, or

in any way encouraged to assert what contradicts history, or to override facts by pious beliefs, or in any form to hold "the thing that is not."

When we reflect on points susceptible of improvement in our beloved Mother Church, it is well to betake ourselves to prayer; well also to give thanks for her grace of sincerity, and to sue out, each one of us for himself, his own individual share of so fundamental a grace.

If we are not truthful one by one, we shall never add up as a truthful community.

March 19.

WATCH yet a while,
Weep till that day shall dawn when thou shalt smile:
Watch till the day
When all save only Love shall pass away.

Then love rejoicing shall forget to weep,
Shall hope or fear no more, or watch or sleep,
But only love and stint not deep beyond deep.
Now we sow love in tears, but then shall reap.
Have patience as True Love's own flock of sheep:
Have patience with His love
Who served for us, Who reigns for us above.

March 20.

IT is good to be last not first
    Pending the present distress,
It is good to hunger and thirst
    So it be for righteousness.
It is good to spend and be spent,
    It is good to watch and to pray,
Life and Death make a goodly Lent
    So it leads us to Easter Day.

March 21.

FEAST OF ST. BENEDICT, ABBOT. Born about the year 480; died standing at the foot of the Altar of Monte Cassino, and beside his twin sister's grave opened to receive him, 543.

THIS is that great and holy Benedict, by birth noble, the Patriarch of Western Monachism. About the age of fourteen he fled from the world and its delights, and in a cave near Subiaco as a most austere hermit conquered first himself; afterwards waxing mighty to conquer a multitude of souls for Christ. Disciples flocked around him. Yet a while, and he removed with a small body of his spiritual sons to Monte Cassino, and there founded the renowned monastery. whence he migrated no more.

Amongst his chief glories ranks the conciliatory influence whereby he promoted amity between the barbarian conquerors of Italy and the down-trodden sons of that lovely land.

He was a " repairer of the breach," a " restorer of paths to dwell in." To God be the praise, through Jesus Christ our Lord. Amen.

March 22.

CHRIST'S Heart was wrung for me, if mine is sore ;
　　And if my feet are weary, His have bled ;
　　He had no place wherein to lay His Head ;
If I am burdened, He was burdened more.
The cup I drink, He drank of long before ;
　　He felt the unuttered anguish which I dread ;
　　He hungered Who the hungry thousands fed,
And thirsted Who the world's refreshment bore.

If grief be such a looking-glass as shows
  Christ's Face and man's in some sort made alike,
    Then grief is pleasure with a subtle taste :
    Wherefore should any fret, or faint, or haste?
Grief is not grievous to a soul that knows
  Christ comes,—and listens for that hour to strike.

March 23.

IN common parlance Strong and Weak are merely relative terms : thus the " strong " of one sentence will be the " weak " of another.

We behold the strong appointed to help the weak : Angels who " excel in strength," men. And equally the weak the strong : woman " the weaker vessel," man.

This, though it should not inflate any, may fairly buoy us all up. For every human creature may lay claim to strength, or else to weakness : in either case to helpfulness. " We that are strong," writes St. Paul, proceeding to state a duty of the strong. *We* who are weak may study the resources of the weak.

Of our Divine Lord a prophetic Psalm speaking in His Person saith : " I am feeble and sore smitten," and this in close connexion with that almighty work of Atonement, whereby He took our place, and bore our guilt and our penalty.

And following afar off in Christ's footsteps, the many-sided St. Paul asks : " Who is weak, and I am not weak? "

Now helpfulness being constituted our privilege, of necessity it becomes likewise our duty. The dignity entails the charge.

How, then, can you or I help? One obvious un-answerable answer is, " By prayer " : yet must we not make of prayer a lazy substitute for other forms of help.

By peering all round us (in hopes of seeing and not of *not seeing*) we may very likely discern quite unforeseen openings for rendering assistance for spending and being spent. For instance: Can a child save his country? Hear what a boy only eight years old did.

He was I suppose a Dutch boy, doubtless aware in his childish way of the all-importance of dams and dykes. One evening returning home from a visit, he noticed a dribble through one of those flood-barriers. How cope with this literal "letting out of water"? Some might have fetched help: not so he. He thrust his eight-year-old finger into the leak, and all night long held it there, plugging out the advancing ruin. In the morning there he was found, worn indeed, but not worn out.

"Who follows in his train?"

March 24.

Vigil of the Annunciation.

THE month of March is liable to frost and to boisterous wind, yet its sun has acquired strength, and its earth puts forth violets.

Such a world as March favours seems the very world for this vigil: rich in firstfruits of life, rich in promise, yet withal cold and full of unrest; visited by strong sunshine to remind us how the Archangel Gabriel, "the strength of God," came down from heaven bearing to this groaning and travailing creation a message of consolation and revival; and putting forth violets with bowed heads, veiling leaves, exquisite fragrance, to set before us in a symbol the Virgin "Handmaid of the Lord" in the loveliness of her gifts and graces.

March 25.

" BEHOLD the handmaid of the Lord ; be it unto me according to thy word." Thus, as on this day, " the choice one of her that bare her" answered the angelic announcement that she should bring forth the Son of God.

An Archangel visited a Saint, a Saint received an Archangel.

We discern, so to say, nothing but angels and saints taking sweet counsel together and walking in that house of God as friends ; their thoughts engrossed by God, their hearts set not on themselves or on each other, but on God.

If the approach of Christ wrought up these twain to such a height of piety, whereunto cannot His indwelling exalt us?

St. Paul wrote : "I live ; yet not I, but Christ liveth in me ;" and again : "I can do all things through Christ which strengtheneth me."

March 26.

A BURDENED heart that bleeds and bears,
   And hopes and waits in pain,
And faints beneath its fears and cares,
   Yet hopes again.

Wilt Thou accept the heart I bring,
   O gracious Lord and kind,
To ease it of a torturing sting,
   And staunch and bind?

Alas, if Thou wilt none of this,
　　None else have I to give:
Look Thou upon it as it is,
　　Accept, relieve.

Or if Thou wilt not yet relieve,
　　Be not extreme to sift:
Accept a faltering will to give,—
　　Itself Thy gift.

March 27.

By the Mosaic Law fish were omitted and honey was excluded from sacrifice.

Beasts and birds appear privileged, fish humiliated; flour, oil, exalted, honey abased.

Look again.

The only time that we are distinctly told what ordinary food it was which Christ partook of, was when accepting from His disciples "a piece of a broiled fish, and of an honeycomb," He did eat before them.

Christ, God of God, Very God of Very God.

This life is full of shallow judgments and one-sided estimates.

If in this world Apostles were "the offscouring of all things," we may well hope that much besides of the overlooked refuse of earth will reappear amongst the treasure of heaven.

We may well hope that it will reappear. "Let us also fear," lest we be not there to recognise it.

March 28.

Is it any disadvantage when the performance of duty is attended by unavoidable pain or difficulty, and so by an involuntary tinge of disrelish?

Not necessarily a disadvantage. Grievous besetments may turn to our greater edification and profit, so long as we guard against difficulty breeding discontent, or pain a grudge.

Such a point was once illustrated to me in conversation :—

A vigorous man strolls a couple of miles along country lanes to call on an acquaintance : the act is friendly, and as such it is accepted. The same man, grown gouty, hobbles his two miles on tortured feet, reluctant, yet eager, because he "loveth at all times." Which walk gives the higher proof of love? Which will most endear him to his friend?

March 29.

LIE still, my restive heart, lie still :
God's Word to thee saith, " Wait and bear."
The good which He appoints is good,
The good which He denies were ill :
Yea, subtle comfort is thy care,
Thy hurt a help not understood.

"Friend, go up higher," to one: to one,
"Friend, enter thou My joy," He saith :
To one, "Be faithful unto death."
For some a wilderness doth flower,
Or day's work in one hour is done,—
"But thou, could'st thou not watch one hour?"

March 30.

I.

ONCE in Scotland, while staying at a hospitable friend's castle, I observed, crossing the floor of my bedroom, a rural insect. I will call it, though I daresay it was not one in strictness, a pill millepede.

Towards my co-tenant I felt a sort of good will not inconsistent with an impulse to eject it through the window.

I stooped and took it up, when in a moment a swarm of baby millepedes occupied my hand in their parent's company.

Surprised, but resolute, I hurried on, and carried out my scheme successfully; observing the juniors retire into cracks outside the window as adroitly as if they had been centenarians.

Pondering over this trifle, it seems to me a parable setting forth visibly and vividly the incalculable element in all our actions. I thought to pick up one millepede, and behold! I was transporting a numerous family.

If thus we cannot estimate the full bearing of action, how shall we hope to estimate the full extent of influence? I thought to catch one millepede, and an entire family lay at my mercy!

March 31.

2.

In that self-same bedchamber I used to answer matutinal taps, supposing myself called: and lo! it was only a tapping of jackdaws or of starlings lodged in the turrets.

Winged creatures they were, but neither angel visitants nor warning summoners. How many fancied calls or omens are in fact no more significant than jackdaws or starlings?

On the other hand: to him "that hath ears to hear," any good creature of God may convey a message.

April 1.

A Castle-builder's World.
"The line of confusion, and the stones of emptiness."—(Isaiah xxxiv.11.)

UNRIPE harvest there hath none to reap it
  From the misty, gusty place ;
Unripe vineyard there hath none to keep it
  In unprofitable space.
Living men and women are not found there,
  Only masks in flocks and shoals;
Flesh-and-bloodless hazy masks surround there
  Ever wavering orbs and poles ;
Flesh-and-bloodless vapid masks abound there,
  Shades of bodies without souls.

April 2.

I HAVE an impression (for I will not relate my adventure quite positively) that in my youth, being at that time too ignorant to appreciate such a rarity, in one of my country walks I found what I can only call a four-leafed trefoil.

Perhaps I plucked and so destroyed it : I certainly left it, for most certainly I have it not.

Not that I thought nothing of it : I thought it curious, pointed it out, I daresay, to my companion, and left it.

Now I would give something to recover that wonder : *then*, when I might have had it for the carrying, I left it.

Once missed, one may peer about in vain all the rest of one's days for a second four-leafed trefoil.

No one expects to find whole fields of such : even one, for once, is an extra allowance.

Life has, so to say, its four-leafed trefoils for a

favoured few : and how many of us overlook once and finally our rare chance !

Well, whether literally or figuratively, but one thing then remains for us to do : to walk humbly and thankfully among this world's whole fields of three-leafed trefoil.

April 3.

FEAST OF ST. RICHARD, Bishop of Chichester. Born about the year 1198, died 1253.

ST. RICHARD had his share of public troubles faced and borne as became a Christian ; and lightened to him doubtless by the support of Divine Grace, even more than by that kindly and affectionate heart, which having endeared his person to his familiars, now endears his memory to ourselves.

As in life, so in death, he edifies us :—

"When he was standing hearing Mass, he fell down in a fit, and was carried into his bed in the ward of the hospital. On coming to himself, he told his chaplain that he would never rise again from that bed, and he bade him secretly prepare everything for his funeral. His old friend, Master Simon de Terring, who had entertained him during the time that the property of the see was confiscated, drew near the bed ; St. Richard turned his peaceful face towards him, and said, 'I was glad when they said unto me, We will go into the house of the Lord.'"

April 4.

FEAST OF ST. AMBROSE, Confessor and Bishop of Milan. Born about the year 340, died 397.

TWO glorious deeds stand out prominently in the career of St. Ambrose. He put the Emperor Theodosius to public penance for a horrid massacre whereby

he had stained his soul: and he became God's instrument in the conversion to the true faith of St. Augustin,
afterwards Bishop of Hippo.

No less venerable does he appear as a defender of
the Catholic Church against the Arian heresy, and as
a Father and Doctor whose writings form part of that
Church's permanent dowry of wisdom.

A pretty story is related of his infancy: how a
swarm of bees alighted on his mouth while he slept,
and took wing again leaving him unhurt. Which
incident conveyed to paternal affection an augury of
his mature eloquence.

Thus lips for the moment speechless, and creatures
permanently destitute of speech, combined to deliver
an intelligible message to one who had love for an
interpreter.

All creation would teach us spiritual lessons and
gladden us by heavenly meanings, if we cherished
that same interpreter.

"Beloved, let us love one another: for love is of
God; and every one that loveth is born of God, and
knoweth God."

April 5.

HEAVEN'S chimes are slow, but sure to strike at last:
  Earth's sands are slow, but surely dropping through:
  And much we have to suffer, much to do,
    Before the time be past.

Chimes that keep time are neither slow nor fast:
  Not many are the numbered sands nor few:
  A time to suffer, and a time to do,
    And then the time is past.

April 6.

WEIGH all my faults and follies righteously,
   Omissions and commissions, sin on sin;
   Make deep the scale, O Lord, to weigh them in;
Yea, set the Accuser vulture-eyed to see
All loads ingathered which belong to me:
   That so in life the judgment may begin,
   And Angels learn how hard it is to win
One solitary sinful soul to Thee.
I have no merits for a counterpoise:
   Oh vanity my work and hastening day,
What can I answer to the accusing voice?
     Lord, drop Thou in the counterscale alone
   One Drop from Thine own Heart, and overweigh
   My guilt, my folly, even my heart of stone.

April 7.

"I HAVE prayed for thee, that thy faith fail not," spake our Adorable Almighty Lord to St. Peter.

Yet the Apostle's faith failed, not finally indeed, but with a pitiable temporary lapse.

Wherefore does our Lord thus, by His Evangelist, declare to His whole cherished Church that even His own intercession was not at once and to the full efficacious?

Surely not for our discouragement, but rather to uphold us by the strong consolation of an inexhaustible hope.

He, perfect in wisdom, power, love, waited patiently for His prayer's fulfilment, enduring for the moment that it should apparently fail.

If in the light of His Example we cannot wait patiently, and thus waiting cannot pray and pray again for those we love trembling, if we will not endure rebuffs, and hope against hope, yea, and though God slay us and ours still trust in Him, then is our own faith faltering if it has not already failed.

How reinforce it? There may be higher and better ways, yet I think this humble way will not displease Him: by an appeal for that gift of faith without which it is impossible to please God, and on the very ground that without it we cannot offer up availing intercessions.

April 8.

"Then shall the land enjoy her sabbaths, as long as it lieth desolate; ... even then shall the land rest, and enjoy her sabbaths."—(LEV. xxvi. 34.)

NOW this territory whereof the text speaks was the Holy Land, the abode of the Holy Nation.

Viewed in reference to each other, it was the nation that sanctified the land rather than the land the nation: and this, because it appertains to the higher and not to the lower element to consecrate its fellow.

It was so, that is, in theory. In practice, Israel oftentimes and widely desecrated their hallowed dwelling-place. They, living, were the nobler element; she, lifeless, whilst filled with them became defiled by their defilements; emptied of them, recovered her passive proper sanctity.

They were like the soul, she like the body.

Let us thus think of all our dead, reverencing and hoping for them. Be they what they may, their bodies are for the present keeping sabbath: and "if Thou, Lord, wilt be extreme to mark what is done amiss, O Lord, *who* may abide it?"

"He that judgeth me is the Lord. Therefore judge nothing before the time, until the Lord come, Who both will bring to light the hidden things of darkness, and will make manifest the counsels of the hearts: and then shall every man have praise of God."

It was again a holy nation which at last re-entered its own holy land of promise.

" He putteth his mouth in the dust; if so be there may be hope."

April 9.

REST remains, when all is done,
　　Work and vigil, prayer and fast,
　　All fulfilled from first to last,
　　All the length of time gone past
And eternity begun.

Fear and hope and chastening rod
　　Urge us on the narrow way:
　　Bear we now as best we may
　　Heat and burden of to-day,
Struggling, panting up to God.

April 10.

ONE day long ago I sat in a certain garden by a certain ornamental water.

I sat so long and so quietly that a wild garden creature or two made its appearance: a water rat, perhaps, or a water-haunting bird. Few have been my personal experiences of the sort, and this one gratified me.

I was absorbed that afternoon in anxious thought, yet the slight incident pleased me. If by chance people noticed me they may have thought how dull and blank I must be feeling: and partly they would have been right, but partly wrong.

Many (I hope) whom we pity as even wretched, may in reality, as I was at that moment, be conscious of some small secret fount of pleasure: a bubble, perhaps, yet lit by a dancing rainbow.

I hope so and I think so: for we and all creatures alike are in God's hand, and God loves us.

April 11.

AMONG duties which are characteristically Christian there is not one more plainly prescribed than the love of enemies. Moreover, this duty once laid down commends itself forthwith to man's noblest sympathies: it appears ravishingly lovely, irresistibly attractive, to eyes inured to gaze on Christ.

Most people, I assume, have no private and personal enemies of their own: but so long as they themselves are ranged on God's side, God's enemies become theirs.

All sinners, all shortcomers, all criminals, all are to be beloved, if not as friends then as enemies.

But which of us is the lover and which the beloved in this connexion? The best of us is a sinner, the worst of us may become a saint.

If we love all, we shall be the less likely to class erroneously either ourself or our neighbour.

April 12.

"His heart is established, he shall not be afraid, until he see his desire upon his enemies."—(Ps. cxii. 8.)

WHAT desire? The Psalmist does not say.

But Christians are privileged to read the sentence in the light of Gospel perfection: to us Christ has said: "Love your enemies."

What then is a worthy desire for enemies? The same as for friends. As St. Paul writes to his beloved Corinthians: "We are glad . . . when ye are strong : and this also we wish, even your perfection."

But mounting higher he writes to the Romans: "God commendeth His love toward us . . . when we were enemies, we were reconciled to God by the death of His Son."

Yet far above, as it were even out of St. Paul's sight, Christ Himself ascends when He calls those same enemies friends, saying: "Greater love hath no man than this, that a man lay down his life for his friends."

"Now if any man have not the Spirit of Christ, he is none of His."

"Go, and do thou likewise."

April 13.

A COLD wind stirs the blackthorn
    To burgeon and to blow,
Besprinkling half-green hedges
    With vegetable snow.

Through coldness and through keenness,
    Dear hearts, take comfort so :
Somewhere or other doubtless,
    These make the blackthorn blow.

April 14.

To be a saint at all, man must become like God : to be at all like God, man must become a saint.

I suppose there is no Divine Perfection more

vividly reflected in the dim human mirror than the
Divine Love of sinners.

In the purest, loftiest, most spiritual heart of man
or woman, oftentimes next to God Supreme, sits enshrined some one beloved sinful soul.

Sinful, I mean, among sinners: for if any of us
"say that we have no sin, we deceive ourselves, and
the truth is not in us."

On behalf of such cherished souls no gift is grudged:
not tears, or prayers, or agony of fear, or anguish of a
lifetime. For their sakes hearts more precious than
most precious alabaster are broken and pour forth
fragrance, and drain out the last drops of life, and
would and can keep back nothing, if so be their sacrifice may win acceptance.

Of those who "love much," many love thus: and is
not theirs a life worth living, leading up, and not down,
to a death worth dying?

April 15.

I HAVE never forgotten the courageous reverence
with which one to whom a friend was exhibiting prints
from the Book of Job, avowed herself afraid to look at
a representation which went counter to the Second
Commandment, and looked not at it.

A host of us talk "as seeing Him Who is invisible:"
she so acted.

Blessed she who then set to her seal that God is
true, and since then has "died in faith."

Oh! what is earth, that we should build
Our houses here, and seek concealed
Poor treasure, and add field to field,

And heap to heap, and store to store,
Still grasping more, and seeking more,
While step by step Death nears the door?

April 16.

SOME people have it as their lifelong characteristic to rank not first but second in their particular world, circle, career, groove.

Such persons may be positively good, comparatively inferior : positively liked, comparatively unloved.

They are the Ajax Telamons of everyday life.

Amongst the few familiar to me, Ajax Telamon stands out as one of the noblest and most pathetic figures of mythical (?) antiquity. As a warrior unsurpassed, except by rapid-footed Achilles. Mighty to hoist and hurl a rock, yet at the game of hurling outdone by Polypoetes. Gigantic in strength, yet at a trial of strength foiled by adroit Ulysses ; who subsequently contested with him and won the Vulcanian Arms. Losing heart at last and self-destroyed, the victim of sheer shame.

But after all I fancy that some of us (I certainly for one) care more now for Ajax than for those who at some point excelled him. The comparative aspect has faded away, the positive remains.

If even time lasts long enough to reverse a verdict of time, how much more eternity?

Let us take courage, secondary as we may for the present appear. Of ourselves likewise the comparative aspect will fade away, the positive will remain.

"Our soul loatheth this light bread."—(NUMBERS xxi. 5.)
" Is there any taste in the white of an egg?"—(JOB vi. 6.)

THAT first is the speech of certain carnal Israelites concerning the Manna: that last, of one sorely tried Saint concerning the natural food in question.

Manna, we know on Divine authority, is a type of the Blessed Sacrament of Christ's Body and Blood (*see* St. John vi. 26–58). An egg (though not by revelation) is one commonly accepted symbol of the Resurrection. Thus both combine in bearing a reference to the same life-sustaining Sacrament.

And, alas! if the two symbols bear such a reference, so also do the two murmurs. Still the natural man craves not for spiritual nourishment of his spiritual self, but rather for gross relishing bodily indulgence: and still many a harassed saint feels in silence—God grant to us all the grace at least of *silence*—that there is no "taste" for him in "the Life of the world."

Let us turn to a different discouragement: perhaps one may throw light upon the other.

I suppose I do not stand alone in feeling (at least on unreasoning impulse) as if our Blessed Lord in the days of His mortality, whilst man's eyes could look upon and his hands handle that living and breathing "Word of Life," appeared more winningly accessible, less awe-striking, less overwhelming than He does now. The element of doubt was in great measure excluded from Face to face intercourse with Him. Men, women, children could see and hear, and in some degree could estimate His inviting Aspect, His gracious Voice: when He said "Come unto Me," "Follow Me," His Will and pleasure were spoken plainly and not in parables.

We ourselves, on the contrary, look forward to never beholding Him until He comes "to be our Judge," revealing that Face from which earth and heaven shall flee away. Meanwhile we approach His Altar in dimness: our own sinfulness comes home to us by every channel of conviction; "Him we see not."

O Lord, make us even as those Thy beloved blind men who first beheld Thy Face of Love when their eyes were opened, but on whom Thy Face of Love was also bent while they beheld it not. Amen.

April 18.

I REMEMBER rising early once to see the sun rise.

I rose too early, and waited wearily and impatiently.

At length the sun rose.

At length? Scarcely. The sun kept time, though I kept it not: the sun lagged not because I hurried.

If the material sun fails not, much more is that supreme "Sun" infallible whereof we read: "Unto you that fear My Name shall the Sun of Righteousness arise."

Therefore, neither doth our Lord delay His coming, however the Church expectant may reiterate, "Why is His chariot so long in coming? why tarry the wheels of His chariots?"

"Beloved, be not ignorant of this one thing, that one day is with the Lord as a thousand years, and a thousand years as one day. The Lord is not slack concerning His promise, as some men count slackness; but is longsuffering to usward, not willing that any should perish, but that all should come to repentance."

April 19.

FEAST OF ST. ALPHEGE, ARCHBISHOP OF CANTERBURY. Born in Britain, about the year 954; died 1012.

IN early life St. Alphege renounced the world and took up his abode in a monastery. There, with great devotion to God, he carried on the labour of self-conquest. He became an abbot; then Bishop of Winchester; finally, on the death of Archbishop Aelfric, he was translated to the see of Canterbury, in the year 1006.

In his days Denmark scourged England, and by the Danes he met his death. A captive in their hands, he was rated by them at a heavy ransom, but remained resolute that no such sum should for his sake be wrung from his already impoverished country. Which patriotism cost him his life: he was pelted with bones and horns, until one of the Danes (there is room to hope from a merciful motive) struck him dead with an axe.

It has been questioned whether St. Alphege, who died not for the truth's sake, but by an heroic impulse of self-sacrifice, is entitled to be styled a Martyr. St. Anselm, however, acknowledges him as such. In any case we may praise God for him as for one " of whom the world was not worthy."

April 20.

PITEOUS my rhyme is,
What while I muse of love and pain,
Of love misspent, of love in vain,
Of love that is not loved again :
  And is this all then ?

As long as time is
Love loveth. Time is but a span,
The dalliance space of dying man:
And is this all immortals can?
   The gain were small then.

Love loves for ever,
And finds a sort of joy in pain,
And gives with nought to take again,
And loves too well to end in vain:
   Is the gain small then?
   Love laughs at " never,"
Outlives our life, exceeds the span
Appointed to mere mortal man:
That which love is and does and can,
   Is all in all then.

April 21.

ONCE in conversation I happened to lay stress on
the virtue of resignation, when the friend I spoke to
depreciated resignation in comparison with conformity
to the Divine Will.

My spiritual height was my friend's spiritual hillock.

Not that he reproved me : standing on a higher
level he made the way obvious for others also to
ascend.

Now he was a man in continual pain, hindered and
hampered in his career by irremediable ill-health.
And moreover he was in occasional social intercourse
one of the most cheerful people I ever knew.

If only we—if only I were as *resigned* as he was
conformed!

And why not?

April 22.

ONE of the most genuine Christians I ever knew, once took lightly the dying out of a brief acquaintance which had engaged her warm heart, on the ground that such mere tastes and glimpses of congenial intercourse on earth wait for their development in heaven.

Then she knew Whom she trusted : *now* (please God) she knows as she is known.

> Lord, I had chosen another lot,
> But then I had not chosen well ;
> Thy choice and only Thine is good :
> No different lot, search heaven and hell,
> Had blessed me, fully understood ;
> None other, which Thou orderest not.

April 23.

FEAST OF ST. GEORGE, MARTYR; accounted Patron Saint of England. The year 285 has been assigned as the date of his martyrdom; which event, however, has likewise been attributed to the year 303.

BY a conjecture St. George is that certain man (mentioned but unnamed in history) of whom it is related that in the city of Nicomedia he publicly tore to shreds an edict of Diocletian, as impious and unworthy of observance. For this act he forfeited mortal life, and went up to the glory of the life immortal.

Far different from so kindling yet sober a narrative is the career of our saint, according to widespread romantic legend. Who does not think of St. George as a quasi-impossible personage slaying a dragon and rescuing a princess?

And by all means let us so picture him, only turning the wild legend into a parable of truth. Thus the dragon becomes the devil, whom the Christian champion overcame by the Blood of the Lamb and by the word of his testimony, when he loved not his life unto the death; and the princess whom he protected and served appears as no mortal bride of his own, but as the Church, "the bride, the Lamb's wife."

Fabrications, blunders, even lies, frequently contain some grain of truth: and though life at the longest cannot be long enough for us to sift all, one occasionally may repay the sifting.

April 24.

LORD, what have I to offer? sickening fear
    And a heart-breaking loss.
Are these the cross Thou givest me? then dear
    I will account this cross.

If this is all I have, accept even this
    Poor priceless offering,
A quaking heart with all that therein is,
    O Thou my thorn-crowned King.

Accept the whole, my God, accept my heart
    And its own love within:
Wilt Thou accept us and not sift apart?
    — Only sift out my sin.

April 25.

FEAST OF ST. MARK, EVANGELIST; died about the year 68.

POPULAR though not undisputed tradition assigns a Martyr's Crown to St. Mark; a crown won in Egypt, where as Bishop of Alexandria he was done to death by an idolatrous mob : thus the legend imports.

Whether or not this evangelist is the same as " Marcus, sister's son to Barnabas," named by St. Paul, he was presumably that "Marcus my son" mentioned by St. Peter; this Apostle having, it is supposed, supplied materials for St. Mark's Gospel.

But thus St. Mark's personality remains involved in doubt. We know not whether, for aught that is recorded to the contrary, he did not proceed in one unbroken course on his road to perfection: or whether he was once guilty of a grave backsliding narrated in the Book of Acts, and afterwards apparently retrieved.

In the one case, his example inspirits saints to press onward to the goal: in the other, it encourages peni-tents to arise and return into the way of righteousness. Either with Moses at the Red Sea he bids the people go forward : or else with a Greater than Moses beside another sea he tenderly provokes to good works, saying, "Go home to thy friends, and tell them how great things the Lord hath done for thee, and hath had compassion on thee"— Divine words so fully recorded in no Gospel besides his own.

April 26.

WHEN sick of life and all the world—
How sick of all the earth but Thee !—
I lift mine eyes up to the hills,
    Eyes of my heart that see,

I see beyond all death and ills
Refreshing green for heart and eyes,
The golden streets and gateways pearled,
    The trees of Paradise.

"There is a time for all things," saith
The Word of Truth, Thyself the Word,
And many things Thou reasonest of:
    A time for hope deferred,
But time is now for grief and fears;
A time for life, but now is death;
Oh! when shall be the time of love,
    When Thou shalt wipe our tears?

Then the new Heavens and Earth shall be
Where righteousness shall dwell indeed;
There shall be no more blight, nor need,
    Nor barrier of the sea;
No sun and moon alternating,
For God shall be the Light thereof;
No sorrow more, no death, no sting,
    For God Who reigns is Love.

April 27.

"Hope deferred maketh the heart sick: but when the desire cometh, it is a tree of life."—(PROV. xiii. 12.)

WE feel or fancy ourselves quite at home in the first clause of this proverb, whether or not we have deeply and keenly experienced the heart sickness of which it speaks.

But how about the second clause?

Left to myself, I at any rate might never have caught its most blessed meaning. But one from whose words I ought to have imbibed much wisdom, and from whose example many virtues, once pointed out the Cross of Christ Crucified as that Tree of Life which satisfied the world's heartsick hope.

And if it suffices to slake a world's desire, whose desire sufficeth it not to slake?

Even as the Lord hath said: "I, if I be lifted up from the earth, will draw all men unto Me."

"Draw me, we will run after Thee."

April 28.

I.

A FRIEND once vividly described to me how in a country walk he had remarked cobwebs shaped more or less like funnels or tunnels, one end open to the road, while deep down at the other end lay in wait the spider.

I walked a little about the same country, and failed to observe the spider. Fortunately for me I was not a fly.

The spider was on the alert in his sphere, my friend was on the alert in his higher sphere; I alone, it would seem, was not on the alert in either sphere.

If we turn all this into a parable, and magnify the spider to human or superhuman scale, what must become of the wayfarer who strolls along not on the alert in any sphere?

April 29.

2.

THAT funnel web seems to me an apt figure of the world.

It exhibits beauty, ingenuity, intricacy. Imagine

G

it in the early morning jewelled with dewdrops, and each of these at sunny moments a spark of light or a section of rainbow. Woven, too, as no man could weave it, fine and flexible, frail and tenacious.

Yet are its beauties of brilliancy and colour no real part of it. The dew evaporates, the tints and sparkle vanish, the tenacity remains, and at the bottom of all lurks a spider.

Meanwhile a fly has been tempted in through the wide mouth of easy access : a fly who returns no more. What becomes of the fly takes place (happily) out of sight : the less seen of that fly the better.

Or suppose that a pitiful passer by stops and stoops to rescue the fly in mid funnel before the spider clutches it. Out it comes alive indeed, but to what a life!

If its wings are not left behind, they are swathed around it as by a mummy cloth; and if its legs remain, so also are they.

Fine and flexible, frail and tenacious, the web clings to the fly, although the fly clings not willingly to the web.

At the worst, it must lie immovable and starve. At the best, it must live an uncouth, hampered, degraded life, at least for a time.

And this creature that can scarcely, or that cannot crawl, is a creature endowed with wings!

April 30.

" EYE hath not seen :"—yet man hath known and
        weighed
    A hundred thousand marvels that have been :
What is it which (the Word of Truth hath said)
    Eye hath not seen?

" Ear hath not heard :"—yet harpings of delight,
 Trumpets of triumph, song and spoken word,
Man knows them all : what lovelier, loftier might
 Hath ear not heard?

" Nor heart conceived :"—yet hath man now desired
 Beyond all reach, beyond his hope believed,
Loved beyond death : what fire shall yet be fired,
 No heart conceived?

" Deep calls to deep :"—man's depth would be despair
 But for God's deeper depth : we sow to reap,
Have patience, wait, betake ourselves to prayer :
 Deep answereth deep.

May 1.

FEAST OF ST. PHILIP AND ST. JAMES, APOSTLES.

THE Gospel tells us little specially of St. Philip, and
even less of St. James (the Less). Alike in office and
in grace, their careers, according to tradition, differed
widely. St. Philip, father of a family, endured martyrdom in the midst of certain benighted heathen :
St. James, in inviolate celibacy, was done to death at
Jerusalem by his own doubly benighted apostate countrymen.

On their Feast Day they stand before us as it were
hand in hand : " Behold, how good and joyful a thing
it is, brethren, to dwell together in unity!"

Whatever remains uncertain about them, of two
facts we rest assured : they loved God, and therefore
they cannot but have loved one another.

This double yet indivisible point of excellence is
indisputably true of all saints and of each saint. This

G 2

we know of every one, even while of millions we can ascertain nothing besides.

The world will know enough about us, if it know this much: and even if the world know it not, it suffices so long as God knows it.

May 2.

MAN's life is death. Yet Christ endured to live,
Preaching and teaching, toiling to and fro,
Few men accepting what He yearned to give,
Few men with eyes to know
His Face, that Face of Love He stooped to show.

Man's death is life. For Christ endured to die,
In slow unuttered weariness of pain,
A curse and an astonishment, passed by,
Pointed at, mocked again,
By men for whom He shed His blood—in vain?

May 3.

FEAST OF THE INVENTION OF THE CROSS.

ACCORDING to a popular tradition St. Helena, mother of Constantine the Great, "invented" or (as we should now say) discovered the true Cross in the earlier half of the fourth century.

If so, great was the privilege of St. Helena.

She sought (says the legend) for the sacred Cross by removing an idol-temple from the site of the crucifixion, and by causing the hallowed soil to be excavated. Three crosses then came to light, when our Lord's was identified by help of a miracle. If thus she did once for all, she did it of course to the exclusion of all mankind who should come after.

Must then our own privilege be less than hers? Surely it may be far greater.

For our Lord Himself ever since the supreme Day of Pentecost seeks (so to say) for His Cross, not in senseless earth, but in each warm human heart. In yours, in mine, He seeks it : does He find it?

He finds it in every heart that for love of Him suffers patiently, and at the least thankfully, if not joyfully.

We are certain to know what suffering is, this needs no disquisition : but do we know what patience is? If not, He finds not His Cross enshrined in our hearts . . . in my heart.

And if His Cross be not there, "what good shall my life do me?"

May 4.

"One swallow does not make a summer."

A ROSE which spied one swallow
Made haste to blush and blow :
"Others are sure to follow :"
Ah no, not so!
The wandering clouds still owe
A few fresh flakes of snow,
Chill fog must fill the hollow,
Before the bird-stream flow
In flood across the main
And winter's woe
End in glad summer come again.
Then thousand flowers may blossom by the shore,
But that Rose never more.

May 5.

LOVE said nay, while Hope kept saying
　　All his sweetest say,
Hope so keen to start a-maying!—
　　Love said nay.

Love was bent to watch and pray:
　　Long the watching, long the praying:—
Hope grew drowsy, pale and grey.

Hope in dreams set off a-straying,
　　All his dreamworld flushed by May;
While unslumbering, praying, weighing
　　Love said nay.

May 6.

FEAST OF ST. JOHN BEFORE THE LATIN GATE.

WOULD we fain know whether St. John the Apostle and Evangelist did really at the Latin Gate under persecuting Domitian descend into a caldron of boiling oil, and having thus in will endured martyrdom, return to his daily life scatheless and refreshed?

The wish is quite harmless: yet for the present it seems not very profitable. Meanwhile historical probability is brought forward as contrary to the alleged event.

If we knew, we should not be the better: by not knowing, we are none the worse.

One use, however, we can confidently make of a dubious legend, and it is this: we can meditate upon it as one instance (if of nothing else) of the innumerable array of points which lying apart from our vocation we shall not be required to give account of at the Day of Judgment.

About such points we may innocently feel curious, but we should not wax excited or argue obstinately. For if they will not import to us then, neither can they truly import to us now.

"The secret things belong unto the Lord our God."

May 7.

A LOVELY young woman (not then of my acquaintance) went one evening to a concert, her face swollen and bound up, observing that she went not to be seen but to hear.

She had, I believe, a methodical brain in that charming head of hers. Certainly on this occasion she drew the line accurately between what is and what is not essential to a listener. Thus, despite her swollen face, she went with a fair prospect of enjoyment.

Half the mortifications of life (many of them life-long mortifications) spring from a confusion in our own minds as to what the particular occasion, connexion, circumstance, demands of us.

We insist on being attractive, when all that is required of us is to be attracted. edified. or it may be merely entertained. It is not our neighbour's standard but our own we fall short of, if our utmost efforts leave us unsightly, uninteresting.

Our neighbour, according to his (or her) gift, sings, listens, looks beautiful, simply and contentedly.

If only we too would adorn ourselves with simplicity and contentment, at the worst we could sit listening with pleasure and profit. Meanwhile it is very likely that a cheerful, radiant heart would light up even our faces with some charm we hanker after and miss.

A corrosive mind gives plain features no chance.

May 8.

I.

THERE is a design by William Blake symbolic of the Resurrection. In it I behold the descending soul and the arising body rushing together in an indissoluble embrace : and this design, among all I recollect to have seen, stands alone in expressing the rapture of that reunion.

Not more enkindling perhaps, yet potent to stir a tenderer depth, is a passage in the Divina Commedia, which describes a company of the blessed yearning for the Resurrection: not, as Dante conjectures, for their own perfection's sake merely, but likewise for the renewal's sake of beloved ties.

I cannot show you the engraving, but hearken to the poet :—

" Our person shall be dearer in God's face
    From its rebuilding, when the glorious
    And hallowed body it shall re-embrace.
Thence will increase the light gratuitous,
    That Sovran Goodness will on us bestow,
    Light, which on Him to look empowereth us ;
And thereby shall our insight greater grow,
    So shall the ardor, which is thereby lit,
    So shall the rays, that from this ardor flow.
But as you see the brands, that flame emit
    Around them, and their own distinctness hold,
    From their keen whiteness overpowering it,
So must the light, which doth us now enfold,
    Be past in glory by those bodies bright,
    The same that, late and early, mix with mould.

Nor shall we be fatigued by so much light,
    For strong the organs of the new-made men
    Shall wax, to bear all workings of delight.
So prompt and eager both the rings were then,
    That well they seemed to cherish true desires,
    For their cold bodies, when they called Amen,
Perhaps not for themselves, but for their Sires,
    Their Mothers, and for all that had been dear,
    Or ever they became perpetual fires."
                Paradise, canto 14 (Cayley's translation).

May 9.

2.

"A FRIEND loveth at all times."

Let us thank God that this blessed text is without limitation. Once loving, we cannot love too long.

Death and the grave need make no difference. "Out of sight, in mind," would be a proverb worthy of Christians.

Are we trembling, are we in agony, for our beloved dead? Very well; it is God's Will all-holy that so for the present it should be : but this does not by one hair's breadth trench on our privilege of loving "at all times."

What in this case or in that may befit us throughout eternity, we cannot foresee : but all time, to the end of our days, is covered by that word of consolation, "A friend loveth at all times."

May 10.

3.

AND if during our mortal frailty we are thus invited, and so by inference are directed, to " love at all times," we may well thank God and take courage in the trust that such dear saints as on earth loved us, are not because they have been set free from infirmity ceasing to love us.

Purified and perfected, they have become more like Christ : who ever became more like Christ by loving less ?

If love on earth is man's exclusive (because all-inclusive) preparation for heaven, surely the result must be led up to and not led away from by the preparation.

In ordinary education the subject we are set to study is that very subject we shall be examined in, and in which proficiency will be required of us ; the accomplishment we are set to practise is that one in which it is hoped we shall at a future period excel.

And if so in nature, why not so in grace?

May 11.

LORD, when my heart was whole I kept it back,
    And grudged to give it Thee.
Now then that it is broken, must I lack
    Thy kind word " Give it Me "?
Silence would be but just, and Thou art just.
Yet since I lie here shattered in the dust,
With still an eye to lift to Thee,
    A broken heart to give,
    I think that Thou wilt bid me live,
    And answer " Give it Me."

May 12.

1.

An Oriental legend celebrates the beauty of Joseph, son of Jacob, by saying that when the submerged lily of the Nile beheld him, she rose to the surface as at sight of the sun.

A parable, I think.

So human love rises and responds to human beauty, excellence, endearment.

Yet that to which it rises is not a light-giver, but a shadow-caster: is not God, but man.

May 13.

2.

Nay, but there is a brighter side to such a parable!

Even St. Peter in passing by cast a shadow, and in that shadow faith sought, and therefore may well have found healing.

Even the eagle gazes not upon the sun, except under shelter of a special optical guard.

Us, too, shadows will benefit, if faith unseals to us their virtue. Us, too, physical conditions will aid, if through them we seek to find the Uncreated Light.

"Sun of my soul, Thou Saviour dear."

May 14.

Young girls wear flowers,
  Young brides a flowery wreath,
But next we plant them
  In garden plots of death.
Whose lot is best:
The maiden's curtained rest,

Or bride's whose hoped-for sweet
  May yet outstrip her feet?
Ah! what are such as these
To death's sufficing ease?
He sleeps indeed who sleeps in peace
  Where night and morning meet.

Dear are the blossoms
  For bride's or maiden's head,
But dearer planted
  Around our blessed dead.
Those mind us of decay
And joys that fade away,
  These preach to us perfection,
  Long love, and resurrection.
We make our graveyards fair
For spirit-like birds of air,
For Angels may be finding there
  Lost Eden's own delection.

May 15.

I HAVE long remembered a story I was once told
as a party of us sat at luncheon.

The speaker, a General, had had a pet robin, a
tame wild robin if I may call it so, a free familiar
bird, fed and cared for by him and his.

One day coming home from shooting he aimed his
last random shot at a speck in the sky. No startling
result ensued : what should ensue from a shot aimed
at such a safe altitude?

Alas, a presumable result did ensue, not visible, but
unalterably invisible. The tame robin never came
again: and the soldier who loved it, and as he believed shot it, could not, when I listened to him, tell
the story without emotion.

How many of us in heedlessness or in haste have ere now wounded some affection dear to us as our own heart. Perhaps a friend would pardon so grave an offence the more readily did he but realise how much sorer in such a case must be the offender's own wound than any other. Let us have mercy on each other and forgive : even a wronged robin's silence and absence were hard to bear.

May 16.

IF love is not worth loving, then life is not worth
    living,
  Nor aught is worth remembering but well forgot,
For store is not worth storing and gifts are not worth
    giving,
  If love is not ;

  And idly cold is death-cold, and life-heat idly hot,
And vain is any offering and vainer our receiving,
  And vanity of vanities is all our lot.

Better than life's heaving heart is death's heart un-
    heaving,
  Better than the opening leaves are the leaves that
    rot,
For there is nothing left worth achieving or retrieving,
  If love is not.

May 17.

I.

IN many cases the person who annoys and the person who is annoyed are both in the right, or (if you please) are both in the wrong.

An Englishman travelling in the East offered

hospitality to an Arab chief, and they sat down to a meal together.

Each had his national mode of eating, and standard of good breeding.

The host, surprised at foreign manners, contemplated his feeding guest ; until at last, observing him on the point of putting into his mouth a morsel to which a chance hair was attached, he stopped him in the act.

Up rose the stately Arab, saying : " I will not eat with a man who watches his guest so closely that a hair cannot be swallowed unseen."

Were both quite right, or were both a little wrong?

Such questions become important when annoyances befall us : still more, when through us they befall others.

May 18.

2.

I INCLINE to think that the Englishman behaved worse in one way, the Arab in another.

The first presumably stared beyond the limits of good manners. The other took offence where no offence, but a trifling service was intended.

The Englishman gave the provocation, but without ill will. The Arab received it with at least a shade of resentment.

Thus the curiosity deserved rebuke, yet that rebuke came not altogether well from him who administered it.

If only the twain could and would have made allowances for each other, they might have wound up with coffee and sweets !

Why then should not you and I under any such trying circumstances wind up with sweets, if not with coffee?

May 19.

ST. DUNSTAN (according to documents more or less conclusive) was born in the year 925 and died in 968. He ruled the monks of Glastonbury as Abbot, was consecrated Bishop of Worcester, afterwards, though without vacating his actual See, became Bishop of London, and terminated his career as Archbishop of Canterbury. He lived in times troublous for Church and State: as an ecclesiastic he stood forth as champion of a celibate clergy; as a statesman he faced monarchs and factions, and waged battle for the right.

This seems to be a fairly accurate skeleton-sketch of a life full of turmoil and conflict.

But is this, or anything elaborated from such material as this, the picture which rises before our mental eye at the name of St. Dunstan? Surely not. He rises before us as a legendary personage in the act of routing a besetting devil by dint of a pair of tongs!

The historical St. Dunstan will benefit us if we study his career with an impartial love of right, and hatred of wrong, wheresoever found.

But the legendary St. Dunstan? He and such as he will do us no good if, overlooking the grave lesson of self-conquest and sin-conquest, we assimilate nothing but tongs and a devil.

The devil whom St. Dunstan foiled will end by foiling us.

May 20.

THAT Song of Songs which is Solomon's,
    Sinks and rises, and loves and longs,
Through temperate zones and torrid zones,
    That Song of Songs.

    Fair its floating moon with her prongs :
Love is laid for its paving stones :
    Right it sings without thought of wrongs.

Doves it hath with music of moans,
    Birds in throngs and damsels in throngs,
High tones and mysterious undertones,
    That Song of Songs.

May 21.

" THE half was not told me," said Sheba's Queen,
    Weighing that wealth of wisdom and of gold :
" Thy fame falls short of this that I have seen :
    The half was not told.

    Happy thy servants who stand to behold,
Stand to drink in thy gracious speech and mien ;
    Happy, thrice happy, the flock of thy fold.

As the darkened moon, while a shadow between
    Her face and her kindling sun, is rolled,
I depart ; but my heart keeps memory green :
    The half was not told."

An English tourist in Sicily relates how he met with general kindness and hospitality. At one single house, however, the tone, though not the broad basis of hospitality, changed.

The family did not come forward to welcome him, but a depressed staff of domestics received and waited on him.

He lacked nothing, save a welcome. Arriving one day and departing the next, unwelcomed he arrived, and unwelcomed he departed.

This treatment left upon him a gloomy impression. How should meat, drink, shelter suffice and solace an unwelcomed guest?

Yet afterwards he saw cause to revise and reverse his estimate, becoming aware that the undemonstrative family who had harboured him laboured at that very time under the anxiety of a bitter grief. Rejoice with him they could not, burden him with a share of their own misery they would not ; all that they had to give they gave, and hid from their guest an irremediable sorrow.

How often we judge unjustly when we judge harshly. The fret of temper we despise may have its rise in the agony of some great, unflinching, unsuspected, self-sacrifice, or in the sustained strain of self-conquest, or in the endurance of unavowed, almost intolerable pain.

Whoso judges harshly is sure to judge amiss.

" Judge not, and ye shall not be judged : condemn not, and ye shall not be condemned."

H

May 23.

" ARMIAMOCI ed andate." Thus, the story goes, a General preparing for war addressed his soldiers. If only the words could be rendered into neat and pointed English! but this cannot be done: I, at least, cannot do it.

" Let us arm ourselves, and go you." Such a lame translation conveys the meaning stripped of grace. Fortunately it is the meaning I want, not the manner.

So many of us, alas! exhort in the style of that General.

" This heart-rending distress: won't you relieve? This crying evil: can't you remedy?"

It is marvellous what openings invite our neighbour to head forlorn hopes, storm breaches, grapple with sanitary, or social, or spiritual, or what-not foes. Yet more marvellous is it that we do not see our own way even to bringing up the rear of a hopeful hope.

Far from wedging ourselves in breaches, not so much as a door with a practicable approach seems to us to exist within our personal radius.

Many doors have doorsteps, and many doors without doorsteps have their threshold level with the ground. Amongst the cityfull of accessible doors, does not one within our reach stand open? If all are shut, does not one possess a knocker?

May 24.

I.

A CERTAIN Englishman sojourning in the East, and by mishap breaking a valuable pipe, the property of his entertainer, felt abashed, when his host took up the word: " In a stranger the destruction of so costly an article might cause displeasure, but in a friend every action has its charm."

One friend I once possessed who would, I think, on occasion have been capable of such graciousness. But why (if so it be) have I known one such only? and why am I (alas!) not myself the second?

Whoso loves generously need not fall short even of such a standard as this: for to reassure a friend is sweeter than to hoard a treasure. And besides, if all things do really work together for good to them that love God, then amongst "all things" cannot but be included accidents and losses : whence to fret over such must be either to quarrel with a blessing, or to pass sentence on ourselves as not entitled to it.

May 25.

2.

NAY, but, not to dwell on mere social contrarieties, it were well if, with instant and absolute sweetness of acquiescent welcome we comported ourselves towards every direct dispensation of God's most holy Will.

Which of us has the grace to feel on the instant, and heartily to protest: " Every change and chance, disappointment, duty, denial, cross, has its charm "—to feel this at once and for ever, and therein to abide at peace?

" Peace I leave with you, My peace I give unto you : not as the world giveth, give I unto you," says our Divine Master, Whose gift implies a promise of strength to appropriate it.

" The peace of God, which passeth all understanding, shall keep your hearts and minds through Christ Jesus," writes in benediction, by the pen of His apostle, God the Holy Ghost.

"Let him seek peace, and ensue it" sums up in one sentence this our duty with its inalienable privilege.

May 26.

FEAST OF ST. AUGUSTINE, FIRST ARCHBISHOP OF CANTERBURY.

THIS "Apostle of the English," sent on his mission by St. Gregory the Great (Pope), died about the year 605. Of his early life nothing appears to be known. He is rendered illustrious by the great work he wrought for God in converting Ethelbert, King of Kent, with a multitude of the Anglo-Saxons, from heathenism to Christianity : for which blessed achievement we of England may well hold him in honour from generation to generation for ever.

Not at all points does St. Augustine shine, according to one version of his history, which represents him as arrogant and unbrotherly towards a British Hierarchy, his predecessors and fellow-labourers on the same soil. Yet none the less, by all of English race, from his own day down to this very day on which I write, is he to be revered as a benefactor : as such, let us remember him lovingly and gratefully.

Such a rule may safely be observed towards all benefactors, whether spiritual or temporal.

"Thine own friend, and thy father's friend, forsake not."

May 27.

FEAST OF ST. BEDE THE VENERABLE : born about the year 673, died about 735.

THE Venerable Bede was a monk of Jarrow, priest, teacher, writer in various branches of literature. His great work, an Ecclesiastical History of England, remains both as a monument of his ability and industry, and as almost the sole authority on its own subject and for the period in question.

His life, though not entirely exempt from crosses, appears to have been passed in the tranquil happiness of a devout ascetic student. As such let us contemplate him, and (if ought of the kind be our proper gift) humbly try to follow him; to which holy course a few words of his own, uttered towards the close of his life, may inspirit us, our first quotation being poetical :—

" None is wiser than him needeth, ere his departure, than to ponder ere the soul flits, what good, what evil it hath wrought, and how after death it will be judged."

" O Glorious King, Lord of all Power, Who, triumphing this day, didst ascend up above the heavens, leave us not orphans ; but send down on us from the Father the Spirit of Truth, which Thou hast promised. Hallelujah."

" I will not have my pupils read what is untrue, nor labour on what is profitless after my death."

And because by grace he had lived the life of the righteous, therefore by help of that same grace he cheerfully died the death of the righteous :—" Singing ' Glory be to the Father, and to the Son, and to the Holy Ghost,' he breathed his last, as he uttered the Name of the Holy Ghost, and so departed to the heavenly kingdom."

May 28.

THEY lie at rest, our blessed dead :
The dews drop cool above their head,
They knew not when fleet summer fled.

Together all, yet each alone :
Each laid at rest beneath his own
Smooth turf or white allotted stone.

When shall our slumber sink so deep,
And eyes that wept and eyes that weep
Weep not in the sufficient sleep?

God be with you, our great and small,
Our loves, our best-beloved of all,
Our own beyond the salt sea wall.

May 29.

A GLOOMY Christian is like a cloud before the rainbow was vouchsafed.

We all (or almost all) more or less present cloudy
aspects, thanks to tempers, griefs, anxieties, disap-
pointments.

But the heavenliest sort of Christian exhibits more
bow than cloud, walking the world in a continual
thanksgiving ; and " a joyful and pleasant thing it is to
be thankful."

At unequal distances behind and below him tramp
on graduated Christians of every density and tinge :
some with full-coloured bows, some with a faint bit of
broken bow, some with the merest tint of prismatic
colour at a torn edge ; all bearing some sign of God's
gracious covenant with them.

In this company we fail to trace the gloomy Christian, all cloud, no bow.

But if he really and truly is not traceable high or
low among the caravan of pilgrims with their badge of
hope, where is he to be sought for on holy ground ?

May 30.

PARTING after parting,
Sore loss and gnawing pain :
Meeting grows half a sorrow,
Because of parting again.

When shall the day break,
That these things shall not be?
When shall new earth be ours
Without a sea,
And time that is not time,
But eternity?

May 31.

A CIVILIZED man complaining of having little time, an uncivilized man, who heard him, retorted that he supposed he had all there was to be had. So runs the story.

That savage taught not his hearer only, but me also.

Each of us, then, possesses all the time there is for any one : an obvious truth, but one which never struck me so forcibly before.

What is meant by "want of time?" What do I mean by the words ?

It seems that I must mean one of two things : either that I lack time for duties because I devote it to non-duties, or that, devoting it to duties, I feel discontented at lacking leisure for non-duties.

Non-duties may be attractive; they may even appear on occasion heroic or self-devoted : but we may be sure they are not duties so long as there honestly is not time for them.

On the contrary, taking the place of duties, they would degenerate into offences.

If we are bound to pronounce ourselves "unprofitable servants," even when "we have done that which was our duty to do," what are we to be called when we have *not* done so? when we have done something else? or when we have done nothing?

June 1.

FEAST OF ST. NICOMEDE, PRIEST AND MARTYR. First Century.

THIS holy man having first rendered himself conspicuous and obnoxious by bestowing Christian burial
on a virgin martyr, refused to apostatize from Christ
by offering sacrifice to the false gods, and was beaten
to death. His corpse was cast into the Tiber, but
being recovered thence by piety similar to his own,
was after all consigned to consecrated earth.

Thus making good King Solomon's proverb : "He
that watereth shall be watered also himself," and the
Divine sentence of our Lord Jesus Christ : "With the
same measure that ye mete withal it shall be measured
to you again."

June 2.

"As cold waters to a thirsty soul, so is good news from a far country."

"GOLDEN haired, lily white,
    Will you pluck me lilies?
Or will you show me where they grow,
    Show where the limpid rill is?
But is your hair of gold or light,
    And is your foot of flake or fire,
And have you wings rolled up from sight,
    And songs to slake desire?"

"I pluck fresh flowers of Paradise,
    Lilies and roses red,
A bending sceptre for my hand,
    A crown to crown my head.
I sing my songs, I pluck my flowers
    Sweet-scented from their fragrant trees :
I sing, we sing amid the bowers,
    And gather palm branches."

"Is there a path to Heaven
 My stumbling foot may tread?
And will you show that way to go,
 That bower and blossom bed?"
"The path to Heaven is steep and straight
 And scorched, but ends in shade of trees,
Where yet awhile we sing and wait,
 And gather palm branches."

June 3.

I.

"THE bottomless pit" mentioned several times in the Apocalypse is not (I believe) named in any other Book of Holy Scripture. To us Christians it is revealed "for our admonition, upon whom the ends of the world are come."

Whatever other idea we may form of the bottomless pit, whatever other feature we may think to detect within its undefined horror, two points stand out unmistakably: as a *pit* it is a place into which to fall; as *bottomless*, it appears to be one within which to fall lower and lower for ever and ever.

Herein lies one distinct thought for ourselves: an awful thought. A deep fall, indefinitely deep, so long as any bottom at any depth underlies the lapser, must at length be arrested and must stop. However mangled or shattered, and on whatever floor landed, the wretch cannot cease there to lie: self-destroyed, indeed, yet accessible to Mercy and Help if these deign to look so low, and lift with recovering hands, and carry home on shoulders rejoicing.

But in the *bottomless* pit I see a symbol of that eternal antagonism and recession by which created free will seems able to defy and baffle even the

Almighty Will of the Creator. At a standstill any-
where, though on the extreme boundary of time or
space, the sinner might be overtaken by the pursuing
Love of God : but once passing beyond those limits,
eternity sets in ; the everlasting attitude appears taken
up, the everlasting recoil commenced.

Beyond the grave no promise is held out to us of
shipwreck, great fish, dry land, to turn us back towards
the Presence of God from our self-chosen Tarshish.

June 4.

2.

I HAVE read how matter can be exploded, or at the
least can be conceived of as exploded, from the sun,
with such tremendous force as to carry it beyond the
radius of solar attraction.

That attraction which unifies and sways a whole
harmony of dependent planets, recalls not one atom
which has passed beyond the pale.

O Christ my God Who seest the unseen,
    O Christ my God Who knowest the unknown,
    Thy mighty Blood was poured forth to atone
For every sin that can be or hath been.

O Thou who seest what I cannot see,
    Thou Who didst love us all so long ago,
    O Thou Who knowest what I must not know,
Remember all my hope, remember me.

June 5.

FEAST OF ST. BONIFACE, otherwise Winfrid, styled the Apostle of Germany; Archbishop of Mainz, and Martyr. Born at Crediton, near Exeter, about the year 680; slain on a mission and with about fifty companions by certain pagans of East Friesland, 755.

GREAT is England's glory in having given birth to so eminent a hero of the Faith. From early childhood the little Winfrid set his heart on piety and the service of God. At first his father entertained for him secular views, but after a while he sanctioned his son's obvious vocation: the lad assumed a religious habit, took the name of Boniface, and about the age of thirty was ordained priest.

But the safe and peaceful duties of an English priest sufficed not this ardent spirit. Bishop Willibrord, of Utrecht, was labouring among the heathens of Frisia: this Boniface knew, " the fire kindled," and he sailed to join that mission.

His first expedition, however, failing, he returned to his cloister: but only to quit it once more, betake himself to Rome, and solicit from Pope Gregory II missionary powers.

Invested with these, he started anew for Frisia, and entered on those devoted labours which won thousands of converts to Christianity, and at length earned for himself the martyr's unfading palm.

A while he worked under Bishop Willibrord: but when that now aged prelate desired to raise him also to the Episcopate, St. Boniface shunned the dignity and departed to a fresh field. His obedience, however, equalled his self-devotion and humility: and when it became the Pope's expressed pleasure to elevate him to so lofty a sphere of duty, he submitted to undergo consecration at Rome; and returned to his beloved field of toil, not as Bishop of one assigned locality, but as general episcopal pastor of any flock he could gather in that wide German territory.

A man he was of many toils and of much love, faithful to old associations and unforgetful. In need of missionaries he looked to England, and thence received a noble response ; devoted men and devoted women betaking themselves to break up under him the fallow ground, or to occupy the land reclaimed for Christ.

He ordained Bishops, and under his auspices monasteries were founded and throve. He preached the simplest sermons to his rugged converts, teaching them in plain words the lovely Gospel history, instructing them what to do and wherein to sin no more.

At length, in old age, having provided for himself a successor in the See of Mainz, he started afresh on a personal mission into a still heathen portion of Friesland. There for a time his work prospered, and many were converted to Christ. But on a day when the lately baptized should have undergone confirmation, a savage band of pagans bore down on the missionaries and slew them :—"The Archbishop himself, when he saw that his hour was come, took a volume of the Gospels, and making it a pillow for his head, stretched forth his neck for the blow, and in a few moments received his release."

June 6.

HEARTSEASE I found, where Love-lies-bleeding
　　Empurpled all the ground:
Whatever flowers I missed unheeding,
　　Heartsease I found.

Yet still my garden mound
Stood sore in need of watering, weeding,
    And binding things unbound.

Ah, when shades fell to light succeeding.
    I scarcely dared look round :
"Love-lies-bleeding" was all my pleading,
    Heartsease I found.

June 7.

1.

WHO could have foreseen that Manna, type of
"the true Bread from heaven," would have been
withheld on the Sabbath Day, which day prefigures
that final rest which remaineth for the people of
God?

Nay, rather: for that one day the Manna assumed
permanence.

The Israelites no longer gathered, because they
possessed it. On other days they measured it; on
that holyday of rest they no longer measured, but
simply enjoyed it.

Even so throughout the eternal Sabbath there will
be no need of Sacraments, those outward and visible
signs of inward and spiritual grace given unto us ;
because the elect will be once and for ever one with
Christ.

Moreover, since each ·Jewish Sabbath prefigured
that supreme Sabbath Day which was truly an high
day, and which we Christians observe as Easter
Even; therefore it doubly behoved that no Manna
should fall thereon, for Christ Himself hath said :
"The days will come, when the Bridegroom shall be
taken away from them, and then shall they fast in
those days."

June 8.

2.

NEVERTHELESS, although the Manna on six successive days fell within the reach of all, those only who had gathered and stored it on the sixth day of toil, possessed it on the final day of rest.

On that seventh day, any who had it not already laid up could not find it, though they might seek it carefully with tears.

Some who thus sought and found it not, were reproved; and the fault was laid to their own charge.

We Christians in the Sacrament of Christ's Most Blessed Body and Blood, enjoy access to the True Bread from heaven; and to us our loving Lord has said : "This do in remembrance of Me." If in our present day of discipline we neglect thus to lay up Christ in our hearts, and so despise our birthright; on what plea can we lay claim to our blessing, even indissoluble union with Christ, in the day of blessing?

June 9.

ROSES on a brier,
  Pearls from out the bitter sea,
Such is earth's desire
  However pure it be.

Neither bud nor brier,
  Neither pearl nor brine for me :
Be stilled, my long desire ;
  There shall be no more sea.

Be stilled, my passionate heart ;
  Old earth shall end, new earth shall be ;
Be still, and earn thy part
  Where shall be no more sea.

June 10.

WHEREIN lies the saddening influence of mountain scenery? For I suppose many besides myself have felt depressed when approaching the "everlasting hills."

Their mass and loftiness dwarf all physical magnitudes familiar to most eyes, except the low-lying vastness of the ocean and the boundless overarching sky. They touch and pass through those clouds which limit our vision.

Perhaps their sublimity impresses us like want of sympathy.

Well, saddened and probably weary, I ended one delightful day's journey in Switzerland; and passed indoors, losing sight for a moment of the mountains.

Then from a window I faced them again. And, lo! the evening flush had turned snow to a rose, "and sorrow and sadness fled away."

"Yea, though I walk through the valley of the shadow of death, I will fear no evil: for Thou art with me; Thy rod and Thy staff comfort me."

June 11.

FEAST OF ST. BARNABAS, APOSTLE.

THIS Levite of Cyprus bore the name of Joses, until those who were Apostles before him renamed him Barnabas; by interpretation, the Son of Consolation.

His first recorded deed is one of Christian liberality: having land, he sold it, and laid the money at the Apostles' feet.

Afterwards he introduced St. Paul to the mistrustful Church, and vouched for him.

He rejoiced over the conversion of many in Antioch, exhorting them to steadfastness.

He laboured and suffered among the Jews: he laboured and suffered among the Gentiles.

Thus far Holy Writ. Tradition completes his history by martyrdom in his native island of Cyprus.

First and last his career shines and glows with love. For the way of love is that path of the just which is as the shining light that shineth more and more unto the perfect day.

"Lord, . . . how can we know the way? Jesus saith . . ., I am the Way, the Truth, and the Life: no man cometh unto the Father, but by Me."

June 12.

A ROSE, a lily, and the Face of Christ
    Have all our hearts sufficed:
For He is Rose of Sharon nobly born,
    Our Rose without a thorn;
And He is Lily of the Valley, He
    Most sweet in purity.
But when we come to name Him as He is,
    Godhead, Perfection, Bliss,
All tongues fall silent, while pure hearts alone
    Complete their orison.

June 13.

I.

YEARS ago a small party of us crossed the Alps into Italy by the Pass of Mount St. Gotthard.

We did not tunnel our way like worms through its dense substance. We surmounted its crest like eagles.

Or, if you please, not at all like eagles: yet assuredly as like those born monarchs as it consisted with our possibilities to become.

To act like an eagle is so far to emulate an eagle. To act by preference like a worm, is voluntarily to discard any shadow of resemblance to its betters.

Better be the last of eagles than the first of worms.

June 14.

2.

At a certain point of the ascent Mount St. Gotthard bloomed into an actual garden of forget-me-nots.

Unforgotten and never to be forgotten that lovely lavish efflorescence which made earth cerulean as the sky.

Thus I remember the mountain. But without that flower of memory could I have forgotten it?

Surely not: yet there, not elsewhere, a countless multitude of forget-me-nots made their home.

Such oftentimes seems the principle of allotment (if reverently I may term it so) among the human family. Many persons whose chief gifts taken one by one would suffice to memorialise them, engross not those only but along with them the winning graces which endear. Forget-me-nots enamel the height.

And what shall they do, who display neither loftiness nor loveliness? If "one member be honoured, all the members rejoice with it."

Or, if this standard appears too exalted for frail flesh and blood to attain, then send thought onwards.

The crowning summit of Mount St. Gotthard abides invested, not with flowers, but with perpetual snow: not with life, but with lifelessness.

I

In foresight of the grave, whither we all are hastening, is it worth while to envy any? "There is no work, nor device, nor knowledge, nor wisdom, in the grave, whither thou goest." "Grudge not one against another, brethren, lest ye be condemned : behold, the Judge standeth before the door."

June 15.

THE lowest place. Ah, Lord, how steep and high
  That lowest place whereon a saint shall sit !
Which of us halting, trembling, pressing nigh,
  Shall quite attain to it?

Yet, Lord, Thou pressest nigh to hail and grace
  Some happy soul, it may be still unfit
For Right Hand or for Left Hand, but whose place
  Waits there prepared for it.

June 16.

I HAVE read how on one certain occasion, out of a whole shipfull, two men were pious, God-fearing Christians. Only, being of two different nations and languages, it seemed very doubtful whether they ever would make each other out as citizens of the same city.

One day one of them sat reading his Bible, as solitary as Elijah, when he asserted "I only:" till the other's eye lighted on the unmistakable-looking page; when by signs, gestures, anyhow, somehow, he claimed his brother; and they both expressed common joy, reciprocal affection.

Still intercourse was denied them. Until one in exuberant bliss uttered the word Allelujah! Whereunto the other responded Amen.

Speech pithy, pointed, and profitable to mutual edification. "Golden words, silver silence," to recast the popular phrase.

Which phrase is too often illustrated, revised in a second and reverse sense: "Words of dross, alloyed silence:" for idle gossip and detraction and indiscretion ply glib tongues, and their conversational pauses are far from silvery.

Whoso cannot give forth silver words, let him maintain golden silence.

June 17.

FEAST OF ST. ALBAN, styled the Protomartyr of Britain. Beheaded about the year 304.

THIS gracious personage was born at ancient Verulam, hard by the ruins of which important place our city of St. Alban's now stands.

On him lighted down the blessing of one who receives a prophet. He was still living in paganism when he gave shelter to a Christian priest fleeing from persecution : and in guerdon of this good deed Christ was preached to him. Thus each saved the other's life : one the life temporal, the other the life eternal.

The emissaries of death arrived at St. Alban's door on the track of their prey ; but he who had been a soldier of Rome, was not one to flinch as a soldier of Christ. He exchanged cloaks with his guest, sped him on his journey, and in his stead confronted the hostile party. Taken before the governor, his faith armed him against all terrors : scourged, he rejoiced ; led to death, he was satisfied.

The first man appointed to slay him, responding to the sudden call of Divine Grace, avowed himself a

Christian : whereupon the twain were decapitated together.

"The righteous shall be had in everlasting remembrance."

June 18.

FRIENDS, I commend to you the narrow way :
    Not because I, please God, will walk therein,
    But rather for the Love Feast of that day,
The exceeding prize which whoso will may win.
    Earth is half spent and rotting at the core,
    Here hollow death's-heads mock us with a grin,
Here heartiest laughter leaves us tired and sore.
    Men heap up pleasures and enlarge desire,
    Outlive desire, and famished evermore
Consume themselves within the undying fire.
    Yet not for this God made us ; not for this
    Christ sought us far and near to draw us nigher,
Sought us and found and paid our penalties.
    If one could answer " nay " to God's command,
    Who shall say " nay " when Christ pleads all He is
For us, and holds us with a wounded Hand ?

June 19.

THE science of one age proves oftentimes to be the ignorance of a more advanced age. To balance which circumstance, a random guess or flash of insight overlooked or set aside at one moment, does sometimes reappear as the discovery of a later moment.

I know of a little girl who not far from half a century ago, having heard that oil calmed troubled waters, suggested to her Mother its adoption for such a purpose in case of sea storm.

Her suggestion fell flat, as from her it deserved to fall. Yet nowadays, here is science working out the babyish hint of ignorance!

"Precept upon precept; . . . line upon line; here a little, and there a little : " a hundred times over, and in a hundred ways, we are taught how things hidden from the wise and prudent are once and again revealed unto babes.

June 20.

FEAST OF THE TRANSLATION OF ST. EDWARD, KING.
[See also March 18.]

THIS transaction took place in the year 980 (982 ?), when, from an unhallowed grave at Wareham, the young king's body was by Queen Elfrida's order removed to Shaftesbury, and there with due pomp and solemnity laid at rest in a Convent of Benedictine Nuns.

One wicked ambitious woman took away his life, a congregation of devout women honoured his remains. Thus recalling a prophecy of our Lord's own most sacred death and entombment : " He made His grave with the wicked, and with the rich in His death."

Blessed is that life which imitates Christ's Life, blessed that death which is conformed to His Death. How blessed will be that resurrection which shall show forth the likeness of His Resurrection !

" He that endureth to the end shall be saved."

June 21.

O YE, who are not dead and fit
Like blasted tree beside the pit
But for the axe that levels it,—

Living show life of love, whereof
The force wields earth and heaven above:
Who knows not love begetteth love?

Love poises earth in space, Love rolls
Wide worlds rejoicing on their poles,
And girds them round with aureoles.

Love lights the sun, Love through the dark
Lights the moon's evanescent arc,
Lights up the star, lights up the spark.

O ye who taste that love is sweet,
Set waymarks for all doubtful feet
That stumble on in search of it.

Sing notes of love; that some who hear
Far off inert may lend an ear,
Rise up and wonder and draw near.

Lead life of love; that others who
Behold your life, may kindle too
With love and cast their lot with **you.**

June 22.

Darkness instinctively repels, light attracts us.

Yet only according to the good pleasure of God's Will, can either of them help or hinder us: true, both literally and figuratively.

Let us seek for a "treasure of darkness."

We who are born to trouble as the sparks fly upward, cannot, except by a process which consumes us, fly up at all.

To fly up on any terms, on any wings, must be beneficial.

Now we all have seen a literal fire pale and dwindle under strong sunshine, but when screened off into comparative darkness, regain colour and recover strength.

Thus sunshine of earthly happiness may easily prove too exhausting for some souls. And then it will be the good hand of our God upon them which sends darkness of sorrow, even if need be darkness of death.

Nor (except as His Will may ordain for better, for worse) can there as regards ourselves be any in-equality between light and darkness : so long, that is, as instead of murmuring "Peradventure the darkness shall cover me," we conform our own mind to the Divine Mind, and abide ready to sing with adoring David : "Yea, the darkness is no darkness with Thee, but the night is as clear as the day : the darkness and light to Thee are both alike."

June 23.

VIGIL OF ST. JOHN BAPTIST.

ST. JOHN BAPTIST himself, in reference to our Lord, stands as the Vigil to the Feast.

He simply leads to Christ. Except the Lord had followed, he had not come.

His aspect is austere, Christ's winning.

He is the salient figure of repentance : Christ the pure embodiment of Love.

Repentance is valueless, except it ends in love.

What indeed is there of any value, except it foster love ?

And what Saint will profit us one whit, except he helps us nearer to Christ Who is Incarnate Love?

"God is love ; and he that dwelleth in love dwelleth in God, and God in him."

"John stood, and two of his disciples ; and looking upon Jesus as He walked, he saith, Behold the Lamb of God !"

June 24.

FEAST OF THE NATIVITY OF ST. JOHN BAPTIST.

"HE was a burning and a shining light : and ye were willing for a season to rejoice in his light," spake our Blessed Lord, honouring His forerunner.

To whom spake He thus? To Jews, mostly unconverted.

Were then those carnal men capable of rejoicing in a luminary which lit up the valley of humiliation, the penitential pathway unto righteousness? Yea, for the Truth hath said it.

And even thus we read elsewhere of King Herod, how he "feared John, knowing that he was a just man and an holy, and observed him ; and when he heard him, he did many things, and heard him gladly."

Nevertheless, neither the monarch nor his subjects did the one thing needful : they picked and chose amongst their sins ; of which some may have fared like discarded favourites, while the favourites of the hour were retained.

Half-hearted and double-faced such men resemble husbandmen who prune salient twigs from a poisonous plant, by that very pruning strengthening the deepseated unattacked root.

So, after a while, Herod slew the Baptist. And again, after a while, Herod mocked the Lord Christ and the Jews crucified Him.

It is then possible (though possible only up to a certain point) for sinners to admire virtue, practise righteousness, approve things more excellent, extol repentance, skim amendment, yet all the time to abide at enmity with God.

It was possible for many of old : it is possible for ourselves of to-day.

" Try me, O God, and seek the ground of my heart : prove me, and examine my thoughts. Look well if there be any way of wickedness in me : and lead me in the way everlasting."

June 25.

LORD, grant me grace to love Thee in my pain,
  Through all my disappointment love Thee still,
  Thy love my strong foundation and my hill,
Though I be such as cometh not again,
A fading leaf, a spark upon the wane.
  So evermore do Thou Thy perfect Will
  Beloved through all my good, through all mine ill
Beloved though all my love beside be vain.
If thus I love Thee, how wilt Thou love me,
  Thou Who art greater than my heart? (Amen!)
  Wilt Thou bestow a part, withhold a part?
The longing of my heart cries out to Thee,
  The hungering, thirsting, longing of my heart :
What I forewent wilt Thou not grant me then?

June 26.

IF ever I deciphered a " Parable of Nature " surely I did so one summer night at Meads.

The gas was alight in my little room with its paper-less bare wall.

On that wall appeared a spider, himself dark and defined, his shadow no less dark and scarcely if at all less defined.

They jerked, zigzagged, advanced, retreated, he and his shadow posturing in ungainly indissoluble harmony. He seemed exasperated, fascinated, desperately endeavouring and utterly helpless.

What could it all mean? One meaning and one only suggested itself. That spider saw without recognising his black double, and was mad to disengage himself from the horrible pursuing inalienable presence.

I stood watching him awhile. (Presumably when I turned off the gas he composed himself.)

To me this self-haunted spider appears a figure of each obstinate impenitent sinner, who having outlived enjoyment remains isolated irretrievably with his own horrible loathsome self.

And if thus in time, how throughout eternity?

June 27.

A BISHOP's Pastoral Staff has two quaint likenesses among natural objects: a curled-up elephant's trunk, and a young budding frond of fern.

There is a theory that the soul within moulds the outer frame. Hence surface similarity suggests a corresponding similarity underlying the surface.

Whence—at least as a harmless fancy—I infer that the Staff may advantageously study an elephant's trunk as a pattern of delicately discriminating tact, copying its nicety of touch in minute matters and its vigorous hold on things broad and weighty.

While the frond will teach ways of bowing gracefully, of being pliant without weakness, of profiting by light and not losing ground in darkness, of bearing storms from any quarter.

. . . . But Bishops should write for me, not I for Bishops!

For my own behoof therefore I wind up by reflecting that every Christian is constituted "king and priest" in our Father's kingdom : that in consequence some grade of pastoral work devolves on each of us, if not as a dignity yet as a responsibility : and that as regards every soul within reach of our influence we all are in truth our "brother's keeper."

So that we all may meditate profitably on a Pastoral Staff.

June 28.

VIGIL OF THE FEAST OF ST. PETER.

HAD not ambition and pride, jealousy and envy, said their say to the embroilment of the subject and the abashing of the meek, would any impartial ordinary reader call in question that some sort of advantage, precedence, pre-eminence, did according to the inspired Gospel record really and truly appertain to St. Peter?

To deny so much, unless it be false, lands us in Babel, the city of confusion. To acknowledge so much, if it be true, will not by itself "violently turn and toss" us out of our venerable Anglican Mother Church.

This Vigil of St. Peter invites us all to one of two profitable exercises :—whoso holds the truth, let him cleave thereto thankfully : whoso detects or suspects himself as being in error, let him " pray that he may interpret" at least to himself.

Only the envious can be injured by St. Peter's primacy, whatsoever it amounts to.

Only the ambitious can profit by his exaltation above his genuine level.

Now there is nothing injurious in such an injury, nor aught profitable in such a profit.

June 29.

FEAST OF ST. PETER, APOSTLE AND MARTYR.

"LOVEST thou Me more than these? . . . Lovest thou Me? . . . Lovest thou Me? . . ." spake to His Apostle the Lord God, the Wise Master, the injured Friend. " Peter was grieved. . . . And he said unto Him, Lord, Thou knowest all things; Thou knowest that I love Thee."

But if St. Peter knew it, much more Christ. Even throughout the threefold denial, while, it may be, for the moment the fallen saint himself knew it not; yet He who was greater than his heart and knew all things, still knew it.

Then Christ "looked" in love, and Peter went out and wept bitterly. Now Christ questioned in love, and Peter was grieved.

These grievous dealings were the faithful wounds of a friend who loveth at all times: for if the servant loved his Lord, much more that Lord His servant.

Whatever may appear disputable about St. Peter, his love is indisputable. If other branches of study suitable to his Festival are too difficult for us, let us contentedly study love.

But which love, the lesser or the greater? St. Peter himself could by no means love God, except as having been first loved by God.

We shall love St. Peter and all other saints well, when we love our Lord Jesus better still. " Love all

for Jesus, but Jesus for Himself," writes a master in
the science of love.

And whatever may be doubtful, this remains certain :
every man who loves God a little, is loved by Him
much : every man who loves God much, is still loved
by Him more.

June 30.

SAINTS are like roses when they flush rarest,
Saints are like lilies when they bloom fairest,
Saints are like violets sweetest of their kind.
    Bear in mind
This to-day. Then to morrow :—
All like roses rarer than the rarest,
All like lilies fairer than the fairest,
All like violets sweeter than we know.
    Be it so.
To-morrow blots out sorrow.

July 1.

LORD God of Hosts most Holy and most High,
  What made Thee tell Thy Name of Love to me?
What made Thee live our life? what made Thee die?
    "My love of thee."

I pitched so low, Thou so exceeding high,
  What was it made Thee stoop to look at me
While flawless sons of God stood wondering by?
    "My love of thee."

What is there which can lift me up on high
  That we may dwell together, Thou with me,
When sin and death and suffering are gone by?
    "My love of thee."

O Lord, what is that best thing in the sky
   Which makes heaven heaven as Thou hast
     promised me,
Yea, makes it Christ to live and gain to die?
    "My love of thee."

July 2.

FEAST OF THE VISITATION OF THE BLESSED VIRGIN MARY.

THIS Visitation of St. Mary to her cousin "righteous" Elisabeth, was the occasion on which the unborn Baptist did homage to the coming Christ, and the Virgin Mother spake the Magnificat.

Long ago a lover of "things lovely" suggested to me as an appropriate text for the Salutation: "Righteousness and peace have kissed each other."

The dear speaker herself was humble and righteous, and has since then entered (I trust) into peace. Yet not for works of righteousness of man's doing, but according to His mercy God saveth all, both first and last. who are or who shall be saved.

Even the Blessed Virgin said and said truly: "My soul doth magnify the Lord, and my spirit hath rejoiced in God my Saviour. For He hath regarded the lowliness of His handmaiden."

July 3.

LOVE doth so grace and dignify,
   That beggars treat as king with king
Before the Throne of God most High:
Love recognises love's own cry
   And stoops to take love's offering,

A loving heart though soiled and bruised,
    A kindling heart though cold before :—
Whoever came and was refused
By Love? Do, Lord, as Thou art used
    To do, and make me love Thee more.

July 4.

FEAST OF THE TRANSLATION OF ST. MARTIN, BISHOP OF TOURS.

(This saint we shall meet with again, and in person, on November 11.)

As a general proposition, it surely is most pious and most reverential to leave the dead at rest in their graves.

Often, moreover, as in the case of this St. Martin, holy men have loved and observed an ascetic retirement which seems doubly indisposed towards posthumous translation.

Had this well-meant rite been more charily practised, such reticence might at least in some measure have checked that scandalous multiplicity of relics, which has assigned duplicate heads and an overplus of members to the same Saint in the face of abashed Christendom.

Not but what some exhumations for honourable enshrinement may have been praiseworthy : amongst which let us hope this of St. Martin ranks. Indeed, as a case more or less in point and " written for our learning," we read in Genesis how " Joseph took an oath of the children of Israel, saying, God will surely visit you, and ye shall carry up my bones from hence:" which oath being observed, the Patriarch's remains were transported out of Egypt into the Holy Land of Promise. But as bearing on ourselves and on our own practice, surely all Christendom *is* "holy ground."

Now if I have betrayed prejudice, I beg my reader's pardon. Meanwhile I well remember how one no longer present with us, but to whom I cease not to look up, shrank from entering the Mummy Room at the British Museum under a vivid realisation of how the general resurrection might occur even as one stood among those solemn corpses turned into a sight for sightseers.

And at that great and awful day, what will be thought of supposititious heads and members?

July 5.

INNOCENT eyes not ours,
  Are made to look on flowers,
Eyes of small birds and insects small:
  Morn after summer morn,
  The sweet rose on her thorn
Opens her bosom to them all.
  The least and last of things
  That soar on quivering wings,
Or crawl among the grass-blades out of sight,
  Have just as clear a right
  To their appointed portion of delight,
    As Queens or Kings.

July 6.

TWO frogs I met in early childhood have lingered in my memory: I frightened one frog, and the other frog frightened me.

The frightened frog evinced fear by placing its two hands on its head: at least, I have since understood that a frog assumes this attitude when in danger, and my frog assumed it.

The alarming frog startled me, "gave me quite a turn," as people say, by jumping when I did not know it was near me.

My fright was altogether without justifying cause. Not so the first frog's : for presumably my warm finger made the cool creature uncomfortable. Besides, how could it tell what was coming next? although in truth I meant it no harm.

I wish that as regards their intention as much could nowadays be certified for some of the wisest of this world, and that every scared frog were like my scared self, unreasonable.

But seeing that matters are as they are—because frogs and such like cannot in reason frighten us now,—is it quite certain that no day will ever come when even the smallest, weakest, most grotesque, *wronged* creature will not in some fashion rise up in the Judgment with us to condemn us, and so frighten us effectually once for all?

July 7.

CONTEMPTUOUS of his home beyond
The village and the village pond,
A large-souled Frog who spurned each byeway,
Hopped along the imperial highway.

Nor grunting pig nor barking dog
Could disconcert so great a frog.
The morning dew was lingering yet
His sides to cool, his tongue to wet;
The night dew when the night should come
A travelled frog would send him home.

Not so, alas! the wayside grass
Sees him no more:—not so, alas!

K

A broadwheeled waggon unawares
Ran him down, his joys, his cares.
From dying choke one feeble croak
The Frog's perpetual silence broke:
"Ye buoyant Frogs, ye great and small,
Even I am mortal after all.
My road to Fame turns out a wry way:
I perish on this hideous highway,—
Oh for my old familiar byeway!"

The choking Frog sobbed and was gone:
The waggoner strode whistling on.

Unconscious of the carnage done,
Whistling that waggoner strode on,
Whistling (it may have happened so)
"A Froggy would a-wooing go:"
A hypothetic frog trolled he
Obtuse to a reality.

O rich and poor, O great and small,
Such oversights beset us all:
The mangled frog abides incog,
The uninteresting actual frog;
The hypothetic frog alone
Is the one frog we dwell upon.

July 8.

I.

An apter flower for love-lore could scarcely be
selected than the forget-me-not.

It expresses a lofty affection, inasmuch as its corolla
is heavenly blue: but this is picked out with pink, to
stamp it as human and homely. It suggests how good

stands not still, but goes on to become better; for its buds are prevalently pink, its expanded blossoms chiefly blue. Its centre is golden, love being a great giver and giving of its best.

While by a crowning touch of appropriateness, its blossom stalk has a habit of dividing into a double spike of bloom. Thus showing us two that make up but one.

"What therefore God hath joined together, let not man put asunder."

July 9.

2.

I HAVE seen too—once indeed I possessed, so I write from memory—a most exquisite shell, composed of two halves, which joined together make up one flawless heart.

Each separate half is beautiful, shaded with darker and lighter rose tints, worked in grooves and curves, and finished with a notched edge. Yet each by itself remains obviously imperfect and purposeless.

Join them together and notch fits into notch; each brings out, proves, achieves, the perfection of the other.

Does such an illustration seem to excel and shame the possibilities of even the highest and purest human love?

Nay, but St. Paul quoted that same mutual human love in illustration of a Love which is not human merely but Divine also:—

"A man . . . shall be joined unto his wife, and they two shall be one flesh. This is a great mystery; but I speak concerning Christ and the Church."

July 10.

3.

THE less symbolizes the greater, the lower the higher.

Our study of a forget-me-not and of a shell will not entail loss of time—that irreparable loss!—if it helps us to realize that all reciprocal human love worthy of the name, exhibits a tinge of heaven as well as a warmth and colouring of earth.

That it is so far selfless as to be only one harmonious part of a better whole.

That it is faithful, fitting into nothing except its own other self.

And that unless it sets Christ before us at least as in a glass darkly, it were good for it not to have been born.

July 11.

MAN'S life is but a working day
Whose tasks are set aright :
A time to work, a time to pray,
And then a quiet night.
And then, please God, a quiet night
Where palms are green and robes are white,
A long-drawn breath, a balm for sorrow,—
And all things lovely on the morrow.

July 12.

A FONDLING Dog and a fondling Donkey : the old fable tells us how differently they fared.

And thus it ever has been, and thus presumably it ever will be ; but is it thus right and reasonable ?

In a measure it is, in a measure it is not.

If we examine ourselves on the " Dog and Donkey " question, I think many of us may find that not the deed, often not even the manner of doing, but continually the doer, makes all the difference to us. " Dogs " we pet, " Donkeys " we flout.

The Dog may lick us unrebuked : the Donkey must not so much as brush us with his nice hairy long ear.

Or granting that the Donkey *is* clumsy and coarse : can nothing be condoned to his obviously virtuous intention ?

A number of good kind people correspond more or less with the demonstrative Donkey ; but why ? just because they desire to be agreeably sociable. However clumsy their attempts, nothing can disguise the fact that they mean well.

Perhaps, even, they are misled by the success of some general favourite, who says, proposes, does everything with all ingratiating tact.

Wherefore they also aim at repartee, and take to catching us up ; at jocoseness, and jar our nerves. Our pet nerve they grate upon : a hint as broad as a scowl suffices not to suppress them.

Well, dense they may be, but they mean well by all men.

We are highly strung, sensitively refined, our tact amounts to intuition, not one weak point should we exhibit but for super-exquisite delicacy. Only do we, with equal consistency of honest purpose and endeavour, mean well by *all* men?

July 13.

I.

LET none despair of any grace, however remote from their original lot.

I once looked over a fine collection of old Venetian glass vessels.

By no means, I suppose, were any two of these precisely similar, not a mould from without but a breath or a blast from within having shaped them.

Some perhaps might be described as quaint, others certainly as elegant, many, if not all, as beautiful.

But the point of beauty which astonished me was that one or more of the specimens had caught, as it were, a momentary grace such as charms us in many flowers. Such a contour, a curve, an attitude if I may so call it, did here or there one of these old glasses exhibit, as a petrified blossom bell might retain, or as flexibility itself or motion might show forth if these could be embodied and arrested.

Inert glass moulded from within caught the semblance of such an alien grace.

Now God's grace moulds us from within.

July 14.

2.

IN the same collection of glass, but not among the Venetian specimens, stood two antique Greek vases, mended, I believe, though to all intents flawless, portly and oxydised.

What words can describe their beauty? Placed as they were aloft in my friend's drawing-room, one might stand for sunrise, the other for moonrise.

Sunrise was brilliant as the most gorgeous pheasant ; *moonrise* exquisite as the most harmonious pigeon. But, as I said before, words do not describe them : I cannot exaggerate, I can only misrepresent their appearance.

Well, with these unrivalled vases vivid in my memory, I one day rescued from an English roadside ditch a broken bottle : and it was also oxydised ! So, at least, I conclude : for in a minor key it too displayed a variety of iridescent tints, a sort of dull rainbow.

Now my treasure-trove was nothing to those others : yet could not their excess of beauty annul its private modicum of beauty.

There are, I presume, many more English ditches than Greek Islands, many more modern broken bottles than antique lustrous vases. If it is well for the few to rejoice in sunrise and moonrise, it is no less well for the many to be thankful for dim rainbows.

July 15.

FEAST OF ST. SWITHUN, BISHOP OF WINCHESTER. Born presumably towards the commencement of the ninth century : died in the year 862. (Strictly speaking, however, it appears that the 2nd of July is St. Swithun's own day, the 15th the day of the Translation of his remains.)

WE read that in his youth St. Swithun was distinguished by humility. " Before honour is humility." In later life he became the associate and counsellor of kings, directing, assisting, reproving them.

Whatever else we may or may not know of this eminent Prelate, we are almost certain to connect an idea of fine or wet weather with the day of his Translation. The story goes how by a downpour of rain he opposed the removal of his body, although at length that removal was effected.

If we connect this alleged opposition with the saint's humility, the legend will serve to illustrate the virtue. And as everything under the sun may be turned to good account, this story must be susceptible of the process : shall it teach us humility?

July 16.

HAVE I not striven, my God, and watched and
  prayed?
 Have I not wrestled in mine agony?
 Wherefore dost Thou still turn Thy Face from
  me?
Is Thine Arm shortened that Thou canst not aid?
Thy silence breaks my heart : speak though to up-
  braid,
 For Thy rebuke yet bids us follow Thee.
 I grope and grasp not ; gaze, but cannot see.
When out of sight and reach, my bed is made,
And piteous men and women cease to blame,
 Whispering and wistful of my gain or loss ;
 Thou Who for my sake once didst feel the Cross,
 Lord, wilt Thou turn and look upon me then,
And in Thy glory bring to nought my shame,
 Confessing me to angels and to men?

July 17.

I.

To this hour I remember a certain wild strawberry growing on a hedgerow bank, watched day by day while it ripened by a little girl and by my yet younger self.

My elder instructed me not to pluck it prematurely, and I complied.

I do not know which of us was to have had it at last, or whether we were to have halved it. As it was we watched, and as it turned out we watched in vain: for a snail, or some such marauder, must have forestalled us at a happy moment. One fatal day we found it half-eaten, and good for nothing.

Thus then we had watched in vain : or was it altogether in vain? On a very lowly level we had obeyed a counsel of prudence, and had practised self-restraint.

And shall the baulked watches of after-life prove in vain? " Let patience have her perfect work."

July 18.

2.

" HALF-EATEN and good for nothing," said I of the strawberry. I need not have expressed myself with such sweeping contempt.

Some snail may have been glad to finish up that wreck. Some children might not have disdained the final bite.

Yet to confine my reflections to snails and their peers: why should not they have a share in strawberries?

Man is very apt to contemplate himself out of all proportion to his surroundings : true, he is " much better than they," yet have they also their assigned province and their guaranteed dues.

Fruits for man, green herb for other living creatures, including creepers on the earth, is the decree in Genesis. Thus for the Garden of Eden : and why not thus, as regards the spirit of the decree, here and now?

But man, alas ! finds it convenient here to snap off a right and there to chip away a due. Greed grudges

their morsel to hedgerow birds, and idleness robs the
provident hare of his winter haystack, and science pares
away at the living creature bodily, "And what will
ye do in the end thereof?"

July 19.

A Word for the Dumb.

PITY the sorrows of a poor old dog,
    Who wags his tail a begging in his need;
Despise not even the sorrows of a frog,
    God's creature too, and that's enough to plead;
Spare puss, who trusts us, purring on our hearth;
    Spare bunny, once so frisky and so free;
Spare all the harmless tenants of the earth;
    Spare and be spared,— or who shall plead
      for thee?

July 20.

FEAST OF ST. MARGARET OR MARINA, VIRGIN MARTYR. Her
martyrdom took place, perhaps, in the third century.

I READ that no trustworthy authority has come to
light for any details regarding this personage. Even
her existence does not admit of proof.

Her legendary acts represent her as brought up by
a Christian nurse, and as herself a Christian. Wherefore her pagan father disowned her. At length, after
various trials, tortures, and triumphs, she died by decapitation.

Nevertheless—and this undermines meditation—we
cannot feel assured that she lived at all, or died, or
went up to glory. Yet should not her memory, or her
phantom as the case may be, do us some good? Let
her not engross one day in the year for nothing!

On one supposition we can picture her in accordance with her name of Margaret as a modest daisy, growing where for the present we cannot come : or as a pearl not yet brought up from hidden depths to the sun-lighted surface. Or dwelling on her alternative name of Marina, we can look forward to knowing her when both sea and earth render up the dead.

On the other hand should she not exist, we shall yet have gained and not lost if this Feast Day (though it be not her Festival) have led us to think of things pure and lovely, of virtue, and of praise.

July 21.

THE sinner's own fault? So it was.
   If every own fault found us out,
   Dogged us and hedged us round about,
What comfort should we take, because
   Not half our due we thus wrung out?

Clearly his own fault. Yet I think
   My fault in part, who did not pray,
   But lagged, and would not lead the way.
I, haply, proved his missing link.
   God help us both to mend and pray.

July 22.

FEAST OF ST. MARY MAGDALENE. The date of her death is unknown.

A RECORD of this Saint is a record of love. She ministered to the Lord of her substance, she stood by the Cross, she sat over against the Sepulchre, she sought Christ in the empty grave, and found Him and was found of Him in the contiguous garden.

Yet this is that same Mary Magdalene out of whom aforetime He had cast seven devils.

Nevertheless, the golden cord of love we are contemplating did all along continue unbroken in its chief strand: for before she loved Him, He loved her.

Thus love it was which brought Christ and that soul together, and bound them together first and last. Or rather, first and not last: for time must end in eternity, and eternity must end which never endeth, before the mutual love of Christ and His saints shall end.

To love first is God's prerogative. But blessed be He Who humbles not His least saint by loving last.

July 23.

WHO would wish back the Saints upon our rough,
　Wearisome road?
　　Wish back a breathless soul
　　Just at the goal?
　My soul, praise God
For all dear souls which have enough.

I would not fetch one back to hope with me
　A hope deferred,
　　To taste a cup that slips
　　From thirsting lips:—
　Hath he not heard
And seen what was to hear and see?

How could I stand to answer the rebuke,
　If one should say:
　　"O friend of little faith,
　　Good was my death,
　And good my day
Of rest, and good the sleep I took"?

July 24.

VIGILS prepare for Feasts: but Feasts of Saints (mostly) celebrate the Saint's death.

Thus mortal life corresponds with a Vigil, death with a Festival.

We discern this clearly in the case of St. James, and of other such eminent saints; we acquiesce in it cheerfully and are fully persuaded that so it is.

But when ourselves come into question, we seem to see all reversed: our own life, that is, appears as something of a festival, though chequered; our own death as an appalling and beyond experience anxious vigil.

" My brethren, these things ought not so to be. Doth a fountain send forth at the same place sweet water and bitter ? "

July 25.

FEAST OF ST. JAMES THE GREAT, APOSTLE AND MARTYR. Killed with the sword in the year 44.

ST. JAMES, who had craved the Right Hand or the Left Hand seat, and had accepted the cup and baptism proposed to him, was the first of the Apostles to lay down life for his Master's sake.

St. John, who had proffered the same prayer and incurred the same obligation, was the last of them all to die, and that not by martyrdom.

Together they had left nets and boat for Christ. Together they had borne the title of Sons of Thunder. Together they had companied with the Lord Jesus, and afterwards had seen Him ascend into heaven. Together they had received the Gift of the

Holy Ghost, and had preached the Gospel by words and by lives more eloquent than words.

Till a day came when one was taken, the other left : one "followed," the other "tarried." Lovely and pleasant in their lives, in their death they were divided.

Now these twain were princes and great men of the better Israel ; true yokefellows, moreover, and fellow heirs ; set side by side in their high places on the battle-field of the world and in the kingdom of the Church.

Yet each had to finish separately and differently the course begun hand in hand and alike.

Only now once more, and for these eighteen hundred years past, they are together.

Whence we feel vividly that as "circumcision is nothing, and uncircumcision is nothing, but the keeping of the commandments of God," so also life or death, so also even martyrdom or a natural death is "nothing," but the doing or suffering the Will of God.   Amen.

July 26.

FEAST OF ST. ANNE. Mother of the Blessed Virgin Mary.

THAT the Lord's Handmaiden had a mother is indubitable ; that she was blessed with a holy mother is conjecturable.   That this pious mother bore the name of Anne is quite uncertain : but under this name we do well to venerate the memory of her who, bearing whatever name, was privileged to become an ancestress of the Son of God, and so was constituted a link in that providential chain of persons and events which ended in the atoning Cross.

It is comfortable to turn from saints whose history is unauthenticated, to saints whose history is assured, from the Worthies of tradition to the Worthies of Holy Scripture. At every turn that which is human fails or eludes us, that which is Divine endures and suffices.

"Lord, to whom shall we go? Thou hast the words of eternal life."

July 27.

I.

"Simon, Simon, behold, Satan hath desired to have you, that he may sift you as wheat."—(St. Luke xxii. 31.)

THESE words of our Blessed Lord, spoken in the first instance to one Apostle, have ever since warned, and still cease not to warn, each Christian soul.

For though an ordinary Christian is no conspicuous prey, like the College of Apostles, yet Satan deems him well worth a shake of the sieve.

The warning conveyed by our Lord's words is awful : for our " adversary the devil, as a roaring lion, walketh about, seeking whom he may devour." A flesh and blood lion is appalling to human flesh and blood : how tenfold appalling is a spiritual roaring, devouring lion to man's spirit.

But the encouragement in those same precious words rings through and above the alarm they sound. " Satan hath desired " to have us : but of whom ? Of Him to Whom we are as the apple of the eye.

And wherefore does he desire to have us ? That he may sift us as wheat. We are certified as good seed by Satan's desiring permission to sift us : for who ever heard of his desiring to sift tares ?

As to tares, Satan is quite satisfied so long as they grow unmolested, ripen, shed seed, propagate, flourish until the harvest.

Wheat only does he reckon worth his sifting : therefore whatever he sifts is wheat.

2.

TEMPTATION is Satan's sieve: and a wonderful sieve-maker is Satan.

For he can ply as sieves advantages, gifts, even graces.

More than this : he can turn what we have not into an exceptionally searching sieve.

In one case pride, vanity, self-confidence, contempt of others, are likely to come to the surface. In the other case discontent, envy, rebellion. All alike hideous blotches, eating ulcers.

Nevertheless, it is at his own cost that he sifts, and not necessarily at all at ours ; although for the time being it cannot but be at our deadly peril.

For he can never carry his point and destroy us, unless we first make a covenant with death and an agreement with hell : whereas we shall infallibly save our souls alive, if holding fast our profession and our patience, we are careful to maintain good works.

Meanwhile he is doing us an actual service by bringing to the surface what already lurked within. However tormenting and humiliating declared leprosy may be, it is less desperate than suppressed leprosy.

Or rather, nothing is desperate which can and will turn to Christ :—

" There came a leper to Him, beseeching Him, and kneeling down to Him, and saying unto Him, If Thou wilt, Thou canst make me clean. And Jesus, moved with compassion, put forth His Hand, and touched him, and saith unto him, I will ; be thou clean. And as soon as He had spoken, immediately the leprosy departed from him, and he was cleansed."

July 29.

THROUGH burden and heat of the day
　How weary the hands and the feet,
That labour with scarcely a stay,
　Through burden and heat!

　Tired toiler whose sleep shall be sweet,
Kneel down, it will rest thee to pray:
　Then forward, for daylight is fleet.

Cool shadows grow lengthening and grey,
　Cool twilight will soon be complete:—
What matters this wearisome way
　Through burden and heat?

July 30.

"He that hath My commandments, and keepeth them, he it is that loveth Me."—(ST. JOHN xiv. 21.)

SUCH is our Lord's own authoritative definition of His true lover.

But not seldom it would seem as if this His definition fails to satisfy His disciples. Thus one, a self-deceiver, substitutes an emotion for obedience: while another, a self-tormentor, depreciates the obedience he can and (allowing for human frailty) does render, in comparison with emotions he longs after but cannot experience.

The self-deceiver's remedy is simple strenuous obedience, without reference either to sensibility or insensibility.

The self-tormentor's remedy is cheerful trustful obedience "as to the Lord, and not unto men:" for whosoever studies himself in his obedience is—is he

L

not?—obeying as "unto a man" rather than "as to the Lord."

Such an honest scrupulous person may, perhaps, derive comfort from a very homely illustration. When water boils, the bottom of the vessel containing it can be touched with impunity: wherefore? because it lacks heat? on the contrary, because all its heat is carried upward and away from itself.

July 31.

WHY is "the deaf adder that stoppeth her ears" culpable?

Not, surely, because of any involuntary deafness: but because whatever degree of infirmity she may or may not have laboured under, she willed to be and to remain deaf.

Honest difficulties in the way of her hearing may have existed: incomparably beyond them in baneful influence appears to have been the circumstance that she stopped her ears.

We may fairly conclude that had her deafness been absolute she would not have felt any impulse to stop her ears: she could not have apprehended enough to set her against apprehending more.

Because she heard somewhat, she stopped her ears: and because hearing somewhat she took measures to hear no more, therefore she abides condemned.

If because we see her stop her ears we judge and condemn her on that very evidence of her having heard, let us judge ourselves no less honestly.

The responsibility we avoid facing, we have already caught a glimpse of: we are at the least so far cognisant of it as to know that we might ascertain more.

August 1.

LAMMAS DAY. Kept in commemoration of St. Peter's miraculous deliverance "out of the hand of Herod, and from all the expectation of the people of the Jews."

BOTH Lamb-Mass and Loaf-Mass have been proposed as the original form of our word Lammas: which in the first case would allude to a lamb offered annually in York Cathedral; in the second would recall an English festival of first-fruits; both alike belonging to this day.

York Cathedral is dedicated to St. Peter ad Vincula: and our Lord's words to him beside the Sea of Tiberias, "Feed My lambs," have led to the great Apostle's being regarded as patron of lambs.

Yet in the highest sense there is but One Good Shepherd whose own the flock is. All other men, even the holiest, can be but His under shepherds feeding "the flock of God not by constraint but willingly."

Better it is that a lamb should remind us of Christ than of St. Peter: "Behold the Lamb of God!"

And while a loaf may profitably put us in mind to bring forth fruit thirty or sixty or a hundred-fold, it may best dispose us so to do, by setting before us in a figure Christ the Bread of Life. Christ the Corn of Wheat which to quicken us fell into the ground and died.

August 2.

A DIALOGUE.

"THE fields are white to harvest, look and see,
Are white abundantly.
The full-orbed harvest moon shines clear,
The harvest time draws near,
Be of good cheer."

L 2

"Ah woe is me!
    I have no heart for harvest time,
    Grown sick with hope deferred from chime to
        chime."

"But Christ can give thee heart Who loveth thee:
    Can set thee in the eternal ecstasy
    Of His great jubilee:
    Can give thee dancing heart and shining face,
    And lips filled full of grace,
    And pleasures as the rivers and the sea.
    Who knocketh at His door
    He welcomes evermore:
    Kneel down before
    That ever open door
    (The time is short) and smite
    Thy breast, and pray with all thy might."

"What shall I say?"

        "Nay, pray.
    Though one but say 'Thy Will be done,'
    He hath not lost his day
    At set of sun."

August 3.

THERE exists of the mezereon a certain foreign
species whereof the inner bark resembles lace: in-
somuch that the women of the same region do actually
make use of it as lace.

The plant wears its lace within, the women wear
theirs without: the twain seem in some sort to make
up between them one image of that "King's daughter"

who being "all glorious within" is also "brought unto the King in raiment of needlework;" the lace and the needlework in question being alike such as no needle on earth could embroider.

Yet the mezereon clad in its own lace lining, manifests one marked superiority over women arrayed visibly in the same lace: for not they but the plant becomes our emblem of St. Peter's ideal matron "whose adorning let it not be that outward adorning . . . of putting on of apparel; but let it be the hidden man of the heart."

The Creator of all things good has Himself decked a plant with hidden lace. Is the whole of *our* lace on the surface?

August 4.

WHEN I was in north Italy, a region rich in sunshine, heat, beauty, it struck me that after all our English wild scarlet poppies excelled the Italian poppies in gorgeous colour.

I should have expected the direct contrary; the more sunshine. surely the more glow and redness: yet it appeared otherwise when I came to look.

Perhaps sheer stress of sunshine tended to bleach as well as to dye those poppies.

And if so, they aptly symbolize those "always rejoicing" Christians who are, notwithstanding, so sorrowful during the present distress.

For on earth souls need bleaching as well as developing and embellishing. Only in heaven will the sun cease to smite on the just made perfect, and the vehement east wind cease to beat on them.

August 5.

OF each sad word, which is more sorrowful,
 "Sorrow" or "Disappointment?" I have heard
Subtle inflections baffling subtlest rule,
 Of each sad word.

 Sorrow can mourn: and lo! a mourning bird
Sings sweetly to sweet echoes of its dule,
 While silent disappointment broods unstirred.

Yet both nurse hope, where Penitence keeps school
 Who makes fools wise and saints of them that
 erred:
Wise men shape stepping-stone, or curb, or tool,
 Of each sad word.

August 6.

FEAST OF THE TRANSFIGURATION OF OUR LORD.

HEAVEN, Paradise, Earth, each was represented on
the Mount of Transfiguration. For Christ is that Son
of Man Who came down from Heaven and is in
Heaven: Moses and Elias reappeared from whatever
blessed abode enshrined them: St. Peter, St. James,
St. John, still drew mortal breath. If brief that meeting, brief also that parting: long ago (please God) they
met anew to part no more, where none who meet shall
ever part again.

 Well was it for St. Peter that he was not taken at
his word and permitted to set up his "three taber-
nacles." Earth at its loftiest and loveliest is still only
earth: and though God's appointment makes it "good
for us to be here," in itself and compared with the
lowest place in heaven earth is not good.

Yet for a moment the eyes of an Apostle were arrested here, his heart paused here. And no marvel: for where Christ is is the Presence of God, and the Presence of God is Heaven.

August 7.

FEAST OF THE NAME OF JESUS.

JESUS, Lord God from all eternity,
   Whom love of us brought down to shame,
I plead Thy life with Thee,
   I plead Thy death, I plead Thy Name.

Jesus, Lord God of every living soul,
   Thy Love exceeds its uttered fame,
Thy Will can make us whole,
   I plead Thyself, I plead Thy Name.

August 8.

HOLY Scripture bids us " run with patience the race that is set before us."

One might have anticipated that energy or zeal would be the word, rather than patience: but no, it is patience.

If not even a race, then surely nothing that appertains to duty should be done in mere hurry or depend upon impulse. Our race is for life or death, yet must it be run peacefully.

One element of excitement is far removed from it. A race it is, yet only to attain a goal, not to outstrip competitors. On the contrary, there is scarcely a greater help to one's own running than to lend a hand to a halting brother or sister.

Our mighty Forerunner Whom no saint follows except at an infinite distance, even Christ Who in all things hath the pre-eminence, ran His mortal race with glory as of the sun, and alacrity as of a bridegroom, and strength as of a giant: nevertheless He ran it with such peace and patience that He vouchsafed to become as one who carries lambs in his bosom and gently leads the feeble ones.

As of yore to our forefathers, so to-day He saith to us: "Come unto Me, all ye that labour and are heavy laden, and I will give you rest. Take My yoke upon you." Now a yoke is not for standing still, but for toiling forward: and thus He promises us rest while we toil, even as He requires of us patience while we run our race.

> Lord Jesus, who would think that I am Thine?
>   Ah, who would think
> Who sees me ready to turn back or sink,
>   That Thou art mine?
>
> I cannot hold Thee fast, tho' Thou art mine:
>   Hold Thou me fast,
> So earth shall know at last and heaven at last
>   That I am Thine.

August 9.

Yea, if Thou wilt, Thou canst put up Thy sword:
  But what if Thou shouldst sheathe it to the hilt
Within the heart that sues to Thee, O Lord?
  Yea, if Thou wilt.

For if Thou wilt Thou canst purge out the guilt
Of all, of any, even the most abhorred:
  Thou canst pluck down, rebuild, build up the unbuilt.

Who wanders, canst Thou gather by love's cord?
   Who sinks, uplift from the under-sucking silt
To set him on Thy rock within Thy ward?
   Yea, if Thou wilt.

August 10.

FEAST OF ST. LAURENCE, DEACON AND MARTYR.

DURING the persecution under Valerian in the year
258, this heroic saint died a torturing death over a
slow fire.

It is related of him, as of St. Stephen, that while
undergoing his agony his face was glorified as the
face of an angel. His eyes gazed fixedly on heaven,
his countenance remained unruffled.

To so sweet a soul, sorer perhaps than pangs of the
body, had been that pang of parting when three days
earlier his beloved Priest and Pope St. Sixtus went
up before him by the road of martyrdom to the
kingdom of peace.

   To meet, worth living for;
      Worth dying for, to meet;
   To meet, worth parting for,
      Bitter forgot in sweet:
   To meet, worth parting before
   Never to part more.

August 11.

"How think ye? if a man have an hundred sheep, and one of them
be gone astray, doth he not leave the ninety and nine, and goeth into
the mountains, and seeketh that which is gone astray? And if so be
that he find it, verily I say unto you, he rejoiceth more of that sheep,
than of the ninety and nine which went not astray."—(ST. MATT. xviii.
12, 13.)

AND so do we. So, at least, seem oftentimes
to do the most fervent intercessors: red-hot for

the salvation of saints, at white heat for the salvation of sinners.

Whence further it would almost appear that excellent pious people love the guilty more than the innocent, scarlet sinners more than fellow saints.

Are any of us disheartened hereby and driven out of sympathy with our brethren? Nay, there lies an effectual remedy within reach.

Let us but humbly recognise ourselves as the sinners God discerns us to be, and we shall thankfully accept a share in the effectual fervent prayers of those who praying always faint not.

August 12.

I.

"Behold the Lamb of God."—(St. John i. 36.)

LET us study a lamb, in hopes of learning from it something concerning our adorable Saviour. For such similitudes as are employed in Holy Scripture must contain a lesson for us.

The lamb, Divinely appointed for sacrifice, does obviously typify Christ sacrificed as our atonement.

But this is, so to say, the lamb's office, not his essence. So that we may still ask: wherefore was a lamb, rather than another living creature, chosen for so sacred a purpose?

The main answer may indeed lie beyond our reach in a region of mysteries: yet none the less some wisdom within our reach may lie upon the surface.

At first sight, then, a lamb is a picture of innocence. Its woolly white face looks as pure as a snowdrop, its voice has a plaintive tone of perpetual appeal which goes to the heart. It is cheerful, moreover, full of pretty ways and contentment. It is born when earth, arraying herself in renewed verdure, prepares to blossom as a step towards fruitfulness: it inhabits clean green meadows, and drinks sweet clean water.

August 13.

2.

"Behold the Lamb of God, which taketh away the sin of the world."— (St. John i. 29.)

JESUS is no mere picture of innocence, but is very Innocence incarnate. A lamb and all other things innocent and pure are His picture.

That "Voice" which His sheep hear and know is a voice not of command merely but also of winning appeal. He invites us: "Come unto Me, all ye that labour and are heavy laden, and I will give you rest." He urges us: "If any man thirst, let him come unto Me, and drink." He reproaches us: "Ye will not come to Me, that ye might have life." He pleads for us: "Lord, let it alone this year also." He probes our hearts: "Lovest thou Me?"

Well may we read how once even in the synagogue of Nazareth "the eyes of all . . . were fastened on Him . . . And all bare Him witness, and wondered at the gracious words which proceeded out of His Mouth." —"Full of grace are Thy lips."

And if lambs liable to sacrifice were contented and cheerful creatures (though they, indeed, in ignorance), surely "the Lamb slain from the foundation of the world" was far beyond such as they, contented and desirous in His self-sacrifice: "With desire I have desired," said He of the supper; and how not of the

Passion? I once read a work concerning Holy Communion, devout in intention, but (as it struck me) laying stress of such a sort on our Lord's condescension and patience, as suggested that He Who willingly had lived and died for men now found it hard to put up with us sinners, and for our sake to secrete Himself in the Sacrament of His most Blessed Body and Blood. May I have misunderstood the tone of that book!

Lastly, if Christmas as we keep it in December be the actual season of our Lord's birth, then in that (as in the rest) He leaves lambs far behind Him, being born into this world at a more desolate moment than they. Earth at mid-winter is comparatively bare; leaves, blossoms and delights come back with spring.

August 14.

"Fra Modesto non fu mai Priore," say the Italians: or in English, "Brother Modestus never became Prior."

"Brother Modestus was sure to make a mess of it," "Brother Modestus was a fool for his pains,"— exclaim worldly worldlings and worldly churchlings in chorus.

A "mess" and a "fool" undeniably, according to their standard who in their generation are wiser than the children of light.

Inflated bladders, puff balls, loud and hollow drums: such symbols as these tally with too many of the successes and of the successful of this world.

And by comparison, Brother Modestus and his career *are* mere collapse: drum him out of the world!

But behold! he wishes nothing better. He has made his count for nothing to-day, all to-morrow;

nothing on earth, all in heaven. He knows Whom he has believed, and is persuaded that He is able to keep all things committed unto Him against that day.

Now, he that ruleth his spirit is better than he that taketh a city.

August 15.

I.

A PEBBLE dropped into a pool disturbs the water in a circle widening without definite boundary.

Motion displaces air, nor can we assign any limit to the extent of such displacement.

Earth revolving within space carries along with itself its own vast atmosphere.

And more or less like each of these, personal influence is certain and is incalculable; is a mighty engine inseparable from a proportionate burden of responsibility. None are too great, none too small, for this burden. St. Paul laid himself out, moulded himself, spent himself to bear it worthily; as his own words attest:—

"Though I be free from all men, yet have I made myself servant unto all, that I might gain the more. And unto the Jews I became as a Jew, that I might gain the Jews; to them that are under the law, as under the law, that I might gain them that are under the law; to them that are without law, as without law (being not without law to God, but under the law to Christ), that I might gain them that are without law. To the weak became I as weak, that I might gain the weak: I am made all things to all men, that I might by all means save some."

August 16.

2.

IMPOSSIBLE as in reality it is to avoid exercising personal influence, there is yet a restricted sense in which it may be withheld to the grievous hurt of those whose due it is : just as a lantern may be placed so as to hide its light.

But alas! such withholding amounts not to neutrality but to evil influence : the lantern which does not cast light casts shadow. "He that gathereth not with Me," saith the Truth, "scattereth."

On the other hand and for our encouragement, good influence may be at work where no immediate visible result ensues; where the result may not by us be traceable on earth or in time, but only in heaven and throughout eternity.

I have read a story of a date palm which lived a long while green and barren. One year without apparent cause it bore fruit. Wherefore? Because out of sight a remote kindred palm shed its fructifying pollen, and this the wind bore to impregnate the barren tree.

August 17.

WHEN all the overwork of life
   Is finished once, and fallen asleep
We shrink no more beneath the knife,
   But having sown prepare to reap,
Delivered from the crossway rough,
   Delivered from the thorny scourge,
   Delivered from the tossing surge,
Then shall we find—(please God!)—it is enough?

Not in this world of hope deferred,
  This world of perishable stuff;
Eye hath not seen, nor ear hath heard,
  Nor heart conceived that full "enough:"
Here moans the separating sea,
  Here harvests fail, here breaks the heart;
  There God shall join and no man part,
All one in Christ, so one—(please God!)—with me.

August 18.

I.

NOAH being commanded to build an Ark, built it then and there upon (as it seems) the dry ground.

A huge immoveable unprecedented Ark, high and dry on land, when its only conceivable use was for the water!

Presumably the Antediluvians noticed the incongruity: perhaps they enjoyed it: possibly it confirmed them in a theory that no sane man would listen to Noah.

Up to a certain moment that old-world controversy seemed carried on between common sense and shiftless fanaticism, "for the children of this world are in their generation wiser than the children of light."

Only,—there was to be an end of that generation.

The certain moment came, "the flood came, and took them all away," and after all the last word of the controversy fell to Noah.

Thus it was, and thus it is, and thus it ever will be between the world and the Church: "Because the foolishness of God is wiser than men; and the weakness of God is stronger than men."

2.

How did Noah build his Ark?

We may fairly assume that he built it openly, avowedly, without any subterfuges or pretences whatsoever.

For instance. We do not suppose that he kept the Ark looking like a house, or like a land carriage, as long as possible; ingeniously erecting and maintaining scaffolding around the navigable base, but leaving door and windows full in view. Or that when the substructure could no longer be hidden, he opened an artificial creek to suggest that he had ways and means of utilising his ark.

No. We may well believe that as he had faith enough to build his ark, so also he had faith enough not to tone it down, or colour it, or gloss it over by any tinge of imposture.

Now we Christians all of us are (or ought to be) building arks "to the saving of" our souls.

How many of us are building them in unabashed openness and honesty? neither parading our religion, nor keeping it under lock and key: neither falling on our knees to seem devout (as Bishop Jeremy Taylor puts it), nor starting off them to seem indevout (often the keener temptation), if we hear some one coming.

August 20.

I.

INTERRUPTIONS are vexatious.

Granted. But what is an interruption?

An interruption is something, is anything, which breaks in upon our occupation of the moment. For instance: a frivolous remark when we are absorbed, a selfish call when we are busy, an idle noise out of time, an intrusive sight out of place.

Now our occupations spring?... from within: for they are the outcome of our own will.

And interruptions arrive?... from without. Obviously from without, or otherwise we could and would ward them off.

Our occupation, then, is that which we select. Our interruption is that which is sent us.

But hence it would appear that the occupation may be wilful, while the interruption must be Providential.

A startling view of occupations and interruptions!

August 21.

2.

All but, that which is frivolous, selfish, idle, intrusive, is clearly not Providential.

As regards the doer, no: as regards the sufferer, yes.

I think we often quite misconceive the genuine appointed occupation of a given moment. perhaps even of our whole lives. We take for granted that we ought to enjoy a pleasure, or complete a task, or execute a work, or serve some one we love: while what we are really then and there called to is to forego a pleasure, or break off a task, or leave a cherished work incomplete, or serve some one we find it difficult to love.

Interruptions seem well nigh to form the occupation of some lives.

Not an occupation one would choose; yet none the less profitable on that account.

How would saints speak of interruptions? One

might remark, "To me they are not grievous:" and another, "For me they are safe." But would any saint observe, "Interruptions are vexatious," and there stop?

August 22.

In north Italy I observed that whilst the cattle are grand and beautiful beyond our English wont, the pigs are exceptionally mean and repulsive.

Thus in one characteristically lovely land what is fair shows at its fairest, what is ugly shows at its ugliest.

And if thus in the natural sphere, thus likewise in the spiritual sphere.

Christendom exhibits extremes not attainable in the outer world. Its "cattle" excel all cattle : its "swine" wallow beneath all swine.

Foulest of the foul is an unchristian Christian : no better, far worse, than any sow that returns "to her wallowing in the mire."

August 23.

Vigil of St. Bartholomew.

This Saint is concealed from us by, as it were, a double veil. Beyond his name and certain statements in which other persons are associated with him, no unquestionable mention is made of him either in the Gospels or in the Book of Acts : while his name itself, signifying "Son of Tolmai" may in a sense be regarded as no name at all.

Thus then it has pleased God to hide him from us, even in the process of showing him to us. And thus it is that he sets us an example, by becoming the blessed opposite of those who, doing good works to be seen of men, receive then and there their reward.

The Father Who seeth in secret will reward him openly.

"O how plentiful is Thy goodness, which Thou hast laid up for them that fear Thee : and that Thou hast prepared for them that put their trust in Thee, even before the sons of men ! Thou shalt hide them privily by Thine own Presence from the provoking of all men : Thou shalt keep them secretly in Thy tabernacle from the strife of tongues."

August 24.

FEAST OF ST. BARTHOLOMEW, APOSTLE.   Tradition assigns to this
Saint, martyrdom in one of its most appalling forms

HE bore an agony whereof the name
    Hath turned his fellows pale:—
But what if God should call us to the same,
    Should call, and we should fail?

Nor earth nor sea could swallow up our shame,
    Nor darkness draw a veil:
For he endured that agony whose name
    Hath made his fellows quail.

August 25.

1.

"Rooms shalt thou make in the ark"—(GEN. vi. 14): but the literal
Hebrew (*see* margin of Authorised Version) says not "rooms" but
"nests."

NOW without for one moment calling in question that these particular "nests" were rooms, the special word employed does yet suggest a special train of thought.

The Ark : the Church. Destruction without, safety within. "A dispensation of the Gospel" is vouchsafed to man, and woe is us if we accept not the offered salvation.

We do (please God) accept it. However unworthily, we occupy rooms in the spiritual Ark: there we live, and there we hope to die.

The rooms being commodiously and thoroughly furnished unto good works, the tenants are thereby invited to perform such good works as belong to their several vocations.

So to do becomes our duty. And it is constituted no less our privilege, seeing that to crown all it has promise of a reward.

Christian duties, Christian privileges: some honest Christians do much, and upbraid themselves for not doing more. They labour and are heavy laden, they are careful and cumbered; making a task of duty, a task of privilege, a task of life, and a most formidable task of death.

The vastness and still more the loftiness of their "room" overwhelms them: "Who is sufficient for these things?" is their prevalent forlorn feeling. At times they would almost be ready (if they dared) to say: "It were better to dwell in a corner of the house-top."

They comport themselves as if too little for their own greatness. They appear like savage man consumed and dwindling away in the face of a civilisation too high for him.

But wherefore contemplate their allotted room as a lofty and vast palace of well-nigh uninhabitable grandeur: as this, and as nothing more?

Our room, as God builds and makes it for us, is likewise our nest: and a nest is surely the very homeliest idea of a home.

August 26.

2.

A NEST implies, suggests, so much.

A circumference in comfortable proportion to its inhabitants' size.

Warmth and softness: " For so He giveth His beloved sleep."

Pure air, bright sunshine; leafy shade sufficient to satisfy a very Jonah.

A windy branch whereon to rock safely. Wind and rain heard yet little felt. A storm, indeed, sometimes, but as the exception not as the rule.

Most of all by way of comfort a nest suggests an overhanging presence of love. A brooding breast sheltering its cherished nestlings. A love ready to confront death in their defence.

" While we were yet sinners, Christ died for us."

When " room " and way are too great for us, let us think of Him Who prepared our present " nest " and carries His little ones, and Who desires to see in each of us of the travail of His Soul and to be satisfied. And Who eighteen hundred years ago comforted His disciples, saying, " In My Father's house are many mansions : if it were not so, I would have told you. I go to prepare a place for you. And if I go and prepare a place for you, I will come again, and receive you unto Myself ; that where I am, there ye may be also."

August 27.

ONE step more, and the race is ended,
　　One word more, and the lesson 's done,
One toil more, and a long rest follows
　　At set of sun.

Who would fail, for one step withholden?
Who would fail, for one word unsaid?
Who would fail, for a pause too early?
    Sound sleep the dead.

One step more, and the goal receives us,
    One word more, and life's task is done,
One toil more, and the Cross is carried
    And sets the sun.

August 28.

FEAST OF ST. AUGUSTINE, BISHOP OF HIPPO, Doctor of the Church
Born at Tagaste, in Africa, in the year 354; died at Hippo, 430.

AURELIUS AUGUSTINE was son of Patricius, a
pagan of some virtue and afterwards converted, and of
Monica, a Christian saint. In early life an unbaptised
Manichæan heretic of strong passions and unbridled
conduct, Augustine left his mother to watch, pray,
agonise for him, while he rejoiced in his youth, walking in the ways of his heart and in the sight of his
eyes, and not laying to heart that God for all these
things would bring him into judgment.

Divine grace, however, responding doubtless to his
mother's prayers for his soul, proved at length stronger
than his evil will and ways: he cast off his vices as the
serpent casts its skin, professed the Catholic Faith, and
was baptised on Easter Eve in the year 387 by St.
Ambrose, Bishop of Milan.

Thenceforward, allowing for human frailty, he retained of the serpent only its wisdom, and put on harm-
lessness as a dove: yet not, alas! without putting it
off under provocation.

In 391 he was ordained priest; and he submitted

to episcopal consecration at an uncertain date, perhaps in the year 395.

In controversy he opposed both Manichæans, Donatists, and Pelagians; yet incurred suspicion of himself holding unsound views as to the doctrine of predestination: nevertheless he is looked up to as a Doctor of the Church. Despite the Spirit of Love which ordinarily ruled him, he seems to have indulged a cruelly harsh temper against the Donatists.

Yet need we not cavil at the blemishes of a saint who of his own free choice died the death of a penitent:—

"He ceased not to preach and work, till in August he was prostrated by fever; and as he used to say that even approved Christians and priests ought to die as penitents, he excluded his friends from his room, except at certain hours, caused the penitential psalms to be written out and fixed on the wall opposite his bed, and repeated them with many tears; thus by his last acts throwing over the consequences, and with them the principles, advanced in his later dangerous treatises."

August 29.

FEAST OF THE BEHEADING OF ST. JOHN BAPTIST.

KING HEROD and his company did after a fashion anticipate the Church in making of this day a festival. Moreover it was Herod's birthday in one sense, before it became St. John Baptist's in another.

Thus emphatically are there feasts and feasts, birthdays and birthdays.

After that carnal birthday ensued the remainder of mortal life: and after the remainder of mortal life ensued what next to Herod and his crew, to the dancing daughter and the venomous mother?

"The secret things belong unto the Lord our God."

Meanwhile St. John Baptist ended his Vigil and began his Feast, ended his death and began his life.

Now there is no "after" to such a Feast, and no "next" to such a life.

"See, I have set before thee this day life and good, and death and evil."

August 30.

TACT resembles a lubricating oil, by virtue of which needful contact is guarded against degenerating into sore rubs and grazes.

According to the ancient Oriental practice of leech-craft, oil was called in to heal physical wounds.

Hear a story in point :—

The pleasure-grounds of a certain Bishop contained an apparatus for turning on and off artificial waters. One day in honour of guests, the Bishop issued orders to his servants to work the fountains : but finding that this had caused offence, on the next similar occasion he gave leave to his servants to play the fountains. Whereupon all went smoothly.

August 31.

IT was once pointed out to me that in countenance a grey parrot and an elephant resemble each other.

But presumably the creatures themselves remain to this day unconscious of their common type, and inhabit pastures or trees or caravans or cages without a notion that each is (with limitations) the other's looking-glass; thus living and thus dying as utter aliens even when brought face to face.

"Know thyself" is an old-established injunction,

and conveys a hint that probably we do *not* know ourselves.

It is startling to reflect that you and I may be walking about unabashed and jaunty, whilst our fellows observe very queer likenesses amongst us.

Any one may be the observer: and equally any one may be the observed.

Liable to such casualties, I advise *myself* to assume a modest and unobtrusive demeanour.

I do not venture to advise *you*.

September 1.

FEAST OF ST. ÆGIDIUS OR GILES, ABBOT. According to various discrepant dates, he appears to have been born in the seventh, and to have died in the eighth century.

TWO pretty legends are told regarding him.

In his youth, going to Church, he bestowed his coat on a diseased mendicant. The poor man was cured, and our Saint is accounted Patron of Beggars.

Later in life he dwelt as a hermit in a forest cave beside the Rhone, nourished there by milk from a doe. This friendly creature, flying one day for her life, took refuge in his cave, where the hunters overtaking her, found that an arrow shot after the doe had wounded not herself but her associate the venerable hermit. Whereupon the king (for it was a royal hunt) cared for the saint's wound, cultivated his friendship, and caused a monastery to be reared on the site of the woodland cell: of which monastery, famous in after-times, St. Giles was chosen Abbot.

Finally:—"Many witness that they heard the company of angels bearing the soul of him into heaven." [I quote at second hand from "The Golden Legend."]

September 2.

I.

I AM told of certain birds which for protection take up their abode beneath wasps' nests. How it happens that they (as I assume) escape being stung, I do not know; but one sees at once that outside enemies might thus be kept at bay.

A wasps' nest for a canopy ; wasps for neighbours : clearly in itself no attractive neighbourhood. Yet better than the alternative, death, or deadly bereavement. So those birds are wise which, preferring of two evils the less, contrive of stings a shelter.

Similarly those persons are wise who amongst evils choose the less rather than the greater.

Why not accept all our trials as beneficial wasps and wasps' nests?

What is most irritating teaches patience, if we will be taught : what is most overbearing teaches humility, if we will learn.

Patience and humility predispose to faith, hope, charity : and where these are, there is safety.

September 3.

2.

I SAID " I do not know " how birds dwelling near wasps' nests escape stinging. Second thoughts show me that I do know.

God's Providence keeps them safe.

In the same sense as young ravens cry to God, we may think of all other feeble instinctive creatures as trusting in Him :—" Thou wilt keep him in perfect peace, whose mind is stayed on Thee : because he trusteth in Thee."

Even so the rose dwells amidst a guard of thorns, and stands alone in her loveliness.

Surely the rose, our own cherished rose, would lose a fine finishing touch of grace and beauty if divorced from her thorns.

And cannot we, who are so much better than bird or flower, take courage to trust our Heavenly Father implicitly? saying and feeling that if only we are such as love Him, our "wasps" and "thorns" alike are ordained for good; inasmuch as "all things work together for good to them that love God."

September 4.

3.

INDEED, I think we may proceed a step further, and reflect that any who like us like us as we are and not as we are not.

The person with the blemishes which are ours, and the weak points which are ours, is the person that those who love us love.

And conversely we may surely admit that (sin excluded) we also love our own beloved without on the whole wanting them to be different.

They are themselves, and this suffices.

We are quite ready to like something superior, but it contents our hearts to love them.

And when once death has stepped in, dividing as it were soul from spirit, the friend that is as one's own soul from oneself, then half those vanished peculiarities put on pathos. We remain actually fond of the blameless oddities, the plain face abides as the one face we prefer.

Now if persons as imperfect as ourselves can secure

a permanent place in the affection of their fellows (of which everywhere and always we behold proofs), our "vale of misery" turns to a perennial well of very sweet and refreshing water, and it becomes us to be thankful.

September 5.

4.

NOT that human affection, excellent as it is, suffices : only it illustrates and certifies to us beyond a doubt the corresponding Divine Affection.

This it does, even if we receive not its testimony. It is like the celestial luminaries which discourse without speech : its sound is gone out into all lands, and its words unto the ends of the world, declaring the Glory of God.

Nevertheless, as sun, moon and stars have had their worshippers, so human love has engrossed its idolatrous votaries.

It, indeed, is ready to "bless with the spirit," but those others are not edified.

Christ keep us or deliver us from worshipping and serving the creature more than the Creator, Who is Blessed for ever.   Amen.

September 6.

IF I should say "my heart is in my home,"
I turn away from that high halidom
    Where Jesu sits : for no where else
    But with its treasure, dwells
The heart : this Truth and this experience tells.

If I should say " my heart is in a grave,"
I turn away from Jesu risen to save,
   I slight that death He died for me;
   I, too, deny to see
   His beauty and desirability.

O Lord, Whose Heart is deeper than my heart,
Draw mine to Thine to worship where Thou art:
   For Thine own glory join the twain
   Never to part again,
   Nor to have lived nor to have died in vain.

September 7.

FEAST OF ST. ENURCHIUS OR EVURTIUS, BISHOP. Died about the year 340.

ST. ENURCHIUS, a Subdeacon in Roman Orders, went into Gaul as a missionary and was consecrated Bishop of Orleans, or (as I read elsewhere) of Arles : perhaps he was translated from one See to the other. He laboured amongst his pagan flock for more than twenty years, converting " nearly the whole city" to the Christian Faith : and having borne the burden and heat of his day, entered into his rest.

   " Write, Blessed are the dead which die in the Lord from henceforth : yea, saith the Spirit, that they may rest from their labours ; and their works do follow them."

September 8.

FEAST OF THE NATIVITY OF THE BLESSED VIRGIN MARY.

   " WITHOUT controversy, great is the mystery of godliness. God was manifest in the flesh."
   Since it pleased God to regard " the lowliness of

His handmaiden," well may we regard her with loving reverence.

Whereto shall we liken this Blessed Mary Virgin,
Fruitful shoot from Jesse's root graciously emerging?
Lily we might call her, but Christ alone is white ;
Rose delicious, but that Jesus is the one delight ;
Flower of women, but her Firstborn is mankind's one
      flower ;
He the Sun lights up all moons through their radiant
      hour.
" Blessed among women, highly favoured," thus
Glorious Gabriel hailed her, teaching words to us:
Whom devoutly copying we too cry " All hail!"
Echoing on the music of glorious Gabriel.

September 9.

"An alabaster box of ointment of spikenard very precious."—(ST. MARK xiv. 3.)

I HAVE read that both the precious spikenard and an inferior quality of perfume are yielded by the same plant.

The commoner sort is extracted by art. The choicer kind consists of such balsam as exudes from the untouched plant.

One resembles a tax, the other a gift.

Thus, by a figure, even a vegetable demonstrates how much nobler is voluntary than compelled service. For love alone genuinely gives : love turns a levied tax into a free gift, whereas a servile gift dwindles in essence to a mere tax.

Nor least so, in things spiritual. Love transmutes bounden duty into freewill oblation : constraint other than love transmutes even unprescribed offerings into taxes.

September 10.

1.

I HAVE read of an elephant who was set to move an enormous weight, which it behoved him to do by sheer force of his mighty head.

But not even his mighty head could stir it.

This his overseer perceived, whereupon other elephants were summoned to assist.

Then the first elephant seeing them approach, and being bent on carrying his point by himself, put forth so desperate an exertion of strength as fractured his skull.

As an elephant I greatly admire him.

Yet a man moulded on his model would, I fear, turn out a failure. He would be too independent to accept help, or to be set right, and he would sacrifice his cause rather than his pride.

September 11.

2.

MEANWHILE there appears a heroic and exemplary side, as well as a warning side to our elephant.

He stands as a figure of one who prefers his work to himself, his duty to his life.

A somewhat comical figure of a hero, yet none the less pathetic.

Not to be laughed at, but looked up to by such persons as have ever postponed work to self, duty to life.

I, for one, must not laugh at him.

September 12.

TREASURE plies a feather,
  Pleasure spreadeth wings,
Taking flight together,—
  Ah! my cherished things.

Fly away, poor pleasure
  That art so brief a thing:
Fly away, poor treasure
  That hast so swift a wing.

Pleasure, to be pleasure,
  Must come without a wing:
Treasure, to be treasure,
  Must be a stable thing.

Treasure without feather,
  Pleasure without wings,
Elsewhere dwell together
  And are heavenly things.

September 13.

EXHAUST this world and its resources: this done,
if spiritual life survives the soul will learn patience.

Sit aloof and look down on the world; viewed
from aloof and aloft the world's hollowness becomes
apparent: this realised, the living soul strikes root in
patience.

The Book of Ecclesiastes discloses to us the mind
of one who learned patience by the first method.

The Epistle of St. James manifests the spirit of one
who learned it by the second method.

In a certain sense, the result is the same from either

process : patience cannot but be patience. Nevertheless, the patience of a worn out penitent is far different from that of a lifelong saint.

"Vanity of vanities; all is vanity," reiterates the Preacher.

"Behold, we count them happy which endure," writes the Apostle.

For most of us it is too late to aim at that patience which crowns lifelong holiness. For none of us (thank God!) is it too late to acquire that patience which dignifies penitence. Whatsoever we be, the precept is for us: "Let patience have her perfect work." Amen.

September 14.

HOLY CROSS DAY.

I FIND the name of this Festival given in full as the Exaltation of The Holy Cross, and to it is dedicated one of the passion flowers.

The Cross was in truth exalted fully and finally when our Lord Jesus Christ hung thereupon on Mount Calvary. But this Feast Day has a later origin, some persons tracing it to a commemoration of that celestial cross which (as is related) led the Emperor Constantine to victory; others, to a recovery of the captive material cross from Chosroes the Persian by the Emperor Haraclius.

Not one exceptional day, however, but every day, from Baptism onwards is the good Christian's "Holy Cross Day." Even as our Lord proclaims to us all: "If any man will come after Me, let him deny himself, and take up his cross daily, and follow Me."

In the Eastern Church there exists an austere Religious Rule, according to which, "When the last

N

offices are closed, a representation of Christ on His Cross is attached to the foot of the bed, so that the eyes of the dying person may rest upon it, and then all go out, and leave the soul to make its departure in complete solitude, in the presence of none save the symbol of the Redeemer."

"Hold Thou Thy Cross before my dying eyes."

September 15.

In weariness and painfulness St. Paul
    Served God and pleased Him: after-saints no less
Can wait on and can please Him, one and all
    In weariness and painfulness,

    By faith and hope triumphant through distress:
Not with the rankling service of a thrall;
    But even as loving children trust and bless,

Weep and rejoice, answering their Father's call,
    Work with tired hands, and forward upward press
On sore tired feet, still rising when they fall,
    In weariness and painfulness.

September 16.

Once as we descended a mountain side by side with the mountain torrent, my companion saw, while I missed seeing, a foambow.

In all my life I do not recollect to have seen one, except perhaps in artificial fountains; but such general omission seems a matter of course, and therefore simply a matter of indifference. That single natural foambow which I might have beheld and espied not, is the one to which may attach a tinge of regret; because, in a certain sense, it depended upon myself to look at it, yet I did not look.

I might have done so, and I did not: such is the sting to-day in petty matters.

And what else will be the sting in matters all important at the last day?

September 17.

FEAST OF ST. LAMBERT, BISHOP OF MAESTRICHT. Born about the year 637; was murdered early in the eighth century.

HE is described as "a wise youth, of amiable aspect, affable speech, and right conversation; of stately form, strong and swift, agile and stout in war, clear headed, handsome, loving, pure and humble, and fond of reading." Thus he had in him the making either of a soldier or of an ecclesiastic. He chose the higher vocation, obeyed sedulously while under rule, and when himself in authority laboured as sedulously.

He has been styled a martyr; yet I question whether accurately, at least in the fullest sense of the word. Two men, trespassing on the temporalities of Maestricht, were slain by members of the Bishop's family: this occasioned a blood feud in which St. Lambert, amongst others, lost his life. He died with exemplary resignation and piety.

Being told of the approaching foe, " Lambert rose, and grasping his sword, his martial fire suddenly blazing up in him, he stood forth without even slipping on his shoes. But almost immediately he remembered himself, laid aside his sword, and prepared for the worst." To one of his nephews he said: " Remember you are guilty of the murder . . . and God will judge sinners. What you did unjustly, now in justice you must expiate . . ." He retired into his chamber, and having put all forth, he cast himself on the ground, with his arms extended, and wept abundantly. Directly after armed men burst in, killing every one in the house. Lambert's door was fastened from within, wherefore one man mounted the roof and ran him through with a spear, which he flung at him from above.

"But the souls of the righteous are in the hand of God, and there shall no torment touch them . . . For though they be punished in the sight of men, yet is their hope full of immortality."

September 18.

I.

HEAVEN and earth alike are chronometers.

Heaven marks time in light, by the motion of luminaries.

Earth marks time in darkness, by the variation of shadows.

To these chronometers of nature art adds clocks with faces easily decipherable and voices insistently audible.

Nature and art combine to keep time for us: and yet we wander out of time!

We misappropriate time, we lose time, we waste time, we kill time.

We do anything and everything with time, except redeem the time.

Yet time is short and swift and never returns. Time flies.

September 19.

2.

WE read in the Apocalypse :—

"And the angel which I saw stand upon the sea and upon the earth lifted up his hand to heaven, and sware by Him that liveth for ever and ever, Who created heaven, and the things that therein are, and the earth, and the things that therein are, and the sea, and the things which are therein, that there should be time no longer."

Thus St. John describes what he saw and heard.

Whence it seems that time is not lightly thought of by a holy angel whose eternity nevertheless depends not on time. With a great oath and an awful solemnity he announces the ending of that time which is man's period of probation.

And man thinks lightly of time!

September 20.

VIGIL OF ST. MATTHEW.

IF giants, dwarfs, and persons of standard height make up mankind, surely to the mental eye human vocations exhibit as wide a scale of extremes. And this, whether we measure vocations by dignity and lowliness, or by arduousness and ease.

To one man is allotted a domestic life of satisfied affection and multiplied blessings, unaccompanied by crushing trials or difficulties. "God answereth him in the joy of his heart:" moderation and thankfulness rank among his chief duties, and "a joyful and pleasant thing it is to be thankful."

Another man is called to hardship, disappointment,

a life and death struggle with the world, the flesh and the devil.

Or if we glance back to the primitive Church for our specimens. Then all Christians had distinctly and decisively to choose their side in the battle of life. Confessors were common, Martyrs not rare.

Yet among this elect congregation a few were set foremost as Apostles ; and out of these, two were inspired to become Evangelists.

Of these two, St. Matthew is one.

It is vain to meditate ambitiously on his glory : it is unworthy to meditate thereon in a craven spirit of sloth.

Yet inasmuch as his Vigil and Festival bid us have him in remembrance, let us at least in one point emulate his luminous example, for in one point we can.

Christ called him : he forthwith obeyed the call, followed Him, clave to Him, lived for Him, died for Him.

And every one of us by asking aright can obtain grace to do the same.

September 21.

FEAST OF ST. MATTHEW, OTHERWISE NAMED LEVI, APOSTLE AND EVANGELIST.

IN St. Luke's Gospel we read how our Lord " went forth, and saw a publican, named Levi, sitting at the receipt of custom : and He said unto him, Follow Me. And he left all, rose up, and followed Him."

Spirit outspeeds matter ; will, action ; love, everything.

St. Matthew, intent on following, first arose : in like manner his heart's desire and choice outstripped physical possibility, so that he had already "left all" when he "rose up."

Having arisen, he forthwith followed ; being called, he forthwith arose ; yet arising forthwith, had in will already relinquished all. Few are they on whom his mantle has descended.

Reluctantly *we* hear a conscience-call : we mean to rise, but later on ; to start, but at a future moment. Perhaps, when grudgingly and of necessity we have at last accomplished both acts, our heart may slowly and drearily (for habit is second nature) get weaned from its first love—say, a money bag—and mount resignedly to higher interests.

But if this result impend only "after a long time." God in mercy grant that the Lord (though also "after a long time") arrive not first to reckon with His sordid servants.

"From sudden death, Good Lord, deliver us."

September 22.

LORD, what have I that I may offer Thee?
Look, Lord, I pray Thee, and see.

What is it thou hast got?
Nay, child, what is it thou hast not?
Thou hast all gifts that I have given to thee :
Offer them all to Me,
The great ones and the small,
I will accept them one and all.

I have a will, good Lord, but it is marred ;
A heart both crushed and hard :
Not such as these the gift
Clean-handed, lovely saints uplift.

Nay, child, but wilt thou judge for Me?
I crave not thine, but thee.

Ah, Lord, Who lovest me!
Such as I have now give I Thee.

September 23.

I.

I HAVE read that such plants as produce a cruciform flower are all alike free from poison.

Life has its blossoming season preparatory to its season of fruit.

And many lives by bereavement, disappointment, pain, hope deferred, blossom, so to say, with crosses.

A choice and blessed blossom, if it correspond with nature's emblem and harbour no venom. For one day the cross petals will drop off, and only the good fruit remain.

September 24.

2.

CHRIST, " for the joy that was set before Him, endured the cross, despising the shame, and is set down at the right hand of the Throne of God."

For our sakes the cruciform blossom of His mortal life was agony and shame : for our sakes the salutary fruit of His life immortal is glory and grace.

And now He looks down from heaven, from the habitation of His holiness and of His glory, if so be He may in us see of the travail of His Soul and be satisfied.

Once He looked, and there was no man. Once He looked, and one penitent went out and wept bitterly.

Now He looks on you, on me.

September 25.

SORROW hath a double voice,
    Sharp to-day but sweet to-morrow:
Wait in patience, hope, rejoice,
    Tried friends of sorrow.

Pleasure hath a double taste,
    Sweet to-day but sharp to-morrow:
Friends of pleasure, rise in haste,
    Make friends with sorrow.

Pleasure set aside to-day
    Comes again to rule to-morrow:
Welcomed sorrow will not stay,
    Farewell to sorrow!

September 26.

FEAST OF ST. CYPRIAN, ARCHBISHOP OF CARTHAGE. The date of his birth is unknown; he died a Martyr, being beheaded about the year 258.

ST. CYPRIAN began life as a lawyer, nor was he baptized till of ripe age. He was chosen Bishop of Carthage by the general voice in the year 248; and though he shrank out of sight to evade the dignity, was finally constrained to obey that call of God conveyed by the mouth of the people.

Even before his consecration he had embarked on the sea of controversy; and amid those stormy waters he toiled year after year, opposing diverse errors, pronouncing judgment on points of faith or of discipline.

From the persecution under Decius he sought shelter by flight, deeming it his duty so to do, yet from afar shepherding his forlorn flock. A second persecution found him immovable in his See, exhorting, sustaining, comforting the souls committed to his charge.

It was not till for the third time he was summoned to face persecution that he joined the noble army of martyrs; nor even then, before he had endured an eleven months' exile from Carthage. Galerius Maximus, Proconsul under the Emperors Valerian and Gallienus, recalled him from banishment, and on his steadfastness in the faith, pronounced his death doom. " Thanks be to God," then said holy Cyprian.

He was led to a field, where he prayed and made ready. The bandage he bound over his own eyes, and two of his friends bound his hands. Whereupon the stroke of the headsman set him free, and sent him home at once and for ever.

He has bequeathed many holy writings to the Church Universal : let us treasure two sentences :—

" He flies not alone who hath Christ the companion of his flight. He is not alone who beareth about with him everywhere the temple of God, and hath God ever within him."

September 27.

"Dust shalt thou eat all the days of thy life;" thus saith the Truth at the beginning : and thus again towards the end ; " Dust shall be the serpent's meat."

Dust the symbol of death : the residuum of death : as it were, the essence of death.

The serpent brought death into the human family, turning life into death : and dust of death is his dole.

Nought besides dust, nought besides death, as it seems : " His delight was in cursing, and it shall happen unto him."

Nothing, then, that retains true vitality shall be his

final prey : nothing but what is dead, utterly, irreversibly lifeless.

O God, Who wouldest not the death of a sinner, but rather that he should be converted and live, convert us, give us life, revive our life, keep us alive, for Christ's sake, Who broke not the bruised reed nor quenched the smoking flax. Amen.

September 28.

OUR life is long—Not so wise Angels say,
Who watch us waste it, trembling while they weigh
Against eternity one squandered day.

Our life is long—Not so the Saints protest,
Filled full of consolation and of rest :
" Short ill, long good, one long unending best."

Our life is long—Christ's word sounds different :
" Night cometh : no more work when day is spent."
Repent and work to-day, work and repent.

Lord, make us like Thy Host, who day nor night
Rest not from adoration, their delight,
Crying " Holy, Holy, Holy," in the height.

Lord, make us like Thy Saints who wait and long
Contented : bound in hope and freed from wrong
They speed (may be) their vigil with a song.

Lord, make us like Thyself, for thirty-three
Slow years of toil seemed not too long to Thee
That where Thou art there Thy Beloved might be.

September 29.

ALL Angels, like All Saints, occupy a Festival Day; unlike men, they give no cause for an introductory Vigil. For sin it is which necessitates vigils, death, all else that is sorrowful.

Their perfection hinders not their sympathy with us: the lack of sympathy is on our side, because so also is the imperfection.

For sin is the only essentially grievous thing in the universe. God, Ever Blessed, had never (that we can conceive) known suffering, if He had not borne " our sins in His own Body on the tree."

Wherefore holy Angels, who neither sin nor bear sins, know not sorrow. Even sympathy, one of our noblest sources of sorrow, is not (so far as we can tell) any source of sadness to them.

They love us, yet cease not to rejoice; care for us, yet observe one unbroken jubilee. How unlike must heaven be to earth, and how unlike the sinless to the sinful.

Yet if they be indeed exempt from sorrow, then Christ is so far like us rather than like them, inasmuch as His experience of sorrow surpasses even our own. He Himself seems to challenge heaven and earth in the words of Jeremiah: " Is it nothing to you, all ye that pass by? Behold, and see if there be any sorrow like unto My sorrow, which is done unto Me, wherewith the Lord hath afflicted Me in the day of His fierce anger."

Good is angelic bliss, for it makes celestial spirits so far like God, All-Good in His perpetual bliss.

Good is human sorrow, for it makes mortal men so far like Christ, Who learnt sorrow for their sakes.

All is good which bears the stamp of a Divine likeness.

Wherefore, while life and joy cease not to be good, grief, vigils, death, have become likewise good; because Christ in His own Person has known them all.

September 30.

FEAST OF ST. JEROME, PRIEST, DOCTOR, AND ASCETIC. Born on the borders of Dalmatia and Pannonia at an uncertain date, perhaps in the year 331; died about 420.

THE Church owes and pays a debt of lasting gratitude to St. Jerome: whose studies in the Hebrew Bible, revision of the Vulgate translation, scriptural comments and polemical writings, establish him as on the whole a vigorous and effective champion of truth.

Yet not altogether without flaw. Of strong natural passions, and still stronger will, he strained that strong will to the uttermost to overcome the natural man; and the desert cell he sometime inhabited witnessed his life and death struggle with evil, his occasional ecstasy, his hard-won triumph.

No marvel that a strength which sufficed to trample down self occasionally ran, as it did, into ruggedness, asperity, unseemliness, in the field of controversy.

Yet had this formidable athlete a tender, accessible heart, affectionate towards the saints he trained amongst Rome's noblest matrons and maids; warm and wide to receive and entertain in his monasteries, in his very cell, fugitives from the once Imperial City when overthrown by an inundation of barbarians.

So this great man wrestled and laboured: on the whole, emitting a trumpet voice of no uncertain sound, and a light to lighten all who would come into that holy house which is the Church of God.

As his life, so his death had both a stormy side and a side of enduring peace. Factious Christians burnt the two monasteries he had partly founded, and chased him thence : yet were his emaciated remains buried in his monastic grotto, and that monastery was at Bethlehem.

Long ago the verdict, whether of friends or of foes, has ceased to affect him. As he himself foresaw when he wrote to the beloved lady Asella : " I know we may arrive at heaven equally with a bad, as a good name."

October 1.

FEAST OF ST. REMIGIUS, ARCHBISHOP OF RHEIMS.   Born about
the year 435; died about 532.

SEVEN feet high and of handsome countenance, as transpires in his after-life, St. Remigius, being then a young man, was sitting in the Church of Rheims, where clergy and people were convened to choose a Bishop, when a ray of light penetrating through the clerestory, illumined his face amid the surrounding comparative darkness, and he was elected by acclamation to the vacant See. Whereupon, he being at the time no more than twenty-two years old, the canonical impediment of youth was waived ; he received Holy Orders, and assumed his allotted dignity.

To him appertains the glory of having instructed and baptized Clovis, King of the Franks, whom at the Font he exhorted in the noble words : " Adore what thou hast burned : burn what thou hast adored."

Various miraculous incidents are narrated in connexion with him. The following forms so striking a parable of the hazard in matters spiritual of ever, under any pretext, reopening a channel once closed against temptation, that either as history or as allegory I transcribe it :—

" A tremendous conflagration broke out at Rheims. St. Remigius came to the rescue when more than half the city was in flames. He went before the raging fire and made the sign of the cross; the flames retreated ; he advanced, and continued making the sign, and the fire backed before him step by step, till he drove it through a gate. Then he ordered the gate to be walled up, and forbade any one ever opening it again. Many years after the owner of the adjoining house, wanting an ash-pit, knocked a hole in the wall that he might shoot his rubbish through it. Instantly out burst the demon of the conflagration and killed the man, his wife, children, and servants."

October 2.

DARKNESS and light are both alike to Thee:
   Therefore to Thee I lift my darkened face ;
Upward I look with eyes that fail to see,
   Athirst for future light and present grace.
   I trust the Hand of Love I scarcely trace.
With breath that fails I cry, Remember me :
   Add breath to breath, so I may run my race
That where Thou art there may Thy servant be.
For Thou art gulf and fountain of my love,
   I unreturning torrent to Thy sea,
      Yea, Thou the measureless ocean for my rill :
      Seeking I find, and finding, seek Thee still :
And oh ! that I had wings as hath a dove,
Then would I flee away to rest with Thee.

October 3.

I HAVE noticed in cold weather how many days a rose will linger in the bud, quarter blown, half blown. When at length, if ever, it expands fully, it will probably not be the most beautiful of roses : still, if far below the finest blossoms at their best moment, it has, on the other hand, lasted longer than they.

Superiority in one point may fairly be set against inferiority in another : duration against quality.

And if this is equitable in estimating flowers, it is no less equitable in estimating people.

Many lives pass in chills and in shadows which preclude certain fine finishing touches of loveliness : their resource will be to excel in endurance.

And in the long run surely the livers of such lives will be ready to sing with David : " The lot is fallen unto me in a fair ground : " for " he that shall endure unto the end, the same shall be saved."

October 4.

I.

No thing is great on this side of the grave,
    Nor any thing of any stable worth :
    Whatso is born from earth returns to earth :
No thing we grasp proves half the thing we crave :
The tidal wave becomes the ebbing wave :
    Laughter is folly, madness lurks in mirth :
    Mankind sets off a-dying from the birth :
Life is a losing game,—with what to save ?
Thus I sat mourning like a mournful owl,
    And like a doleful dragon made ado,
        Companion of all monsters of the dark :
When lo ! the light shook off its nightly cowl,
    And up to heaven flashed carolling a lark,
    And all creation sang its hymn anew.

October 5.

2.

WHILE all creation sang its hymn anew,
  What could I do but sing a stave in tune?
  Spectral on high hung pale the vanishing moon,
Where a last hint of stars hung paling too.
Lark's lay—a cockcrow—with a scattered few
  Soft early chirpings,—with a tender croon
  Of doves,—a hundred thousand calls, and soon
A hundred thousand answers, sweet and true.
These set me singing too at unawares:
  One note for all delights and charities,
    One note for hope reviving with the light,
  One note for every lovely thing that is,
Till while I sang my heart cast off its cares,
  And revelled in the land of no more night.

October 6.

I.

FEAST OF ST. FAITH, VIRGIN MARTYR.   Third century.

WHILE Dacian governed Spain on behalf of the
Emperor of this visible world, and persecuted the
Church on behalf of the arch-emperor of the fallen
invisible world, Faith, a noble maiden of Aquitain,
"fought a good fight, kept the faith," and from a bed
of fire went home to that rest, which the wicked cannot trouble.

Yet some have surmised that this " St. Faith " is no
real flesh and blood person, but an embodiment of that
indomitable Virtue of the same name which in a host
of martyrs has laughed to scorn the impotent power
of the enemy.

O

Whichever she was, let us profit by her.

If she was a weak maid, which of us cannot by Divine Grace become as strong as a weak maid?

If she was a Christian Virtue, which of us is not vowed to have and to hold fast in life and in death that same Christian virtue?

October 7.

2.

LYING a-dying,—
Have done with vain sighing:
Life not lost but treasured,
God Almighty pleasured,
God's daughter fetched and carried,
Christ's bride betrothed and married.
Our tender little dove,
Meek-eyed and simple,
Our love goes home to Love:
There shall she walk in white,
Where God shall be the Light,
And God the Temple.

October 8.

3.

LET us seek to extract one more lesson from St. Faith.

As I was yesterday, so I remain to-day, in doubt as to the existence of this Saint. Wherefore, so far as my exposition of her claims is concerned, we cannot but admit that our ignorance outstrips our knowledge.

Ignorance, then, rather than knowledge, must (it

would seem) feed our souls on certain occasions. What nourishment can we derive from ignorance?

Thus much, at least :—

We find that for practical purposes we do after all know enough of St. Faith : inasmuch as we know enough to enable us to follow the suggestion of our Mother Church, by honouring her (contingent) memory.

And if in the same spirit of faith and obedience we betake ourselves devoutly to search the Scriptures, we shall surely find that, despite our manifold ignorances, we yet do know enough of the Divine Revelation to understand and keep God's commandments.

And "blessed are they that hear the word of God, and keep it."

October 9.

FEAST OF ST. DENYS, BISHOP, accounted Patron Saint of France. Assigned to the third century.

So much has to be set aside as incredible, or at the least as untrustworthy in the history (?) of this personage, that we shall not, I think, memorialise him amiss by reflecting thankfully that one who presumably bore his name was undoubtedly constituted God's instrument in converting to Christianity certain firstfruits of the great and noble French nation.

St. Denys of Paris—for Paris is assigned as the field of his labours, and Montmartre as the scene of his martyrdom—has, erroneously as it appears, been identified with St. Paul's adherent, "Dionysius the Areopagite:" while both together have become confused with the author of certain works belonging to a later century, and popularly and perhaps correctly ascribed to (a third) Dionysius.

Tradition represents St. Denys as beheaded : and

then as arising and carrying his head a considerable distance.

Now, without pretending to pronounce on this particular legend, let us lay to heart St. Paul's injunction: "Refuse profane and old wives' fables, and exercise thyself rather unto godliness."

October 10.

1.

ALL heaven is blazing yet
  With the meridian sun:
Make haste, O sun, make haste to set;
  O lifeless life, have done.

I choose what once I chose;
  What once I willed, I will:
Only the heart its own bereavement knows,
  O clamorous heart, lie still.

October 11.

2.

THAT which I chose, I choose;
  That which I willed, I will;
That which I once refused, I still refuse:
  O hope deferred, be still.

That which I chose and choose
  And will is Jesu's Will:
He hath not lost his life who seems to lose:
  O hope deferred, hope still.

October 12.

A GOOD unobtrusive Christian of my own intimate circle told me that in her worried life—and a worried life it has been—she has derived comfort from the reflection that no day lasts longer than twenty-four hours.

To a good worried Christian this certainty affords legitimate comfort.

But, as it cannot certify comfort to all classes of worried persons, it seems safe for most of us not to wish time shortened.

If time is short, many tempers are yet shorter.

Even a Psalmist prays: "O spare me a little, that I may recover my strength: before I go hence, and be no more seen."

And most of us have very much besides strength to recover.

October 13.

FEAST OF THE TRANSLATION OF ST. EDWARD THE CONFESSOR, KING OF ENGLAND. Born about the year 1002; anointed and crowned on Easter Day 1042; died on the Eve of the Epiphany 1066.

"HE was a mild, pious, but feeble prince: his heart, weaned from the world, sought comfort in religion, and the cares of government were a painful distraction to a mind musing on heavenly things. From his infancy he had been addicted to prayer . . . He was modest in his comportment and sparing in his words."

Such is the character I read of him.

His reign was chequered by troubles, yet these not of such magnitude as to undermine his throne. His family affections seem to have been thwarted if not naturally tepid. His gratitude to the Normans, who entertained him at a period of his depressed fortune, worked prosperously for them, but at the cost apparently of his own native subjects. He gave away his crown by promise, contrary, as is alleged, to an established law of the realm : and, although his own career closed in peace, days of bloodshed and years of civil heartburning and animosity overtook England after him.

I accept him on trust as Saint and Confessor : for, by studying the brief summary I write from, I discern him not as such by aid of my own faculties.   Indeed, I do not perceive that "confessorship" was at all in question : for who challenged his faith?

Nevertheless, charity and obedience alike bid me question my own questionings and mistrust my doubts: and so I do.

"We know in part . . . But when that which is perfect is come, then that which is in part shall be done away."

October 14.

A SENSUAL Christian resembles a sea anemone.

In the nobler element, air, it exists as a sluggish unbeautiful excrescence.

In the lower element, water, it grows, blows and thrives.

The food it assimilates is derived not from the height, but from the depth.

It possesses neither eyes nor ears, but a multitude of feelers.

It squats on a tenacious base, gulps all acquisitions into a capacious chasm, and harmonises with the weeds it dwells amongst.

But what will become of it in a world where there shall be no more sea?

October 15.

1.

TOGETHER once, but never more
  While Time and Death run out their runs:
Though sundered now as shore from shore,
  Together once.

  Nor rising suns, nor setting suns,
Nor life renewed which Springtide bore,
  Make one again Death's sundered ones.

Eternity holds rest in store,
  Holds hope of long reunions:
But holds it what they hungered for
  Together once?

October 16.

2.

WHATSO it be, howso it be, Amen.
  Blessed it is, believing, not to see.
Now God knows all that is; and we shall, then,
  Whatso it be.

  God's Will is best for man whose will is free.
God's Will is better to us, yea, than ten
  Desires whereof He holds and weighs the key.

Amid her household cares He guides the wren,
  He guards the shifty mouse from poverty,
He knows all wants, allots each where and when,
  Whatso it be.

October 17.

FEAST OF ST. ETHELDREDA, VIRGIN QUEEN AND ABBESS. Her death took place in the year 679, on the 23rd of June; the day appointed as her Festival in the Anglican Calendar being the anniversary of the (first) translation of her remains in 695.

THIS Princess, daughter of Anna King of East Anglia, was twice given in marriage. Her first husband, Prince Tombert, appears either to have shared her spirit of self-devotion or to have loved her better than himself, for, in compliance with her will, he forbore to enforce his marital rights during their three years' union. Left a widow she hoped for freedom : yet was constrained by family influence to marry Prince Egfrid, heir of the kingdom of Northumbria. Still, however, she adhered to her former resolution ; and, after twelve years of successful contest, ended strife by separating from her enamoured husband; yet not without first obtaining his reluctant consent.

Thus she fought the battle of life : thus she triumphed. Egfrid, indeed, not enduring her absence pursued her ere long to the monastery of Coldingham : whence however she fled and escaped him.

Finally, she built a monastery for men and women in the Island of Ely, which island she inherited from her first husband. She ruled her Community piously, performed many good deeds, and died (we are informed) still young :—

"At the last moment, surrounded by the brothers and sisters of the numerous community in tears, she spoke to them at length, imploring them never to let their hearts rest on the earth, but to taste beforehand, by their earnest desires, that joy in the love of Christ which it would not be given to them to know perfectly here below."

October 18.

FEAST OF ST. LUKE, EVANGELIST.

IT is not certain that St. Luke died a martyr; but we cannot doubt that he lived a saint.

Setting aside a question easily raised and not easily answered, whether the "Luke" or "Lucas" named three times by St. Paul is or is not this Evangelist, and assuming such identity, we notice how very tenderly he is mentioned as "Luke, the beloved physician:" and again, with a brevity more expressive than a multitude of words, "Only Luke is with me."

But in St. Luke's Gospel, and in his Book of Acts, his own name occurs not so much as once. In the Gospel it seems impossible to trace him, except perhaps by help of tradition: in the Acts we infer his presence on certain occasions only from his use of the word "we" and its derivatives.

Thus St. Luke illustrates for our edification one of King Solomon's noble Proverbs: "Let another man praise thee, and not thine own mouth; a stranger, and not thine own lips."

October 19.

How can one man, how can all men,
 How can we be like St. Paul,
Like St. John, or like St. Peter,
  Like the least of all
  Blessed Saints? for we are small.

Love can make us like St. Peter,
 Love can make us like St. Paul,
Love can make us like the blessed
  Bosom friend of all
  Great St. John,—though we are small.

Love which clings and trusts and worships,
　Love which rises from a fall,
Love which teaching glad obedience
　Labours most of all,
　Love makes great the great and small.

October 20.

I.

As I am nothing of an ornithologist, any small out-door bird with forked tail and black and white plumage may pass with me as a swallow or as a martin. When mud nests are not in sight, then it becomes a swallow.

Once at the seaside I recollect noticing for some time a row of swallows perched side by side along a telegraph wire. There they sat steadily. After a while, when some one looked again, they were gone.

This happened so late in the year as to suggest that the birds had mustered for migration and then had started.

The sight was quaint, comfortable looking, pretty. The small creatures seemed so fit and so ready to launch out on their pathless journey: contented to wait, contented to start, at peace and fearless.

Altogether they formed an apt emblem of souls willing to stay, willing to depart.

Only I fear there are not so many " willing " souls as " willing " swallows.

October 21.

2.

THAT combination of swallows with telegraph wire sets in vivid contrast before our mental eye the sort of evidence we put confidence in and the sort of evidence we mistrust.

The telegraph conveys messages from man to man.

The swallows by dint of analogy, of suggestion, of parallel experience, if I may call it so, convey messages from the Creator to the human creature.

We act eagerly, instantly, on telegrams. Who would dream of stopping to question their genuineness?

Whilst often we act reluctantly, often we act not at all, on the other sort of messages. We dwell anxiously on the thousand contingencies of life, tremblingly on the inevitable contingency of death. We call everything in question, except the bitter certainty of suffering, the most bitter certainty of death.

Who, watching us, could suppose that the senders of telegrams are fallible; and that the Only Sender of Providential messages is infallible?

October 22.

I.

ONE of the prettiest Japanese carvings I ever saw represented an elephant.

Quite a little elephant done in ivory, yet as elephantine as Jumbo himself. Altogether an exquisite work of art.

Still, its finishing touch of excellence resided (to my thinking) neither in trunk nor in knowing eye; but rather in the subtle artistic instinct which had placed that elephant well back on his ivory stand, so as to leave him room to walk on.

The position spoke for itself. There stood the elephant able and willing to take his walk, and to all intents and purposes about to start.

Thus the unique charm of that immovable elephant lay in his expression of progress.

I fear many of our moveable selves so reverse the marvel that the last idea conveyed by our expression is any promise of progress.

But if so, why so?

October 23.

2.

PERHAPS we may gather a hint of the " why " from that same elephant's platform : smooth, and of ivory.

He rose superior to the snare. But we, I think, are often hampered by what may be termed the ivory smoothness of our surroundings and circumstances.

Beautiful things and comfortable things tempt one to loiter, if not absolutely to stand stock still.

Meanwhile the Bible bids us go on unto perfection, and press toward the mark.

To loiter cannot be to press forward : to stand still cannot be to go on.

Which will we forego : smoothness without, or perfection within? a house of ivory here, or the City of Gold hereafter?

October 24.

A WORLDLY Christian resembles a chameleon which possesses two independent eyes addicted to looking in opposite directions.

One eye, let us say, peers frankly downwards fly seeking.

The twin eye peers skywards.

A chameleon used to enjoy the credit of living on air : surely an all but angelic reptile !

Such was the verdict of ignorance. The verdict of knowledge, nowadays, is that the chameleon simply lives on insects.

His downward eye contemplating earth hunts a walking fly. His upward eye scouring heaven presumably hunts a floating fly, but still a fly.

There remains no difference worth speaking of between his upward eye and his downward eye.

October 25.

FEAST OF ST. CRISPIN, MARTYR ; accounted Patron of shoemakers. The year 285 is perhaps the date of this saint's martyrdom. His brother St. Crispinian suffered and triumphed with him. But so much of their legendary history fails to carry conviction with it, that every alleged particular may prudently be held under correction.

THESE pious brothers, then, were Roman shoemakers working at Soissons. An alternative account makes them Roman nobles. Whatever they were in this world's social scale, they are pourtrayed to us as such men as " the King delighteth to honour ; " and where they now dwell, earth and earthly rank alike have dwindled to nothing.

And if " to nothing " there, can they be any great thing here?

October 26.

OF all the downfalls in the world,
   The flutter of an Autumn leaf
   Grows grievous by suggesting grief :
Who thought, when Spring was first unfurled,
Of this? The wide world lay empearled ;
Who thought of frost that nips the world?
            Sigh on, my ditty.

There lurk a hundred subtle stings
  To prick us in our daily walk :
  An apple cankered on its stalk,
A robin snared for all his wings,
A voice that sang but never sings ;
Yea, sight or sound or silence stings.
             Kind Lord, show pity.

October 27.

VIGIL OF ST. SIMON AND ST. JUDE, APOSTLES.

" THE harvest is past, the summer is ended," writes
the Prophet Jeremiah.

Even so this vigil overtakes us in the waning natural
year, with harvest past and summer ended.

What has been sown has also been reaped. After
the reapers the gleaners have followed : the last ears
have been gathered in. It is too late now to sow,
whether or not we have sown long ago ; or to reap,
whether or not we have already reaped.

" The harvest is past, the summer is ended, and we
are not saved," writes the Prophet Jeremiah.

And wiser than he, and more full of tenderness,
Christ wept over Jerusalem, saying, " If thou hadst
known, even thou, at least in this thy day, the things
which belong unto thy peace ! but now they are hid
from thine eyes."

Nevertheless, to-day, while it is called to-day, He
still calls us, saying, " The time is fulfilled, and the
kingdom of God is at hand : repent ye, and believe
the Gospel."

October 28.

FEAST OF ST. SIMON AND ST. JUDE, APOSTLES.

TRADITION, but not with unanimous voice, proclaims that St. Simon was martyred in Persia, being sawn asunder: that St. Jude similarly "fell asleep," hanging pierced upon a cross at Edessa.

St. Jude has enriched the Church with the General Epistle which bears his name : of St. Simon no writings remain to us.

The inspired Gospel narrative records little of either Saint beyond his name, except that of course both are included in statements which speak of "the Twelve."

Thus we behold two illustrious Apostles contented scarcely to be mentioned in Holy Scripture: which celestial partial eclipse is followed up by their sharing one Festival between them.

Truly they learnt of Him Who is "meek and lowly in heart;" and now they know by blessed experience that it is enough for the disciple to be as his Master, and the servant as his Lord.

October 29.

WHO has not rejoiced at the ever familiar, ever marvellous aspect of the stars? Those resplendent orbs remote, abiding.

But now science, endeavouring to account for certain recurrent obscurations of one or more such luminaries, suggests that among them and with them may be revolving other non-luminous bodies; which interposing periodically between individuals of the bright host and our planet, diminish from time to time the light proceeding from one or other ; and again, by advancing along an assigned orbit, reveal their original brightness.

" Such knowledge is too wonderful and excellent for me : I cannot attain unto it."

Yet none the less does the physical hypothesis suggest a spiritual analogy.

If certain stars which present mere dimness and obstruction to our eyes are notwithstanding genuine celestial bodies fulfilling their proper revolution in their legitimate orbit, may not some human fellow creatures who to us exhibit no sign of grace, yet be numbered among the children of God, and have their lot among the saints ?

God grant that so it may be, and grant me fellowship with them.

October 30.

WHO is this that cometh up not alone
  From the fiery-flying-serpent wilderness,
Leaning upon her own Beloved One,
  Who is this?

Lo, the King of King's daughter, a high princess,
Going home as bride to her Husband's Throne,
  Virgin queen in perfected loveliness.

Her eyes a dove's eyes and her voice a dove's moan,
  She shows like a full moon for heavenliness,
Eager saints and angels ask in heaven's zone:
  Who is this?

October 31.

VIGIL OF ALL SAINTS.

THIS Vigil is commensurate with the duration of Christendom, for the life of every Christian is this vigil : so ought yours to be, so ought mine.

A vigil is a period wherein to fast, pray, watch; repent of the past, amend the present, prepare and long for the future.

Such is a vigil. Is my life such?

" The night is far spent, the day is at hand."

November 1.

FEAST OF ALL SAINTS.

As grains of sand, as stars, as drops of dew,
   Numbered and treasured by the Almighty Hand,
   The Saints triumphant throng that holy land
Where all things and Jerusalem are new.
We know not half they sing or half they do,
   But this we know, they rest and understand ;
   While like a conflagration freshly fanned,
Their love glows upward, outward, through and through.
Lo ! like a stream of incense launched on flame
   Fresh Saints stream up from death to life above,
     To shine among those others and rejoice.
What matters tribulation whence they came ?
   All love, and only love, can find a voice
Where God makes glad His Saints, for God is Love.

November 2.

I.

" Unstable as water,"—(or according to an alternative rendering)— " Bubbling up as water, thou shalt not excel."—(GEN. xlix. 4.)

THESE prophetic words of doom spoken against one such individual seem to apply to all persons of the " watery " type : to such persons, that is, as are born unstable and excitable.

P

So far, of course, as the mere natural disposition goes, no fault attaches to them. Only they will have to work under the condition of (at the least) a predisposition towards inferiority.

Which predisposition invites the virtue of humility.

Now where humility lays deep the low-lying foundation, the superincumbent structure can safely and permanently tower aloft unto heaven.

Whence we perceive how by God's grace a predisposition towards inferiority may be reclaimed as a vantage ground for the achievement of excellence.

November 3.

2.

ONE only process there is which renders water stable in itself: the process of freezing.

A second resource exists whereby for practical purposes it can be coerced into acting as if stable: dams, dykes, an impervious channel, restrain its laxity, husband its volume, accumulate and direct its strength.

To freeze suggests discipline rather than indulgence: to be straitened seems less enjoyable than to wander at large.

If we be " watery " characters we may not improbably need chills and shadows of life to harden us: full, unbroken, cloudless sunshine might evaporate us altogether, so that even if sought, our place should nowhere be found.

Or perhaps our lot will be cast in a narrow galling groove. Yet better this, surely, than that we should dribble in all directions into mere slush and mire, come to worse than nothing ourselves, and swamp our neighbourhood.

November 4.

3.

THE instability of liquids can on occasion be counteracted by promptitude at full speed : thus an expert knows how to turn topsy-turvy and up again an open vessel of water without spilling one drop.

Whence it appears probable that unhesitating promptitude will prove a corrective virtue for the limp cold-watery character. "Whatsoever thy hand findeth to do, do it with thy might," urges the experienced Preacher. "While I am coming, another steppeth down before me," declares the hope-sick paralytic.

But while promptitude appears remedial for the cold-watery character, it threatens to heap fuel on the flame of the bubbling-up type.

Touching this latter, I venture not to offer any hint here, beyond quoting a suggestion I have met with elsewhere. When a pailful of water is being carried, wood floating on the surface steadies it : and in this wood that devout author saw the Cross.

Let us excitable people try the efficacy of the Cross applied to our hearts by love. I will not despair of its steadying and calming the unquietest heart amongst us,—yours, or mine.

November 5.

4.

"AND now, Lord, what is my hope? truly my hope is even in Thee."

One unfailing comfort of all who start in life "as water" consists in this : that water is constituted an eminent type of God the Holy Ghost.

P 2

The mist which refreshed Eden, the spring of Hagar
(Gen. xxi. 19), the water which in twelve wells awaited
wayfaring Israel, the desert fountain which called forth
a song, set Him before us "merciful and gracious:"
the water which streamed by the way of Edom to
preserve perishing life, the "pure River of Water of
Life, clear as crystal, proceeding out of the Throne of
God and of the Lamb," set Him before us "plenteous
in goodness."

And they who by His indwelling become moulded
to His likeness, show forth His gracious loveliness, and
are "in the midst of many people as a dew from the
Lord, as the showers upon the grass, that tarrieth not
for man, nor waiteth for the sons of men:" and their
recompense is themselves also to "be like a watered
garden, and like a spring of water whose waters fail
not."

"Wherefore lift up the hands which hang down,
and the feeble knees; and make straight paths for
your feet."

November 6.

FEAST OF ST. LEONARD, HERMIT AND CONFESSOR. Died
about the year 559.

ST. LEONARD was son to a Frankish nobleman and
Godson to King Clovis. Preferring a life of devotion
to the career of a courtier he, after some experience in
a monastery, retired to a forest not far from Limoges,
and there subsisted on herbs and fruits.

In this forest a king. perhaps Theodebert of Aus-
trasia, whose territory included the Limousin, sometimes followed the chase. On one such occasion he was
accompanied by his queen, who then and there gave
birth to a healthy baby, but not before the royal husband's anxiety had been awakened: St. Leonard, how-

ever, arriving opportunely, all went well with mother
and child.   In gratitude to St. Leonard the king
made him a grant of land, whereon our saint raised
a monastery, naming it Noblac, in honour of so noble
a gift, and ruling its inmates until he died.

St. Leonard is accounted the Patron of Prisoners,
Clovis (it is said) having empowered him to release
every prisoner he visited.   If so, we may associate with
his memory the Divine words spoken through Isaiah :—
"Is not this the fast that I have chosen? . . . to let
the oppressed go free, and that ye break every yoke?"

November 7.

ONE of the dearest and most saintly persons I ever
knew, in foresight of her own approaching funeral, saw
nothing attractive in the "hood and hatband" style
towards which I evinced some old-fashioned leaning.
"Why make everything as hopeless looking as possible?" she argued.

And at a moment which was sad only for us who
lost her, all turned out in harmony with her holy hope
and joy.

Flowers covered her, loving mourners followed her,
hymns were sung at her grave, the November day
brightened, and the sun (I vividly remember) made a
miniature rainbow in my eyelashes.

I have often thought of that rainbow since.

May all who love enjoy cheerful little rainbows at
the funerals of their beloved ones.

November 8.

OUR heaven must be within ourselves,
  Our home and heaven the work of faith
All through this race of life which shelves
  Downward to death.

So faith shall build the boundary wall,
  And hope shall plant the secret bower,
That both may show magnifical
  With gem and flower.

While over all a dome must spread,
  And love shall be that dome above;
And deep foundations must be laid,
  And these are love.

November 9.

A COVETOUS, grasping Christian is like a quicksand : the surface smooth, the depth unceasingly on
the suck and gulp.

Everything goes down, nothing comes up again :
yet is the quicksand apparently none the fuller, neither
does it cease from engulphing.

In fact—whether or not one may attribute ideas to
a quicksand—it seems at any rate to entertain no idea
of ever becoming satisfied. Its aim appears to be not
to attain repletion, but to exercise an unbounded
swallow.

In this world, crews, cargoes, ships, waifs and strays,
respond to the " Give, give " of the quicksand ; while
objects of proportionate bulk and quality often respond
to the unuttered " Give, give " of the covetous man.

Thus in this present world, both ; but how in the
next world, either?

November 10.

SCARCE-TOLERABLE life which all life long
  Is dominated by one dread of death,—
  Is such life, life? If so, who pondereth
May call salt sweetness or call discord song.

Ah me, this solitude where swarms a throng!
  Life slowly grows and dwindles breath by breath:
  Death slowly grows on us; no word it saith,
Its cords all lengthened and its pillars strong.
Life dies apace, a life that but deceives:
  Death reigns as though it lived, and yet is dead:
Where is the life that dies not, but that lives?
  The sweet long life immortal, ever young,
  True life that wooes us with a silver tongue
Of hope, much said and much more left unsaid.

November 11.

FEAST OF ST. MARTIN, BISHOP OF TOURS. Born probably at
  Sabaria in Pannonia about the year 320; died, about 400.

AT the age of fifteen St. Martin started in life as a
heathen soldier in the Roman army, though already
he had felt the attractive influence of Christianity.

One winter's day, noticing a poor tattered beggar
he divided with him his cloak. And the next night,
in a dream, he saw our Lord enthroned in glory,
arrayed in the half cloak and saying, "Behold the
mantle given Me by Martin." After this dream, at
the age of eighteen, Martin was baptised. Some two
years later, he seems to have demanded his discharge
from military service at a moment of impending
battle: his commander, Julian, the future apostate
Emperor, denied his request with contempt, only to
be answered, "Post me in the forefront of the army,
without weapons or armour; but I will not draw
sword again. I am become the soldier of Christ."

It may have been some years later that he resorted
to St. Hilary of Poitiers by whom he was ordained
exorcist. Ere long filial affection carried him back
to Pannonia, where his piety was rewarded by the

conversion from paganism of his mother, though not, alas! of his father: where, moreover, protesting against the heresy of certain Arian bishops, he was publicly beaten and expelled from his (assumed) birthplace Sabaria.

We next behold him as a hermit in a Milanese solitude, exchanged later for a little solitary island. Still later he founded a monastery in the vicinity of Poitiers.

At length, about the year 371, the See of Tours falling vacant, the people of Tours by stratagem and force conducted him to his consecration as their Bishop. But he who had been monk and hermit before such elevation, monk and hermit remained in spite of it. First he occupied a cell near the Church; but afterwards he removed to a more lonely hut of branches on the bank of the Loire, where with eighty disciples he led an ascetic life.

He waxed great as promulgator of the Faith among his heathen neighbours, great as champion of the Truth against internal errors, great as contender that the weapons of Church warfare must be spiritual, not carnal. In this last particular he showed himself a faithful disciple of his teacher St. Hilary, whose noble words on the same point I quote (at second hand):— "God will not have a forced homage. What need has He of a profession of faith produced by violence? We must not attempt to deceive Him; He must be sought with simplicity, served by charity, honoured and gained by the honest exercise of our free will."

Even at the end of his long life St. Martin expressed willingness to live on, if for the good of others; but this final sacrifice was not required of him, "for God took him."

November 12.

"LIFT up your hearts"—"We lift them up"—Ah
    me!
I cannot, Lord, lift up my heart to Thee:
Stoop, lift it up, that where Thou art I too may be.

"Give Me thy heart"—I would not say Thee nay,
But have no power to keep or give away
My heart: stoop, Lord, and take it to Thyself to-day.

Stoop, Lord, as once before now once anew
Stoop, Lord, and hearken, hearken, Lord, and do,
And take my will and take my heart and take me too.

November 13.

FEAST OF ST. BRITIUS, BRICTIUS OR BRICE, BISHOP OF TOURS.
Born in the fourth century; died about the year 443.

BRITIUS was brought up by St. Martin of Tours
and succeeded him in that See.

In youth he appears to have been headstrong and
worldly, and accusations beset him in after-life. According to one version of his story these accusations
were refuted; yet his flock appears to have lost, if it
ever had entertained, confidence in him: another
Bishop superseded him in his diocese, and was followed by yet another, while Britius spent seven penitential years in Rome. Thence he travelled home-
wards with letters recommendatory from Pope Sixtus
III; the See once more fell vacant, and he resumed
his former charge and dignity, holding them for another seven years until death removed him. Meanwhile he had acquired a saintly reputation.

I have seen a different colouring given to his story but I follow the more favourable account.

" Charity . . . rejoiceth not in iniquity."

November 14.

IT seems an easy thing
Mayhap one day to sing,
Yet the next day
We cannot sing or say.

Keep silence with good heart,
While silence fits our part :
Another day
We shall both sing and say.

Keep silence, counting time
To strike in at the chime ;
Prepare to sound :—
Our part is coming round.

Cannot we sing or say?
In silence let us pray,
And meditate
Our love-song while we wait.

November 15.

FEAST OF ST. MACHUTUS, BISHOP OF ALETH. I notice his date as assigned to either of two centuries, involving a difference of about sixty years. The earlier date proposed fixes his death in the year 564 or 565.

THIS Machutus, Maclovius, Maclou, or Malo, seems most familiar under the name of St. Malo ; which last form connects him with the locality where he lived, though not with his native land which, it appears, was Wales.

Various legends embalm his memory. In boyhood he fell asleep on the seashore, and would have been drowned by the rising tide had not the sand and weed on which he lay floated upward with him.

Later on, when he had assumed the monastic habit, it was his office to light the candles for matins. No fire was within reach : he placed extinct cinders in his bosom, and drew them out aglow.

He died, apparently, while acting, not as Bishop of Aleth, but as Monastic Superior at Archambray.

His life was passed not without vicissitudes, but seems to have closed in peace.

November 16.

THE goal in sight! Look up and sing,
　Set faces full against the light,
Welcome with rapturous welcoming
　The goal in sight.

　Let be the left, let be the right :
Straight forward make your footsteps ring
　A loud alarum through the night.

Death hunts you, yea, but reft of sting ;
　Your bed is green, your shroud is white :
Hail! Life and Death and all that bring
　The goal in sight.

November 17.

FEAST OF ST. HUGH, BISHOP OF LINCOLN. Born in Burgundy
in the year 1140; died in London, 1200.

HAVING passed through a grave and pious childhood, Hugh, at the age of nineteen, visited the Grande
Chartreuse, near Grenoble, and became enamoured of
its spiritual beauty enshrined amid marvellous natural
beauties of the Alps. Assuming there the Carthusian
habit, he spent ten years under that austere but congenial rule. Then Henry II of England summoned
him to govern a Carthusian Priory at Witham: he
obeyed, and by kindly virtues won the love of his
new neighbours.

In 1186 he was consecrated Bishop of Lincoln: in
which character he withstood or rebuked first Henry
II, afterwards Richard Cœur de Lion, earning the
nickname of Hammer-King by his intrepidity.

He died during the reign of King John, having
returned from an embassy of peace with which that
monarch had charged him to Philip Augustus of
France.

Humility, sweetness, courage,—virtues not always
combined—were united in St. Hugh.

At Witham he was pleased himself to carry stones
and knead mortar for building work.

At Lincoln he made friends with a swan which
frequented his Palace moat; he fed it, and was habitually greeted by it.

Concerning him, Richard Cœur de Lion is reported
to have said: "If all the Bishops in my realm were
like that man, kings and princes would be powerless
against them."

By our saint's own command his deathbed was

made on the floor, being composed of ashes strewn in the form of a cross.

But after his death, we read how "his body was embalmed, and conveyed with great pomp to Lincoln, where it was met by king John of England and king William of Scotland ... The two kings put their shoulders under the bier as it was carried into the church."

November 18.

WE know not when, we know not where,
  We know not what that world will be,
But this we know: it will be fair
  To see.

With heart athirst and thirsty face
  We know and know not what shall be :—
Christ Jesus bring us of His grace
  To see.

Christ Jesus bring us of His grace,
  Beyond all prayers our hope can pray,
One day to see Him face to face,—
  One day.

November 19.

"Cursed is the ground for thy sake ; ... thorns also and thistles shall it bring forth to thee."—(GEN. iii. 17, 18.)

SHORT of reprobation, there is no Divine curse upon sin within which does not lurk a blessing ready for penitents. And this, although "God is not a man, that He should lie ; neither the son of man, that He should repent :" yea, rather, even because He is that Lord Who changeth not, therefore we are not consumed.

Which truth the penal thorn illustrates : for a veritable thorn it is which bears the rose.

November 20.

FEAST OF ST. EDMUND, STYLED MARTYR, KING OF EAST ANGLIA. Born in the year 841; died in battle with the Danes, or was slain after the same battle, 870.

ACCORDING to one account King Edmund, finding himself unequal to resisting the Danish invaders, offered his own person as their prisoner if so his people might be spared. The Danes, however, after tempting him in vain to apostatise from the Christian Faith, treated him barbarously, and ended by shooting him to death with arrows. The town of Bury St. Edmund's is the place of his sepulture.

Another account simply states that he fell in battle against the same invaders.

" The righteous perisheth, and no man layeth it to heart : and merciful men are taken away, none considering that the righteous is taken away from the evil to come. He shall enter into peace : they shall rest in their beds, each one walking in his uprightness."

November 21.

EVERYTHING that is born must die :
　Everything that can sigh may sing :
Rocks in equal balance low or high
　Everything.

Honeycomb is weighed against a sting,
Hope and fear take turns to touch the sky,
　Height and depth respond alternating.

O my soul spread wings of love to fly,
Wings of dove that soars on homebound wing :
Love trusts Love, till Love shall justify
Everything.

November 22.

FEAST OF ST. CECILIA OR CICELY, ROMAN VIRGIN AND MARTYR.
Third century.

LEGEND, if not history, represents St. Cecilia as given in marriage to a young man named Valerian ; whom she converted to Christianity by holding out to him, on that condition, a hope of beholding an Angel who protected her. Valerian, returning from Baptism, beheld Cecilia at her prayers ; and with her, an Angel who crowned the pair with roses and lilies before vanishing. Another version of the story shows us the Angel seated at an organ when the young husband lighted upon him. Tiburtius, brother of Valerian, noticing the flowers and understanding their source, was converted likewise. After which all three laid down life for the faith.

St. Cecilia ranks as patroness of music. Her name, too, whether we say Cecilia or Cicely, is musical. Her story exhibits that good and pleasant thing, a family dwelling in harmonious unity and angelic fellowship.

Music may surpass our powers : harmony and the communion of saints even we ourselves also can compass.

November 23.

FEAST OF ST. CLEMENT, BISHOP OF ROME. Died, perhaps by martyrdom, about the year 100.

ST. PAUL writes to the Philippians (iv. 3) :— "Clement also, and . . . other my fellowlabourers, whose names are in the Book of Life."

Notwithstanding some alleged difficulty in the way of identification, this saint, certified as such by the voice of inspiration, is considered to be the same as the St. Clement we memorialise to-day, and who is counted either as the immediate or as the third successor of St. Peter.

His own writings survive as his worthy monument. Otherwise, despite its remaining historically uncertain whether or not he attained the martyr's palm branch, a legend assigns to him as monument a beautiful chapel raised by angels beneath the sea and enshrining his body. For, according to this tradition, he had been exiled from Rome to the marble quarries of Pontus; where he found and encouraged fellow Christians, and converted pagans: for which latter good work he was condemned to be drowned with an anchor fastened to his neck. Afterwards, in answer to prayer, the sea receded and disclosed the angelic erection.

Another pretty legend relates how in his place of banishment water could only be procured from a spring six miles distant, adding to the weary toil of the quarries. "One day Clement saw a lamb scraping at the soil with one of its forefeet. He took it as a sign that water was there; dug, and found a spring."

Yet what matter mistakes or silence of earthly records concerning any "whose names are in the Book of Life?" Of all such we know assuredly that they shall thirst no more, but the Lamb which is in the midst of the Throne shall lead them unto living fountains of waters, where there shall be no more sea.

November 24.

IN that world we weary to attain,
    Love's furled banner floats at large unfurled :
There is no more doubt and no more pain,
    In that world.

There are gems and gold and inlets pearled ;
There the greenness fadeth not again ;
    There no clinging tendrils droop uncurled.

Here incessant tides stir up the main,
    Stormy miry depths aloft are hurled :—
There is no more sea, or storm, or stain,
    In that world.

November 25.

FEAST OF ST. CATHARINE OF ALEXANDRIA, VIRGIN MARTYR.

THIS blessed maiden seems to have been born late
in the third century, as her death is assigned to the
year 307.

The Emperor Maxentius, conceiving for her an
unworthy passion and remaining baffled by her in-
flexible virtue, confiscated her wealth and banished
her. Thus far history.

Legend adds that her wisdom proved victorious in
an argumentative contest which she held with fifty
philosophers, all of whom she converted to Christianity. She converted, moreover, the Empress Faus-
tina, and a certain Porphyrius, who in his turn won to
the Faith two hundred soldiers. All these personages
alike were graced by martyrdom, though not all after
one manner of death.

For St. Catherine herself a fourfold wheel of horrid

structure was prepared, but it proved inoperative against her. She died by decapitation; after having prayed that her body might be kept intact from profane hands, and that the world might be converted. In reference to the first petition, angels are said to have carried her corpse to Mount Sinai: whilst the second was followed by that victory of Constantine over Maxentius, whereby Christianity became established as the dominant religion of the world.

St. Catherine is honoured as Patroness of Learning: doubtless of sound learning. As such, one cannot help surmising that sundry legends may lie outside her patronage.

November 26.

I.

"A just man falleth seven times, and riseth up again."—(PROV. xxiv. 16.)

FULL of comfort as is this text, of encouragement, of Divine good will and Fatherly lovingkindness, its comfort yet hath a limit.

We must not rearrange the proverb and say: He that falleth seven times is a just man. He may or may not be so: but the proverb speaks to a different point.

All this is obvious, and would not be worth noting down but for our tendency to appropriate promises and revelations of mercy without adequately scrutinizing the conditions on which they depend. "Peace, peace; when there is no peace," is a fallacy as old as the Prophets.

The just man at his sixth fall is perhaps less likely to quote the proverb in question, than is the unjust man at his eighth.

2.

ONE thing is certain: the hero of this proverb is one who having fallen any number of times, riseth up again.

Not the fall but the arising forms our clue to his identity. Not any number of falls, few or many, but that selfsame number of arisings proves him just.

Saul the persecutor was not reconciled to God until he had obeyed the word of Ananias: "And now why tarriest thou? arise . . ." Thenceforward we revere him as St. Paul.

Following whom at an unmeasured distance, even as he at an immeasurable distance followed Christ, "I will arise and go to my Father, and will say unto Him, Father, I have sinned against heaven, and before Thee, and am no more worthy to be called Thy son."

November 28.

"A MERRY heart is a continual feast."
  Then take we life and all things in good part:
To fast grows festive while we keep at least
  A merry heart

  Well pleased with nature and well pleased with
      art;
A merry heart makes cheer for man and beast,
  And fancies music in a creaking cart.

Some day, a restful heart whose toils have ceased,
  A heavenly heart gone home from earthly mart:—
To-day, blow wind from west or wind from east,
  A merry heart.

November 29.

"IN honour preferring one another."

Thus did St. Andrew when he brought to the Messias his own brother Simon, when he mentioned to our gracious Master that lad whose were the five loaves and the two small fishes, when in concert with St. Philip he approached our Lord Jesus with the request of certain Greeks.

Presumably in his mortal day, and evidently down to this our own day, St. Andrew appears eclipsed by the lustre of St. Peter. But how the two will stand in comparison with one another at the last great Day, only that day will declare.

Nevertheless, this we know already and assuredly : that saint who on earth grudged not a brother's superiority, will never grudge it in heaven if in heaven so it be.

"Love as brethren," writes St. Peter : and he who had St. Andrew for a brother might well write the precept.

November 30.

FEAST OF ST. ANDREW, APOSTLE; accounted Patron Saint of Scotland.

ACCORDING to tradition St. Andrew preached the Faith in Achaia, and there laid down his life for it.

A special X-shaped cross is assigned to him as the instrument of his martyrdom. This cross, we read, he saluted in a rapture of devout love to Jesus : on it he hung two days testifying to the assembled people, and then having prayed he died.

To read of saint after saint and triumph after

triumph might drive us to despair, if we looked to the saints only and not in them and through them to the King of Saints. But thus looking, any such temptation vanishes, giving place to indomitable hope. For these were men of like passions with ourselves: and if they now seem too far in advance for us ever to overtake them, what must their own case have appeared who were called not to follow one another, but immediately to follow Christ Himself? and who being called at sundry times and in divers manners, all alike left all and followed Him.

> " They climbed the steep ascent of heaven
>   Through peril, toil, and pain :
> O God, to us may grace be given
>   To follow in their train."

December 1.

I.

DR. NEALE, in the Introduction to his " Mediæval Preachers and Mediæval Preaching," quotes from one of St. Augustine's Paschal Homilies the following curious mystical interpretation of the hundred and fifty-three Fishes of the Second Miraculous Draught :—

" This number signifies the thousand thousands of the Saints and of the faithful. But why did the Lord vouchsafe to signify by these figures the many thousands who shall enter into the kingdom of heaven? Hear why. Ye know that the Law was given by Moses to the people of God ; and that in that Law the Decalogue forms the chief part... These ten precepts no man accomplishes by his own strength, unless he is helped by the grace of God. If, therefore, none can fulfil the Law unless God assist with His Spirit, ye must remember that the Holy Ghost is set forth to us by the number seven. . . . Since, then, we need the Spirit to fulfil the Law, add seven to ten, and you have seventeen. Now, if you count from one to seventeen, you obtain one hundred and fifty-three. I need not count this up for you; count it for yourselves, and reckon thus: one and two and three and four make ten. In like manner add up the other numbers to seventeen, and you will have the holy number of the faithful and of the saints that shall be in heavenly places with the Lord."

This same calculation St. Augustine, we are informed, repeated substantially in a second and again in a third sermon: whence we may infer that however quaint such comments may appear to some hearers or readers, in others they arouse interest and promote edification.

December 2.

2.

By a different process of arithmetic and of argument (if argument it can be termed) the same result may be reached :—

Once more in our search for the " hundred and fifty-three" brought safe ashore, if so be they indeed prefigure the completed number of the elect, we start from the Decalogue.

To fulfil each of the ten commandments man needs the full grace of God's Most Holy Spirit; which fulness of grace let us represent by the sacred number seven.

Multiply each commandment by the grace needed for its observance, one by seven; and this seven again by ten, the number of the commandments: and seventy appears.

Now as Joseph said unto Pharaoh, "For that the dream was doubled unto Pharaoh twice ; it is because the thing is established :" therefore we will express final perseverance by doubling seventy, and obtain one hundred and forty.

But he who is wholly sanctified by God the Holy Ghost is truly owned and saved by the Most Holy Trinity in Unity : wherefore we place the Decalogue under favour of the Divine number Three ; making up an additional thirteen.

Which thirteen and hundred and forty added together amount to the required hundred and fifty-three.

December 3.

3.

THERE remains on the foregoing subject one anxious question for us to ask and for our consciences to answer : are such speculations profitable, or are they trivial ?

Profitable they are, if and so far as they encourage any poor soul to tread the path of obedience.

And perhaps they may effect this, because either line of thought (such as it is) tends to testify : that election is certified, and final perseverance is achieved, by one and the same process open to us all alike,— by simple obedience.

The mystery of predestination or of election may baffle our intellects : obedience will assuredly not transcend our powers.

And there is a second way in which our problem may, I hope, prove helpful : *this* shall we do, and leave weightier matters undone? We should have been—or at least, I should have been disappointed not to reach an accurate intelligible result by the foregoing calculation. A degree of shame often adds a sting to disappointment; for often we have ourselves, our own rashness or negligence to thank for our failures.

What will it be to have misstated or misworked the whole problem of life; to behold at length the perfect number of the elect made up to the last man, woman, child; and ourselves (God forbid!) to be left out in shame and everlasting contempt?

December 4.

I ONCE heard an exemplary Christian remark that she had never been accused of a fault without afterwards recognising truth in the accusation.

And if she, how not I?

At the least her words should make me cautious not to rebut any charge in anger or in haste.

And if me, why not you?

December 5.

BURY Hope out of sight,
   No book for it and no bell;
It never could bear the light
   Even while growing and well;
Think if now it could bear
The light on its face of care
And grey scattered hair.

No grave for Hope in the earth,
   But deep in that silent soul
Which rang no bell for its birth
   And rings no funeral toll.

Cover its once bright head ;
Nor odours nor tears be shed :
It lived once, it is dead.

Brief was the day of its power,
    The day of its grace how brief:
As the fading of a flower,
    As the falling of a leaf,
So brief its day and its hour :
No bud more and no bower
Or hint of a flower.

Shall many wail it? not so:
    Shall one bewail it? not one:
Thus it hath been from long ago,
    Thus it shall be beneath the sun.
O fleet sun, make haste to flee ;
O rivers, fill up the sea ;
O Death, set the dying free.

The sun nor loiters nor speeds,
    The rivers run as they ran,
Through clouds or through windy reeds
    All run as when all began.
Only Death turns at our cries :—
Lo, the Hope we buried with sighs
Alive in Death's eyes!

December 6.

Feast of St. Nicolas, Bishop of Myra. Fourth century.

Thus much and no more I find vouched for by my
usual chief authority.

Legends, however, augment our scanty store of
knowledge, and furnish St. Nicolas with a miraculous

babyhood, pretty if uncertain.   An ecstasy seized him
in his first bath: and while still a suckling he voluntarily fasted on Wednesdays and Fridays.

At a more mature period of his life he saved three
sister maidens from temptation and peril by casting
three bags of gold, one at a time, through the window
of their home, thereby providing their father with
dowries for them.

Popularly he is supposed to have concurred in the
Council of Nicaea, where amongst all the assembled
Bishops " he shone . . . with so great clarity and
opinion of sanctity, that he appeared like a sun
amongst so many stars."   Nevertheless carried away
by zeal he smote Arius, and thereby incurred a heavy
ecclesiastical penalty.

Each legend may teach us something, at any rate by
suggestion.

Not to marvel at miraculous babies, but to nurse
natural ones for God, is our at least *as* blessed privilege.   And though grace "cometh not with observa-
tion" we may feel as certain that Divine Grace takes
possession of them in the Baptismal Font, as we could
possibly feel if we beheld them rapt in visible
ecstasy.

We may study both matter and manner in the
incident of the triple dower: the matter, liberality;
the manner, delicacy.

While the Council sets before us how much may be
lost in one hasty moment.

" Be not highminded, but fear."

December 7.

"And the twelve gates were twelve pearls; every several gate was of one pearl."—(REV. xxi. 21.)

A NATURAL pearl is produced by the disease of an oyster.

Being such, who would have looked to find pearls in the holy and eternal New Jerusalem?

Whatever the "pearls" of heaven may stand for—for Bible language doubtless condescends to our present ignorance—one thing seems clear: since we read of pearls, pearls have a lesson for us.

These pearls form the gates of the celestial city. Gold and gems compose its foundations, its walls, its streets: but all its gates are pearls.

And because pearls stand connected with disease, that is, with one form of suffering, therefore (I think) we may view them as representative of the precious fruits of all worthily borne human suffering: and because they form gates of entrance—exit, thanks be to God, is not in question—they connect themselves vividly with that "great tribulation" out of which came the general assembly of the saints as St. John beheld them in vision:—

"Lo, a great multitude, which no man could number, of all nations, and kindreds, and people, and tongues, stood before the Throne, and before the Lamb, clothed with white robes, and palms in their hands; and cried with a loud voice, saying, Salvation to our God which sitteth upon the Throne, and unto the Lamb. . . . And one of the elders answered, saying unto me, What are these which are arrayed in white robes? and whence came they? And I said unto him, Sir, thou knowest. And he said to me, These are they which came out of great tribulation, and have washed their robes, and made them white in the Blood of the Lamb. Therefore are they before the Throne of God, and serve Him day and night in His Temple." (Rev. vii. 9–15.)

December 8.

FEAST OF THE CONCEPTION OF THE BLESSED VIRGIN MARY.

ST. MARY whom all generations call blessed, we so call.

Who bore the Saviour of all mankind, we cherish in grateful memory.

Whom God the Son deigned to honour, we aspire to honour.

She whom God sanctified is holy: she who responded to God's call is "called and chosen and faithful."

Her gifts are His gifts to her, her graces His graces in her.

"Glory to God in the highest, and on earth peace, good will toward men."

December 9.

Is any grieved or tired? Yea, by God's Will:
 Surely God's Will alone is good and best:
 O weary man, in weariness take rest,
O hungry man, by hunger feast thy fill.
Discern thy good beneath a mask of ill,
 Or build of loneliness thy secret nest;
 At noon take heart being mindful of the west,
At night wake hope for dawn advances still.

At night wake hope. Poor soul, in such sore need
  Of wakening and of girding up anew,
  Hast thou that hope which fainting doth pursue?
    No saint but hath pursued and hath been faint:
Bid love wake hope, for both thy steps shall speed
  Still faint yet still pursuing, O thou saint.

December 10.

I.

" IF any man will do His Will, he shall know of the doctrine, whether it be of God," said Jesus Christ our Lord.

Blessed on all sides is this infallible promise.

It assures us that, at least in the long run, we shall by working faithfully get clear of doubt and darkness.

Obedience, then, is the key of knowledge.

That was a masterstroke of guile by which the serpent cajoled Eve into believing disobedience to be the key of knowledge.

Disobedience may (indeed and alas!) be the key to many of our own beliefs and opinions. Yet even thus, if we will, we can turn it into a genuine though base-metal key of knowledge.

For that which disobedience teaches us is false, either in its essence or in its aspect as regards ourselves.

Wherefore since disobedience unlocks not truth, whatsoever it unlocks is thereby certified as falsity.

For each key fits its own lock and no other.

December 11.

2.

A FURTHER beatitude comforts us in those Divine words of promise: "If any man will do His Will, he shall know of the doctrine, whether it be of God."

For by implication they take account of doubt and ignorance as being no bar to obedience; and therefore as being no irremovable bar to knowledge.

Obedience they enjoin upon us at once: all else may stand over.

Now many have said, and for the time being have said honestly, "I do not know;" or even, "I cannot believe."

But who ever said honestly, "I cannot obey"?

Not that obedience any more than disobedience can of its own proper virtue instruct us: only it has attached to it this promise of God's enlightening grace. And if we desire a second "immutable thing" for our encouragement, Christ hath said, "My grace is sufficient for thee: for My strength is made perfect in weakness."

December 12.

HAVE dead men long to wait?—
There is a certain term
For their bodies to the worm
And their souls at Heaven gate.
Dust to dust, clod to clod,
These precious things of God,
Trampled underfoot by man
And beast the appointed years.—

Their longest life was but a span
For change and smiles and tears:
Is it worth while to live,
Rejoice and grieve,
Hope, fear, and die?
Man with man, truth with lie,
The slow show dwindles by:
At last what shall we have
Besides a grave?

Lies and shows no more,
No fear, no pain,
But after hope and sleep
Dear joys again.
Those who sowed shall reap:
Those who bore
The Cross shall wear the Crown:
Those who clomb the steep
There shall sit down.
The Shepherd of the sheep
Feeds His flock there,
In watered pastures fair
They rest and leap.
"Is it worth while to live?"
Be of good cheer:
Love casts out fear:
Rise up, achieve.

December 13.

FEAST OF ST. LUCY, VIRGIN MARTYR OF SYRACUSE. Slain by
the sword in the year 303 or 304.

HER legend further describes her as by birth noble
and wealthy. Her widowed mother educated her in
the Christian Faith, and very early the maiden vowed

herself to Christ. Sought in marriage by a heathen suitor, she rejected him; and afterwards dispensed her dowry among the poor. Then the man's love turned to anger, and through his denunciation she was put to death.

If "the tender mercies of the wicked are cruel," what oftentimes is their love?

Jesus said: "By this shall all men know that ye are My disciples, if ye have love one to another."

December 14.

I.

THE blood of the Paschal Lamb was to be struck "on the two side posts and on the upper door post of the houses" it guarded: *not* on the threshold. Thus setting forth by a material figure the awful spiritual warning long afterwards delivered unto us "upon whom the ends of the world are come:"

"He that despised Moses' law died without mercy .... of how much sorer punishment, suppose ye, shall he be thought worthy, who hath trodden under foot the Son of God, and hath counted the Blood of the covenant, wherewith he was sanctified, an unholy thing, and hath done despite unto the Spirit of grace? ... It is a fearful thing to fall into the hands of the Living God."

"From all blindness of heart, from hardness of neart, and contempt of Thy Word, Good Lord, deliver us."

December 15.

2.

THE blood of the Paschal Lamb struck on the lintel and on the two side posts, guarded Israel against the stroke of destruction from above or from either hand.

Even so Christ our Passover guards us Christians against overwhelming evil and irresistible temptation. The enemy shall not be able to do us violence, whether that enemy be "the prince of the power of the air" defiling high places by spiritual wickedness, or our fellow man stationed on our own level. The "lintel" and the "side posts" form our impregnable bulwark so long as we hold fast our profession. "I am persuaded, that neither death, nor life, nor angels, nor principalities, nor powers, nor things present, nor things to come, nor height, nor depth, nor any other creature, shall be able to separate us from the love of God, which is in Christ Jesus our Lord."

A single point remained unguarded: the threshold. Whence we learn that the one foe whom we ourselves alone can grapple with; whom even Christ our Head. although He deigns to work in us and with us, will not in our stead put down with a high hand; is the one who crosses the threshold of our house, that is, our own self.

Words of Divine tender lamentation certify to us this distinction:—"Oh that My people had hearkened unto Me, and Israel had walked in My ways! I should soon have subdued their enemies, and turned My hand against their adversaries."

December 16.

"O SAPIENTIA."

These words form the opening of a Latin Anthem which runs as follows :—

"O Wisdom, Who comest out of the mouth of the Most High, reaching from one end to another mightily, and sweetly ordering all things, come and teach us the way of understanding."

This anthem is the first of a series continued daily till Christmas Eve, according to an old use common (with some variation) to Rome, Paris, and England, though now by us discontinued.

Thus, then, did our forefathers celebrate our Lord and His Advent.

" O Sapientia "—"O Wisdom:" that is, " Christ . . . the Wisdom of God." Whom we adore not only as the Wisdom of God, but also as "Christ Jesus, Who of God is made unto us Wisdom."

Nor can we by guidance of any other wisdom use profitably our Advent Seasons on earth. And least of all can we. except in the might and light of that only true Wisdom, make ready for the Lord's second Advent from heaven, as we read :—

" Then shall the kingdom of heaven be likened unto ten virgins, which took their lamps, and went forth to meet the Bridegroom. And five of them were wise, and five were foolish. They that were foolish took their lamps, and took no oil with them : but the wise took oil in their vessels with their lamps. While the Bridegroom tarried, they all slumbered and slept. And at midnight there was a cry made, Behold, the Bridegroom cometh ; go ye out to meet Him. Then all those virgins arose, and trimmed their lamps. And the foolish said unto the wise, Give us of your oil ; for our lamps are gone out. But the wise answered, saying, Not so ; lest there be not enough for us and you : but go ye rather to them that sell, and buy for yourselves. And while they went to buy, the Bridegroom came ; and they that were ready went in with Him to the marriage : and the door was shut. Afterward came also the other virgins, saying, Lord, Lord, open to us. But He answered and said, Verily I say unto you, I know you not. Watch, therefore, for ye know neither the day nor the hour wherein the Son of Man cometh."

December 17.

EARTH grown old yet still so green,
  Deep beneath her crust of cold
Nurses fire unfelt, unseen,—
  Earth grown old.

We who live are quickly told:
Millions more lie hid between
  Inner swathings of her fold.

When will fire break up her screen?
  When will life burst through her mould?
Earth, earth, earth, thy cold is keen,
  Earth grown old.

December 18.

I.

"And the tables were the work of God, and the writing was the writing of God, graven upon the tables. . . . And the Lord said unto Moses, Hew thee two tables of stone like unto the first: and I will write upon these tables the words that were in the first tables, which thou brakest."—(Ex. xxxii. 16; xxxiv. 1.)

THOSE first tables correspond with Adam, being like himself wholly and exclusively the handiwork of God. The unbroken commandment graven materially on the one, spiritually on the other, added glory to both.

Adam by one sin broke the whole law: offending in one point he became guilty of all.

Then did the Divine sentence as it were take him up and cast him down, breaking him in pieces when it decreed, " Dust thou art, and unto dust shalt thou return."

The second tables, partly of Divine workmanship while partly also of human, correspond with our Lord Jesus Christ, Son of God and Son of Mary. These second tables (so far, I think, as Holy Scripture records) never were broken; but abode intact and sacred, like unto His perfect nature and exhaustive obedience.

Yet as Moses in an access of holy indignation cast the former tables out of his hands and brake them beneath the Mount, so on Mount Calvary " it pleased the Lord to bruise " His sinless Son, not for His own sake, but for the sake of us sinners.

That as in Adam all die, even so in Christ may all be made alive.

December 19.

2.

AGAIN. Those second tables prepared by Moses, written upon, and so completed by God Himself, appear further as a figure of regenerate humanity, recreated by God and Man in unison, even by our Lord Jesus Christ. He puts His Spirit within us, reviving, moulding, beautifying us: He renews in our hearts His perfect law: He feeds us with His own Body and Blood: He guides us with His counsel, and after that (if so be we persevere) He will receive us with glory.

He on the Cross is our Beginning, He at the Right Hand of the Majesty on High is our End.

" If I climb up into heaven Thou art there."

Amen: for "Whom have I in heaven but Thee? and there is none upon earth that I desire in comparison of Thee."

December 20.

VIGIL OF ST. THOMAS.

ST. THOMAS doubted.

Scepticism is a degree of unbelief : equally therefore it is a degree of belief. It may be a degree of faith.

St. Thomas doubted, but simultaneously he loved. Whence it follows that his case was all along hopeful.

If we are spirit-broken by doubts of our own, if we are half heart-broken by a friend's doubts, let us beg faith for our friend and for ourself; only still more urgently let us beg love.

For love is more potent to breed faith than faith to breed love. Because there is no comparison between the two: "God is Love;" and that which God is must rank higher, and show itself mightier than aught which God is not.

Nevertheless, faith also is required of us, and faith overflows with blessings.

"If thou canst believe, all things are possible to him that believeth . . . Lord, I believe; help Thou mine unbelief."

"Elisha prayed, and said, Lord, I pray Thee, open his eyes, that he may see. And the Lord opened the eyes of the young man; and he saw."

December 21.

FEAST OF ST. THOMAS, APOSTLE.

THIS Feast occurs on the shortest day of the year. The day which having least light has yet light sufficient, harmonizes with the Apostle whose faith indeed ran short, yet by Christ's help lasted out.

Light at its lowest ebb can increase, so long as its source is the sun : for the sun faileth not.

Faith at its dimmest spark can rekindle, so long as it keeps Christ in view: for much more than the natural sun, that Sun of Righteousness faileth not.

"Jesus saith unto him, Thomas, because thou hast seen Me, thou hast believed : blessed are they that have not seen, and yet have believed."

"Who is among you that feareth the Lord, that obeyeth the voice of His servant, that walketh in darkness, and hath no light? let him trust in the name of the Lord, and stay upon his God."

"I will give thee the treasures of darkness, and hidden riches of secret places, that thou mayest know that I, the Lord, which call thee by thy name, am the God of Israel."

December 22.

SHALL not the Judge of all the earth do right?
　　Yea, Lord, although Thou say me nay.
Shall not His Will be to me life and light?
　　Yea, Lord, although Thou slay.

Yet, Lord, remembering turn and sift and see,
　　Remember though Thou sift me through,
Remember my desire, remember me,
　　Remember, Lord, and do.

December 23.

ONE day I caught myself wishing what I felt convinced would not be the case,—that a certain occupation at once sad and pleasant and dear to me, and at that very moment inevitably drawing towards a close, could have lasted out through the remainder of my lifetime.

Perhaps no harm in the instinctive wish,—none, I hope: yet what fallacies lay at its root!

At least two. One, that something different would be better than what Providence ordained: the other, that my life was sure to outlast the dwindling occupation.

Surely I did not mean that my own choice was wiser than the Divine choice, or that my life was death-proof up to a particular date?

Yet what else does such a wish really imply?

"O Almighty God, Who alone canst order the unruly wills and affections of sinful men; grant unto Thy people that they may love the thing which Thou commandest, and desire that which Thou dost promise; through Jesus Christ our Lord. Amen."

December 24.

CHRISTMAS EVE.

CHRISTMAS hath a darkness
    Brighter than the blazing noon,
Christmas hath a chillness
    Warmer than the heat of June,
Christmas hath a beauty
    Lovelier than the world can show,
For Christmas bringeth Jesus
    Brought for us so low.

Earth, strike up your music,
    Birds that sing and bells that ring;
Heaven hath answering music,
    For all Angels soon to sing;

Earth, put on your whitest
   Bridal robe of spotless snow,
For Christmas bringeth Jesus
   Brought for us so low.

December 25.

CHRISTMAS DAY.

A BABY is a harmless thing,
   And wins our hearts with one accord,
And Flower of babies was their King
   Jesus Christ our Lord:
Lily of lilies He
Upon His Mother's knee;
Rose of roses, soon to be
Crowned with thorns on leafless tree.

A lamb is innocent and mild
   And merry on the soft green sod,
And Jesus Christ the Undefiled,
   Is the Lamb of God:
Only spotless He
Upon His Mother's knee;
White and ruddy, soon to be,
Sacrificed for you and me.

Nay, lamb is not so sweet a word,
   Nor lily half so pure a name;
Another name our hearts hath stirred
   Kindling them to flame:
"Jesus" certainly
Is music and melody,—
Heart with heart in harmony
Carol we and worship we.

December 26.

St. Stephen as Protomartyr for Christ takes, in a certain sense, precedence of all other saints whatsoever, be they even Apostles.

He served tables: thus indirectly recalling our Lord's parable of the Guest bidden to a Feast. As Deacon he stood (rather than sat down) in the lowest room; and to him in his lowliness came betimes the gracious word. "Friend, go up higher."

Now and for evermore hath he worship in the presence of them that sit at meat with him; whether this be in communion with just men made perfect, or with members of the Church still militant here in earth.

To St. Stephen, then, we see granted one exclusive dignity withheld from St. John the beloved, from St. Peter the chief, from St. Paul the superabundant labourer. Yet is not his or any other man's gain his fellow's lack: every one hath his proper gift of God, Whose ancient promise stands sure to each faithful soul: "Prove Me now . . . if I will not open you the windows of heaven, and pour you out a blessing, that there shall not be room enough to receive it."

Christians whose hands are characteristically never closed, open them wide at Christmas, and Christmas Boxes fall due on St. Stephen's Day. First let us connect our doles with the unapproachable Divine Saviour Who, being rich, for our sakes became poor: and this done, there will be no harm in connecting them further with that exalted St. Stephen who for love of Christ and of souls, was content to minister to the necessities of saints in things temporal.

December 27.

FEAST OF ST. JOHN, APOSTLE AND EVANGELIST.

THE "Disciple whom Jesus loved," the survivor of all the Apostles, an inspired Historian and Epistolizer, the Seer of the Apocalyptic Vision : well might this saint whose lifetime approached, if it did not exceed, a century, answer and say, "Even so, come, Lord Jesus."

"Beloved, let us love one another," says St. John,
  Eagle of eagles calling from above :
Words of strong nourishment for life to feed upon,
  "Beloved, let us love."

Voice of an eagle, yea, Voice of the Dove :
If we may love, winter is past and gone ;
  Publish we, praise we, for lo ! it is enough.

More sunny than sunshine that ever yet shone,
  Sweetener of the bitter, smoother of the rough,
Highest lesson of all lessons for all to con,
  "Beloved, let us love."

December 28.

FEAST OF THE HOLY INNOCENTS.

"If there be first a willing mind, it is accepted according to that a man hath, and not according to that he hath not."—(2 COR. viii. 12.)

BUT these blessed babies seem clearly incapable of the "willing mind : " what, then, did they offer ?

They offered what they could. Nevertheless they offered by proxy, being themselves (as we assume) incapable of will and deed alike.

A dazzling halo of paradoxes surrounds their offering.

They worshipped God, to outward appearance without knowing what they did. They died in Christ's stead, Who afterwards died in theirs. Christians they were not, except as the firstfruits of Christ's martyrs. The proxy by whose hand they offered an acceptable sacrifice, was a man wicked and sacrilegious.

And even as their brief life on earth is involved in marvels, so surely to our apprehension is their eternal life in the better country.

For if we are at a loss to conceive the blessedness of ripe saints in heaven, what conception can we form of the blessedness of these whose sanctity was latent, and even whose natural faculties were undeveloped?

They set off speechless, ignorant, with do-nothing hands, helpless feet, vacant minds: for who would lay stress on the speech, or knowledge, work, or walk, or intelligence of infants "from two years old and under"?

And now they have more understanding than many teachers, and are wiser than many aged.

"Jesus rejoiced in spirit, and said, I thank Thee, O Father, Lord of heaven and earth, that Thou hast hid these things from the wise and prudent, and hast revealed them unto babes: even so, Father; for so it seemed good in Thy sight."

December 29.

LOVE came down at Christmas,
Love all lovely, Love Divine,
Love was born at Christmas,
Star and Angels gave the sign.
Worship we the Godhead,
Love Incarnate, Love Divine,
Worship we our Jesus,—
But wherewith for sacred sign?
Love shall be our token,
Love be yours and love be mine,
Love to God and all men,
Love the universal sign.

December 30.

"It was told the king of Egypt that the people fled."—(Ex. xiv. 5.)

NAY, but on the contrary the Truth certifies us that "the children of Israel went out with an high hand" (ver. 8).

On the supposition (apparently) that they fled, Pharaoh summoned his army and pursued after them.

Who told him that they fled? We know not, nor from what motive. To inform him of the unvarnished truth on such a subject would have been a formidable undertaking: possibly some one on whom the duty devolved softened his version of the transaction for royal ears. The people were clean gone: what mattered it whether their exodus was described as a triumph or as a flight?

Yet in the long run it did clearly matter, when Pharaoh and his host ended their chase in the Red Sea.

An awful lesson against time-serving untruths, and all verbal inaccuracy. In this life we cannot always —can we ever?—track a lie to its ultimate issue.

"Deliver my soul, O Lord, from lying lips, and from a deceitful tongue."

December 31.

FEAST OF ST. SILVESTER. Elected Bishop of Rome in the year 314, died 335.

ST. SILVESTER became Pope about two years after the decisive battle of Saxa Rubra had secured Constantine on the Imperial Throne. To this Pontiff, therefore, "the Donation of Constantine" (now challenged as a forgery) purports to have been made, conferring upon "the Chair of Peter . . . imperial power and honour"

St. Silvester is held to have originated various rites
and ceremonies of the Roman use; and during his
pontificate the Lateran Church, magnificent with gold
and silver, was erected by Constantine. This Emperor is reported to have offered our saint a golden
and jewelled diadem, which, however, was refused.

St. Silvester attained a good old age. He lived to
send legates to the Council of Nicaea, being himself
incapacitated from attending it.

The story of his baptising the Emperor Constantine
is, at the least, disputed. Some allege that that
monarch received Baptism on his deathbed from
Eusebius, Arian Bishop of Nicomedia.

Looking back along life's trodden way,
　Gleams and greenness linger on the track:
Distance melts and mellows all to-day,
　Looking back.

Rose and purple and a silvery grey,
　Is that cloud the cloud we called so black?
Evening harmonises all to-day,
　Looking back.

Foolish feet so prone to halt or stray,
　Foolish heart so restive on the rack!
Yesterday we sighed, but not to-day,
　Looking back.

APPENDIX.

Readings for certain movable Holy Days.

Advent Sunday.

BEHOLD, the Bridegroom cometh:—go ye out
With lighted lamps and garlands round about
To meet Him in a rapture with a shout.

It may be at the midnight black as pitch
Earth shall cast up her poor, cast up her rich.

It may be at the crowing of the cock
Earth shall upheave her depth, uproot her rock.

For lo, the Bridegroom fetcheth home the Bride:
His Hands are Hands she knows, she knows His
    Side.

Like pure Rebekah at the appointed place,
Veiled she unveils her face to meet His Face.

Like great Queen Esther in her triumphing,
She triumphs in the presence of her King.

His Eyes are as a Dove's, and she's Dove-eyed;
He knows His lovely mirror, sister, Bride.

He speaks with Dove-voice of exceeding love,
And she with love-voice of an answering Dove.

Behold, the Bridegroom cometh:—go we out
With lamps ablaze and garlands round about
To meet Him in a rapture with a shout.

Advent: Ember Wednesday.

A HOLY man once suggested as a motive for joining in the service for the Churching of Women, that that single occasion might be our only opportunity for praying on behalf of the particular person in question.

Could we but summon up such a spirit of charitable good will to set us praying on Ember Days! And surely if on no other Ember Days, yet at least on these three in Advent, when ringing in our ears are the solemn words "The day is at hand."

Our own souls stand in jeopardy every hour. This we know, this we acknowledge, this at times becomes a burdensome knowledge well-nigh greater than we can bear. But if our own, how pre-eminently theirs who march as champions before our army, as leaders of our forlorn hopes.

It is folly indeed to keep looking for discouragements away from our own misdeeds and shortcomings. Yet if we do look round and do feel discouraged because neither Clergy nor candidates for Holy Orders are all unselfish saints and undaunted heroes, can we hold ourselves altogether guiltless of their defects? May not they in turn look round and wonder that there are so few intercessors, so few to uphold the men "subject to like passions as we are," of whom we complain fluently and for whom we pray in stammers?

Let us pray.

Advent: Ember Friday.

IF we prayed for the Clergy last Wednesday, we then gained a step towards praying more efficaciously for them to-day: prayer being indeed an inspiration, but also an art.

Bishops, Priests, Deacons, all need and all invite our prayers. Bishops whose charge is the widest and most responsible under the sun : for they oversee not the flock of God merely, but specially the overseers of that flock. Priests whose dignity is the highest conferred on mortal man : for they consecrate the Sacrament of the Body and Blood of Christ; and to whom much is given, of him shall be much required. Deacons who are mounting the first step of the loftiest ladder : and which of us knows not the momentous character of a first step?

But some one may retort upon me that Bishops are not in question to-day. Be it so. We shall find a vast field of prayer left, even when we restrict our intention to Priests and Deacons. These things done, the field narrowed and the concentrated prayers offered up, we shall in fact have interceded for the Bishops of the future : nor do I think we shall then be of all persons the least likely to add a petition for the much-tried Bishops of the present.

Let us pray.

Advent: Ember Saturday.

REVERED or not revered, loved or not loved, our Pastors will have to stand together with us before the Judgment Seat of Christ, — venerable or contemptible, lovely or unlovely.

Now there can be no doubt that on the whole the Clergy pray for their people. Many lavish their warmest, deepest human affections in intercessory prayer, travail in birth for souls, fill up that which is behind of the afflictions of Christ for His Body's sake the Church. This by the grace of God they do for us.

And we in our degree can do the same for them. Let us pray for all. To-day for those especially whose life or death race is yet to run.

Let us pray.

Ash Wednesday.

My God, my God, have mercy on my sin
For it is great; and if I should begin
   To tell it all, the day would be too small
     To tell it in.

My God, Thou wilt have mercy on my sin
For Thy Love's sake; yea, if I should begin
   To tell this all, the day would be too small
     To tell it in.

Lent: Ember Wednesday.

ALL time is entrusted to us for the performance of duty. With this aim in view, Lent stands foremost in the ranks of time.

Prayer, Fasting, Almsgiving, being incumbent upon all Christians, prayer on Ember Days naturally betakes itself to the channel of intercessory prayer on behalf of candidates for Holy Orders.

Nor can we thus help them much more appropriately than by praying that they also and in far fuller measure may receive the spirit of prayer, and especially of intercessory prayer. Christ prays for us in heaven: the Holy Ghost prays for us and in us on earth. Christ, Who is God Almighty made Man, dispenseth not Himself from prayer: the Holy Ghost, Who is God Almighty tabernacling in man, dispenseth not Himself from prayer: wherefore those who " pray without ceasing " may above their fellows affirm,

S

"Truly our fellowship is with the Father, and with His Son Jesus Christ."

By imploring so great a boon for others, we secure a portion of it to ourselves.

Lent: Ember Friday.

(St. Mark ix. 28, 29). "This kind can come forth by nothing, but by prayer and fasting," spake our Lord to His disciples after they had failed to cast out a devil.

Hence we are certified by implication that Christ our pattern fasted as well as prayed.

While by direct statement we are certified that neither fasting nor prayer can be dispensed with in the work of expulsion.

Fasting is under one aspect an easy duty : we know distinctly in what it consists, and we know positively whether we are or are not performing it. Under another aspect it is a difficult duty ; because it goes counter flesh and blood, counter much that is innocent, and still more that is natural. Fasting is peculiarly painful, and therefore peculiarly repugnant, to young persons ; so full as they are of spirit, so rich in the faculty of enjoyment.

Now, while, as a rule, the candidates for Holy Orders are young, yet fast they must on pain of remaining incompetent for full spiritual ministrations ; whereas the Man of God is called to "be perfect, throughly furnished unto all good works."

They will need their own earnest prayers for grace to fast, and in many other ways to mortify self. They will need both prayers and example of their fathers and brethren, mothers and sisters in the Church. To pray and fast with one heart and mind binds us into

communion with one another, into the Communion of
Saints: and the Communion of Saints is fellowship
with Christ.

Lent: Ember Saturday.

LIKE Prayer and Fasting, Almsgiving is a duty of
general obligation. To each of the three words
attaches a narrower and also a wider signification.

Prayer, strictly petition, is used as a compendious
term for all devotion.

Fasting, strictly abstinence from food, stands for all
self-mortification.

Almsgiving, strictly a dispensing of charitable doles,
embraces, according to its more extensive meaning,
all practical lovingkindness between men: a wide
field this, even if we consider it covered by the Seven
Temporal and Seven Spiritual Works of Mercy, so
concisely summed up by Bishop Andrewes:—
  "Visit: give drink: give meat: redeem the slave:
  Clothe: tend the sick: and lay the dead in grave.—
  Counsel: rebuke: instruct in wisdom's way:
  Console: forgive: endure unmov'd: and pray."
The Christian Ministry is the Grand Almoner of
the Christian community. To bring this about, the
candidates for Holy Orders have first to offer up
themselves for the glory of God and the good of
souls. Thus, and not otherwise, our "lack of service"
is supplied. Shall they do this for us, and shall we
grudge our substance, our co-operation, our sympathy,
our prayers, to them?

Palm Sunday.

ON the Jewish Day of Atonement, that great day
of foreshadowings and gracious mysteries, the goat of

the sin offering and the scapegoat alike typified our Redeemer, Jesus Christ, the true and only "Lamb of God, Which taketh away the sin of the world."

Alike, yet with a difference.

The goat of the sin offering, slain and consumed, aptly prefigured the sacred Body sacrificed and slain for us: He "bare our sins in His own Body on the tree."

The scapegoat seems no less apt a figure of our Lord's immortal Soul made "an offering for sin." For this goat was by no means to be slain, but laden with the iniquities of all Israel was to be sent away into the wilderness, into a land not inhabited.

Thus, the Soul of Christ having with His precious Body and Blood united to His Divinity made atonement for all mankind, was pleased to depart into Hades, a land uninhabited save by disembodied souls, and it may be bodiless spirits, and whereof holy Job of old said: "The land of darkness and the shadow of death; a land of darkness, as darkness itself; and of the shadow of death, without any order, and where the light is as darkness."

Monday in Holy Week

"The Voice of my Beloved."

ONCE I ached for thy dear sake:
Wilt thou cause Me now to ache?
Once I bled for thee in pain:
Wilt thou rend My Heart again?
Crown of thorns and shameful tree,
Bitter death I bore for thee,
Bore My cross to carry thee,
And wilt thou have nought of Me?

Tuesday in Holy Week.

BY Thy long drawn anguish to atone,
Jesus Christ, show mercy on Thine own:
Jesus Christ, show mercy and atone,
Not for other sake except Thine own.

Thou Who thirsting on the cross didst see
All mankind and all I love and me,
Still from Heaven look down in love and see
All mankind and all I love and me.

Wednesday in Holy Week.

"Kiss the Son, lest He be angry, and so ye perish from the right way."—(Ps. ii. 12.)

THE "kiss" enjoined being a spiritual kiss of loving fealty, we of this nineteenth century, while still on earth, can as readily and as truly offer it to Christ in heaven, as could St. Peter or St. John to that same Divine Master when on blessed Feet He trod the weary ways of Palestine.

For the literal kiss is the symbol, the spiritual kiss the reality.

This last cannot but be precious. The other depends for value on the temper from which it springs: for a gulph divides the sinful woman who because "she loved much" ceased not to kiss our Lord's Feet, from Judas Iscariot who betrayed the Son of Man with a kiss.

In like manner the spiritual embrace excels the literal embrace; this being but the symbol, that the reality.

As we learn from our Saviour's words to St. Mary Magdalene in the Garden of the Sepulchre. " Touch Me not; for I am not yet ascended to My Father," said He to His beloved and loving worshipper: denying her—who can doubt it?—the lower blessing, that He might bestow upon her the higher.

Those who crucified Him handled Him, yet spiritually they touched Him not. Even as aforetime the multitude who "thronged and pressed" Him, touched Him not.

Thursday in Holy Week.

"And the Vine said, . . . Should I leave my wine, which cheereth God and man, and go to be promoted over the trees?"—(JUDGES ix. 13.)

THE great Vine left its glory to reign as Forest
       King :—
" Nay," quoth the lofty forest trees, " We will not
       have this thing ;
We will not have this supple one enring us with its
       ring ;
Lo, from immemorial time our might towers shadow
       ing ;
Not we were born to curve and droop, not we to
       climb and cling ;
We buffet back the buffeting wind, tough to its
       buffeting.
We screen great beasts, the wild-fowl build in our
       heads and sing,
Every bird of every feather from off our tops takes
       wing :
I a king, and thou a king, and what king shall be
       our king ?"

Nevertheless the great Vine stooped to be the Forest
      King,
While the forest swayed and murmured like seas that
      are tempesting :
Stooped and drooped with thousand tendrils in
      thirsty languishing ;
Bowed to earth and lay on earth, for earth's re-
      plenishing ;
Put off sweetness, tasted bitterness, endured time's
      fashioning ;
Put off life and put on death : and lo ! it was all
      to bring
All its fellows down to a death which hath lost the
      sting,
All its fellows up to a life in endless triumphing,—
I a king, and thou a king, and this King to be our
      king.

Good Friday.

LORD Jesus Christ grown faint upon the Cross,
  A sorrow beyond sorrow in Thy look,
    The unutterable craving for my soul,
      Thy love of me sufficed
To load upon Thee and make good my loss
  In face of darkened heaven and earth that shook :—
    In face of earth and heaven, take Thou my whole
      Heart, O Lord Jesus Christ.

Easter Even.

THE tempest over and gone, the calm begun.
  Lo, "it is finished," and the Strong Man sleeps:
All stars keep vigil watching for the sun,
    The moon her vigil keeps.

A garden full of silence and of dew,
   Beside a virgin cave and entrance stone:
Surely a garden full of Angels too,
    Wondering, on watch, alone.

They who cry "Holy, Holy, Holy," still
   Veiling their faces round God's Throne above.
May well keep vigil on this heavenly hill
    And cry their cry of love,

Adoring God in His new mystery
   Of Love more deep than hell, more strong than
      death;
Until the day break and the shadows flee,
    The Shaking and the Breath.

Easter Day.

WORDS cannot utter
   Christ His returning :—
Mankind, keep jubilee,
   Strip off your mourning,
Crown you with garlands,
   Set your lamps burning.

Speech is left speechless ;—
   Set you to singing,
Fling your hearts open wide,
   Set your bells ringing :
Christ the Chief Reaper
   Comes, His sheaf bringing.

Earth wakes her song birds,
　Puts on her flowers,
Leads out her lambkins,
　Builds up her bowers:
This is man's spousal day,
　Christ's day and ours.

Easter Monday.

A BEAUTIFUL type of the Resurrection is furnished by a water lily.

In the evening the white blossom folds up to sink beneath the water.

In the morning it returns above the surface, expands in the air, basks in the sunshine.

Its brief night passes in secrecy and purity: its renewed day is full of light.

Easter Tuesday.

OUT in the rain a world is growing green,
　On half the trees quick buds are seen
　　Where glued-up buds have been.
Out in the rain God's Acre stretches green,
　Its harvest quick though still unseen:
　　For there the Life hath been.

If Christ hath died His brethren well may die,
　Sing in the gate of death, lay by
　　This life without a sigh:
For Christ hath died and good it is to die;
　To sleep whenso He lays us by,
　　Then wake without a sigh.

Yea, Christ hath died, yea, Christ is risen again:
  Wherefore both life and death grow plain
    To us who wax and wane,
For Christ Who rose shall die no more again:
  Amen: till He makes all things plain
    Let us wax on and wane.

Rogation Monday.

OUR Saviour's three Temptations in the Wilderness
suggest thoughts for the three Rogation Days in harmony with the way in which these are often observed
in Anglican Churches.

On Rogation Monday we pray for temporal blessings, particularly for "the kindly fruits of the earth,
that in due time we may enjoy them:" our prayers
thus enlarging and prolonging the perfect petition,
"Give us this day our daily bread."

What we pray for and receive we are virtually
pledged to give thanks for: grace before meals be-
speaks grace after them.

When God blesses our earthly substance it is of His
loving kindness and pity. When He blesses it not,
it is because He is ready to bless us in some higher
way.

If He gives us bread and not stones, it becomes us
to be thankful and to impart to them that have not.

If He gives us stones instead of bread, we may then
go on to learn by experience what already "our fathers
have told us" and our Lord by quoting has doubly
certified, that "Man shall not live by bread alone, but
by every word that proceedeth out of the mouth of
God."

In which words faith and love discern a promise of

that "Bread and Wine" whereby the faithful receive verily and indeed "the Body and Blood of Christ."

It is good, with Asher. to inherit bread and royal dainties : it is better, with Naphtali, to be satisfied with favour and full with the blessing of the Lord.

" Blessed are they which do hunger and thirst after righteousness : for they shall be filled."

" My soul is athirst for God, yea, even for the living God."

Rogation Tuesday.

ON this day we are urged to intercede for foreign missions.

Following the sequence of St. Luke's narrative, the second phase of our Divine Master's threefold temptation sets before us (I humbly think) one snare which in the very nature of such work must more or less beset missionary enterprises, and which if yielded to may render them even worse than useless.

For if, as the proverb asserts, we cannot touch pitch and be clean, it must be perilously difficult to set up one's tent amid Satan's own surroundings and continue in no way the worse for that neighbourhood.

The world and the flesh flaunt themselves in very uncompromising forms in the devil's own territory. And all the power and the glory of them set in array before a man whose work forces him to face and sift them day and night, may well make such an one tremble for himself and betake himself to his knees.

And if he for himself, so we for him : not merely of charity, but strictly also of justice.

For he is our proxy, fulfilling that function which being incumbent upon the Church as a body, many of us cannot, and most of us do not even attempt. It

was no hardship, but a privilege, for Aaron and Hur
to uphold the champion hands of Moses.

And if he and we with one voice beseech for him
and his mission God's grace and benediction, then
doubtless we may look for such an answer to prayer.
as will enable him in peace and safety to go upon
the lion and adder, treading the young lion and the
dragon under foot.

He will stand steadfast upon his watchtower hearken-
ing for God's word to him.

He will be raised up to sit even in heavenly places
in Christ Jesus, and from that "exceeding high mountain" will estimate and despise the world, and the
things of the world.

Vigil of the Ascension: Rogation Wednesday.

OUR Lord's third temptation (still following St.
Luke's order) met Him not in the world at large but
upon a pinnacle of the Temple: and being thus
localized, concerned (apparently) in the first instance,
not the entire human race, but the Jewish nation
represented by such individuals as then and there
were assembled within the sacred precincts; if, that
is, we may assume that the proposed descent was
intended to take place *into* and not *out of* the Temple.

The sign challenged and refused would, then, have
addressed itself to that chosen people. And thus
Christ's example on this occasion throws (I venture
to think) a bright beam of light on our subject for
to-day; on intercession for home missions, with an
eye to the practical carrying on of such missions.

Our great High Priest, His own all-wise all-gracious
Self, was about to enter on His Personal Home

Mission. And at that very moment He quotes Scripture instead of working a miracle, and lays stress not on any personal greatness, but on simple strict obedience.

Whence we cheerfully infer that no personal greatness above our level, or personal power denied us, will be needed for such mission-work as whether we be of the Clergy or of the laity it may please God to call us to.

The Bible will be needed, and that we possess, and can quote ; or if not, the fault is our own.

Personal lowliness will be needed, and whereinsoever we are called we can therein abide content, and work conscientiously. We can work helpfully · with inferiors, teachably with superiors, charitably with all.

And while we thus refrain our souls and keep them low, well may we look up and lift up our heads, for our redemption draweth nigh.

This same Jesus Who is gone into heaven. will so come in like manner as the Apostles saw Him go into heaven.

Not casting Himself down from the pinnacle of a Temple made with hands, but coming with clouds, descending from heaven with a shout, with the voice of the Archangel and with the trump of God.

Then when those who sleep in Jesus return with Him, when those who are alive in Jesus are caught up to meet Him in the air, then, and now, and ever, Good Lord, deliver us.

Ascension Day.

"A Cloud received Him out of their sight."

WHEN Christ went up to Heaven the Apostles stayed
  Gazing at Heaven with souls and wills on fire,
Their hearts on flight along the track He made,
    Winged by desire.

Their silence spake: "Lord, why not follow Thee?
  Home is not home without Thy Blessed Face,
Life is not life.   Remember, Lord, and see,
    Look back, embrace.

Earth is one desert waste of banishment,
  Life is one long drawn anguish of decay.
Where Thou wert wont to go we also went:
    Why not to-day?"

Nevertheless, a cloud cut off their gaze:
  They tarry to build up Jerusalem,
Watching for Him, while through the appointed days
    He watches them.

They do His Will, and doing it rejoice,
  Patiently glad to spend and to be spent:
Still He speaks to them, still they hear His Voice
    And are content.

For as a cloud received Him from their sight
  So with a cloud He will return ere long:
Therefore they stand on guard by day, by night,
    Strenuous and strong.

They do, they dare, they beyond seven times seven
  Forgive. they cry God's mighty word aloud:
Yet sometimes haply lift tired eyes to Heaven,—
    "Is that His cloud?"

Whitsun Eve.

"We wait for Thy lovingkindness, O God : in the midst of Thy temple."

Who cometh? Whom words cannot utter : the All-holy Almighty Spirit, co-equal with the Father and the Son, God Blessed for ever. Amen.

He cometh in Fulness as of wind and Might as of fire. Nevertheless, as a Dove, He cometh to dove-like souls.

Wherewith shall we come before the Lord, and bow ourselves before the High God? Thou, O Lord, fill us and kindle us, that so we ourselves may be made our acceptable offering.

Give us doves to meet Thy Dove : tenderness, sweetness, graciousness, a lowly walk, a heavenward flight.

By Thine Indwelling make us doves : wise as serpents, if it please Thee ; harmless as doves, that we may please Thee. Until that day when Christ Himself shall fetch home His love, His dove, His sister, His spouse.

Whitsun Day.

"When the Day of Pentecost was fully come."

At sound as of rushing wind and sight as of fire,
Lo! flesh and blood made spirit and fiery flame,
Ambassadors in Christ's and the Father's Name,
    To woo back a world's desire.

These men chose death for their life, and shame for
        their boast,
For fear courage, for doubt intuition of faith,
Chose love that is strong as death and stronger than
        death
    In the power of the Holy Ghost.

Whitsun Monday.

"THE fruit of the Spirit is love, joy, peace, long-suffering, gentleness, goodness, faith, meekness, temperance." (Galatians v. 22, 23.)

Blessed be God that these lovely graces are "fruits" not flowers. Flowers might be demanded of us at the dawn of our day of probation, so soon as ever "the Dayspring from on high" had visited us. But for fruits time is allowed ; they form gradually, sweeten gradually, ripen gradually. Even "the husbandman waiteth for the precious fruit of the earth, and hath long patience for it."

Holy Church is that garden of God wherein, according to His many types, God the Holy Ghost deigns to dwell and work. A dove's bower is very peaceful. A watered garden brings forth abundantly. Fruits ripen, sweeten, and are perfected by the sun's blazing fire. The wind blowing "where it listeth" brings out and sheds abroad fragrance, and makes music among bowing branches.

"Come, Holy Ghost, our souls inspire."

Whitsun Tuesday.

LORD Jesus Christ our Wisdom and our Rest
   Who wisely dost reveal and wisely hide,
   Grant us such grace in wisdom to abide
According to Thy Will Whose Will is best.
Contented with Thine uttermost behest,
   Too sweet for envy and too high for pride,
   All simple-souled, dove-hearted, and dove-eyed,
Soft-voiced, and satisfied in humble nest.
Wondering at the bounty of Thy Love

Which gives us wings of silver and of gold ;
Wings folded close, yet ready to unfold
When Thou shalt say,—" Winter is past and gone :"
When Thou shalt say,—"Spouse, sister, love, and dove,
Come hither, sit with Me upon My Throne."

Whitsuntide: Ember Wednesday.

"ASK. and ye shall receive" is the very text for
Whitsuntide : and if for the entire season, eminently
for these three Ember Days.

Whitsuntide is exceedingly brief: it is come and
gone in eight days. We seem to hear once more
proclaimed " Jesus of Nazareth passeth by :" will we
not raise a clamour of entreaty with the blind men of
Jericho? We have no time to lose : this blessed
moment, this moment of blessing " passeth by." Let
us by strength of faith and prayer seize, arrest, per-
petuate it.

Until God the Holy Ghost came down at Pentecost,
the Apostles were in a certain sense themselves but
as candidates for Holy Orders. Spiritual giants,
" men of renown" they were : yet without Him they
could do nothing. Let us with one accord, if not all
in one place, pray for the spiritual ordinary men of
our own day, that according to the blessing on one
Patriarch of Israel, as their days so may their
strength be.

Three things we observe on that unparalleled Feast
of Pentecost : a herald sound, "suddenly there came
a sound from heaven, as of a rushing mighty wind,
and it filled all the house where they were sitting,"—
an accompanying sight, " there appeared unto them
cloven tongues, like as of fire, and it sat upon each of
them,"—and an actual Divine Indwelling, " they were

T

all filled with the Holy Ghost." And since we have as it were a three-storied "house" (to wit, three Ember Days) to "fill" with this Mystery of consolation, let us apportion the three points one by one to the three days.

As the Ineffable Gift was originally bestowed with sound, so must it be given forth again and again with sound. To Christ's ministers first of all were the words spoken : " Freely ye have received, freely give :" and from age to age the Christian ministry is called to teach, preach, rebuke, exhort, lift up a voice like a trumpet. But " if the trumpet give an uncertain sound, who shall prepare himself to the battle?"

Grant, O Lord, we beseech Thee, to all who shall now be ordained to any holy function, that by the Holy Ghost dwelling in them they may know Thy Son Jesus Christ to be the Truth, and that the words spoken by their mouths may never be spoken in vain. For the sake of the same Thy Son, the Word, our Master, Jesus Christ. Amen.

Whitsuntide: Ember Friday.

"CLOVEN tongues, like as of fire."

Words are spoken : deeds and lives speak. The cloven tongues suggest a double lesson. As *tongues* they call for speech from those on whom spiritually they are conferred : as *an appearance of fire* they invite "a burning and a shining" life as their correspondent.

" By the grace of God I am what I am : and His grace which was bestowed upon me was not in vain ; but I laboured more abundantly than they all : yet not I, but the grace of God which was with me,"

writes St. Paul, comparing himself with the other
Apostles.

Now if it was not "Paul" but "grace" which led
that life, performed those deeds, achieved that glory;
what valid reason can any man allege, least of all any
ordained man, for not living in some sort as St. Paul
lived, working as he worked, dying as he died? True,
such an one may be incompetent to preach as he
preached, or write as he wrote. But surely not even
inspired sermons or epistles were foremost in that
chosen vessel's mind when he averred: "To me to
live is Christ, and to die is gain:" or elsewhere: "I
therefore so run, not as uncertainly; so fight I, not
as one that beateth the air: but I keep under my
body, and bring it into subjection, lest that by any
means, when I have preached to others, I myself
should be a castaway."

A spiritual race, an unearthly fight, self-subdual,
Christ-likeness and oneness with Christ, all these
went towards making up that blessed life wherein
St. Paul made himself all things to all men that he
might by all means save some. Amongst these we
recognise no miraculous gifts, but legitimate fruits of
a grace within the reach of all Christians: and we
behold this grace needed and spent by one devoted
minister to edify the Church of God.

Grant, O Lord, we beseech Thee, to all who shall
now be ordained to any holy function, that following
in the luminous track of Thine Apostles they may by
the might of the Holy Ghost so live and walk that
all men may take knowledge of them that they abide
with Jesus. For His sake Who is our Way and our
Life, the same Thy Son Jesus Christ. Amen.

T 2

Whitsuntide: Ember Saturday.

WIND, earthquake, fire, tremendous but empty, ushered in the "still small Voice" which spake to Elijah: "the Lord," we read, "was not" in that wind, that earthquake, that fire.

So when the supreme "Day of Pentecost was fully come," the sound from heaven as of a rushing mighty wind, and the filled house, and the appearance of cloven tongues like as of fire, were all alike awful, but extraneous; appreciable by the senses; outward and visible or audible signs of inward and spiritual grace.

The animated creature is visible, the life abides invisible.

In like manner that which was seen and heard indicated to all men the Advent and Presence of God the Holy Ghost: "but Him they saw not."

This Divine Presence, not those awe-inspiring phenomena, was the essence of all. Had the Almighty Spirit deigned to descend in silence and darkness, the Church would equally have been born, sanctified, glorified.

Manifest signs and wonders addressed, startled, in some happy instances convinced the multitude. The hidden indwelling of God's Most Holy Spirit by itself and alone sanctified the Apostles. Those outward signs forwarded their work: but without the inward reality both work and workers would have been nothing.

Wherefore if hitherto we have prayed that those who aspire to Holy Orders may be endowed with irresistible mouth and wisdom, and with behaviour gracious and acceptable amongst men, much more on this last Ember Day let us pray that their own wills and hearts may be sanctified, and they themselves saved in the great and dreadful day of the Lord.

Grant, O Lord, we beseech Thee, to all who shall now be ordained to any holy function, that Thy Holy Spirit may dwell in them in all fulness, stablishing, strengthening, settling them : making them fair without and fairer within, until having wholly put on Christ they shall rest from their labours, their works following them. For His only sake Who is fairer than the children of men, to Whom Thou gavest not the Spirit by measure, Thy Son our Saviour Jesus Christ. Amen.

Trinity Sunday.

God the Father loved us when He created us, God the Son when He redeemed us, God the Holy Ghost when He took possession of us as His temple.

Three Persons, One God, One Will.

God forbid that we who remain without should cut off our charity from any who have passed before us within the veil. Even if a case appear to us desperate, "who art thou that judgest another man's servant? to his own master he standeth or falleth." Hope against hope is worthy of a Christian. Love strong as death can grapple with despair.

"There is mercy with Thee : therefore shalt Thou be feared."

Trinitytide: Ember Wednesday.

ADVENT bids us look forward and upward, for "Behold, the Bridegroom cometh." Lent turns our eyes backward and inward, for except we repent we shall all likewise perish. Whitsuntide calls on us to seize the actual moment; open our hearts wide and be filled. With Whitsun Day and its "equal" octave Trinity Sunday, our series of exceptional calls and celebrations of particular Divine Mysteries ends or is suspended : is suspended for any who survive till another Advent, is ended for all who survive not.

Trinitytide is a prolonged period wherein to bring forth fruit with patience. All the great things done for us, and revealed to us, ought to have led us up to a simple, earnest, unflagging fulfilment of everyday duties.

And one obvious duty of this Ember season—the last of the ecclesiastical year (in September)—being to pray once again on behalf of the candidates for Holy Orders, let us pray that they may run with patience the race set before them, looking unto Jesus the Author and Finisher of their faith.

For if ordinary lives at ordinary times are liable to become monotonous, tedious, lax, not least so are their lives. It is hard to run on energetically through the burden and heat of the day, and hard to gaze upward steadfastly through the blinding dust and exhaustion of a prolonged race. God grant to them and to ourselves that loving faith which can do all things in Christ's strength.

Trinitytide: Ember Friday.

"Hope maketh not ashamed; because the love of God is shed abroad in our hearts by the Holy Ghost which is given unto us."— (ROM. v. 5.)

NOTHING but the love of God can account for or can justify an indomitable hope. Hope seems the more intimately allied to love, inasmuch as fear, its opposite, will be cast out by perfect love : wherefore? "because fear hath torment."

Hope contrariwise is a pleasure. Hope, like the rainbow, can be evoked out of clouds and gloom to supply a bridge between earth and heaven : but can only be evoked by the sun-like love of God.

The rainbow appears to plant two feet on remote spots of earth, as if for holy souls "from the east and from the west" to mount along its pathway and meet in heavenly places.

Now no class of men can stand in more urgent need of this happy grace of hope than do the members of a ministry who, like Baruch, must not in worldly matters ask "great things" for themselves. They have given their whole substance for love, and henceforward hope as an anchor of the soul sure and steadfast, and which entereth into that within the veil must be their stay. Hope moreover is characteristically natural and very needful to the young, and candidates for Holy Orders (let us not forget it) are for the most part more or less young. St. Paul's blessing on his beloved Roman converts suggests the very prayer we need on behalf of our youthful pastors :—

"Now the God of hope fill you with all joy and peace in believing, that ye may abound in hope, through the power of the Holy Ghost."

Trinitytide: Ember Saturday.

"Now abideth faith, hope, charity, these three; but the greatest of these is charity."—(I COR. xiii. 13.)

IF three days ago we prayed in faith for faith, if yesterday in hope for hope, let us to-day in charity pray on behalf of the candidates for Holy Orders that they may be made perfect in love.

Charity or love includes all graces, all perfections. " Love is the fulfilling of the law." Besides a host of additional excellences, charity "believeth all things, hopeth all things, endureth all things :" so that in charity and not elsewhere faith and hope strike living root, blossom, bear fruit unto life eternal.

" O Lord, Who hast taught us that all our doings without charity are nothing worth ; send Thy Holy Ghost, and pour into our hearts that most excellent gift of charity, the very bond of peace and of all virtues, without which whosoever liveth is counted dead before Thee : grant this for Thine only Son Jesus Christ's sake.   Amen."

OXFORD : HORACE HART, PRINTER TO THE UNIVERSITY

PUBLICATIONS

OF THE

SOCIETY FOR PROMOTING CHRISTIAN KNOWLEDGE.

—·—

HISTORY OF INDIA.

From the Earliest Times to the Present Day. By Captain L. J. TROTTER. With eight full-page Woodcuts on toned paper, and numerous smaller Woodcuts. Post 8vo. Cloth boards, 10s. 6d.

———

SCENES IN THE EAST.

Consisting of twelve Coloured Photographic Views of Places mentioned in the Bible, beautifully executed, with Descriptive Letterpress. By the Rev. CANON TRISTRAM, Author of "Bible Places," "The Land of Israel," &c. 4to. Cloth, bevelled boards, gilt edges, 6s.

———

SINAI AND JERUSALEM; OR, SCENES FROM BIBLE LANDS.

Consisting of Coloured Photographic Views of Places mentioned in the Bible, including a Panoramic View of Jerusalem with Descriptive Letterpress. By the Rev. F. W. HOLLAND, M.A., Demy 4to. Cloth, bevelled boards, gilt edges, 6s.

BIBLE PLACES; OR, THE TOPOGRAPHY OF THE HOLY LAND.

A succinct account of all the Places, Rivers, and Mountains of the Land of Israel mentioned in the Bible, so far as they have been identified; together with their modern names and historical references. By the Rev. CANON TRISTRAM. With Map. Crown 8vo. Cloth boards, 4s.

THE LAND OF ISRAEL.

A Journal of Travel in Palestine, undertaken with special reference to its Physical Character. By the Rev. CANON TRISTRAM. Fourth edition, revised. With Maps and numerous Illustrations. Large post 8vo. Cloth boards, 10s. 6d.

NARRATIVE OF A MODERN PILGRIMAGE THROUGH PALESTINE ON HORSEBACK, AND WITH TENTS.

By the Rev. ALFRED CHARLES SMITH, M.A., Rector of Yatesbury, Wilts, Author of "The Attractions of the Nile," &c. Numerous Illustrations and four Coloured Plates. Crown 8vo. Cloth boards, 5s.

THE NATURAL HISTORY OF THE BIBLE.

By the Rev. CANON TRISTRAM, Author of "Bible Places," &c. With numerous Woodcuts. Crown 8vo. Cloth boards, 7s. 6d.

A HISTORY OF THE JEWISH NATION.

From the Earliest Times to the Present Day. By the late E. H. PALMER, M.A., Author of "The Desert of the Exodus," &c. With Map of Palestine and numerous Illustrations. Crown 8vo. Cloth boards, 4s.

THE ART TEACHING OF THE PRIMITIVE CHURCH.

With an Index of Subjects, Historical and Emblematic. By the Rev. R. St. John Tyrwhitt. Cloth boards, 5s.

AUSTRALIA'S HEROES.

Being a slight Sketch of the most prominent amongst the band of gallant men who devoted their lives and energies to the cause of Science, and the development of the Fifth Continent. By C. H. Eden, Esq., Author of "Fortunes of the Fletchers," &c. With Map. Crown 8vo. Cloth boards, 5s.

SOME HEROES OF TRAVEL;
OR,
CHAPTERS FROM THE HISTORY OF GEOGRAPHICAL DISCOVERY AND ENTERPRISE.

Compiled and re-written by W. H. Davenport Adams, Author of "Great English Churchmen," &c. With Map. Crown 8vo. Cloth boards, 5s.

CHRISTIANS UNDER THE CRESCENT IN ASIA.

By the Rev. EDWARD L. CUTTS, B.A., Author of "Turning Points of Church History," &c. With numerous Illustrations. Post 8vo. Cloth boards, 5s.

HEROES OF THE ARCTIC AND THEIR ADVENTURES.

By FREDERICK WHYMPER, Esq., Author of "Travels in Alaska." With Map, Eight full-page and numerous small Woodcuts. Crown 8vo. Cloth boards, 3s. 6d.

CHINA.

By Professor ROBERT K. DOUGLAS, of the British Museum. With Map, and eight full-page Illustrations on toned paper, and several Vignettes. Post 8vo. Cloth boards, 5s.

RUSSIA: PAST AND PRESENT.

Adapted from the German of Lankenau and Oelnitz. By Mrs. CHESTER. With Map, and three full-page Woodcuts and Vignettes. Post 8vo. Cloth boards, 5s.

Depositories:

LONDON: NORTHUMBERLAND AVENUE, W.C.
43, QUEEN VICTORIA STREET, E.C.

www.ingramcontent.com/pod-product-compliance
Lightning Source LLC
Chambersburg PA
CBHW030626030726
47497CB00006B/1649